Project Duchess

Center Point
Large Print

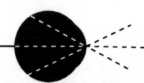

**This Large Print Book carries the
Seal of Approval of N.A.V.H.**

Project Duchess

Sabrina Jeffries

CENTER POINT LARGE PRINT
THORNDIKE, MAINE

This Center Point Large Print edition
is published in the year 2019 by arrangement with
Kensington Publishing Corp.

The text of this Large Print edition is unabridged.
In other aspects, this book may vary
from the original edition.
Printed in the United States of America
on permanent paper.
Set in 16-point Times New Roman type.

ISBN: 978-1-64358-280-1

Library of Congress Cataloging-in-Publication Data

Names: Jeffries, Sabrina, author.
Title: Project Duchess / Sabrina Jeffries.
Description: Large Print edition. | Thorndike, Maine :
    Center Point Large Print, 2019.
Identifiers: LCCN 2019020751 | ISBN 9781643582801 (hardcover :
    alk. paper)
Subjects: LCSH: Large type books. | GSAFD: Love stories.
Classification: LCC PS3610.E39 P76 2019 | DDC 813/.6—dc23
LC record available at https://lccn.loc.gov/2019020751

To Joyce Ratley,
for your many, many fine years of teaching
and caring for our autistic kids and adults.
We'll miss your wisdom and your wonderful ways.
I know you will go on to do even more great
things.

And to my agent,
Pam Ahearn of The Ahearn Agency,
who has supported me for thirty-one years of
good times and bad. Hope we continue
for many more!

Lydia's Husbands

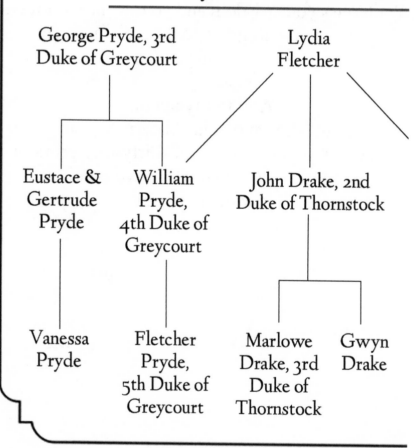

George Pryde, 3rd Duke of Greycourt

Lydia Fletcher

Eustace & Gertrude Pryde

William Pryde, 4th Duke of Greycourt

John Drake, 2nd Duke of Thornstock

Vanessa Pryde

Fletcher Pryde, 5th Duke of Greycourt

Marlowe Drake, 3rd Duke of Thornstock

Gwyn Drake

and Children

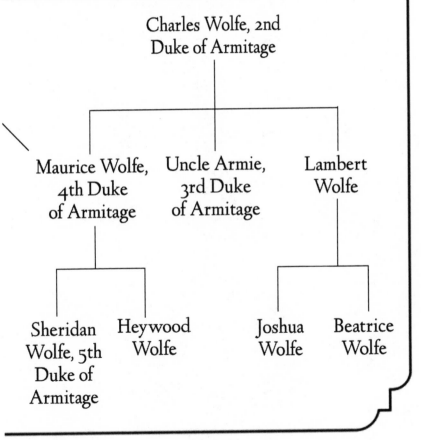

Charles Wolfe, 2nd
Duke of Armitage

Maurice Wolfe,
4th Duke
of Armitage

Uncle Armie,
3rd Duke
of Armitage

Lambert
Wolfe

Sheridan
Wolfe, 5th
Duke of
Armitage

Heywood
Wolfe

Joshua
Wolfe

Beatrice
Wolfe

DOWAGER DUCHESS LOSES
THIRD HUSBAND

As promised, dear readers, we have made haste to bring you the latest on-dit, and a most startling one it is, indeed. The former Lydia Fletcher now has the dubious distinction of having been wed and widowed by three dukes: the 4th Duke of Greycourt, the 2nd Duke of Thornstock, and the newly deceased 3rd Duke of Armitage.

She has also managed to bear each an heir, and in one case, even an heir and a spare—with, it must be said, mixed results. While her son Fletcher Pryde, the 5th Duke of Greycourt, has increased his father's wealth tenfold, he is also rumored to run a secret cabal of licentious bachelors. Given the reserve of this gentleman, one could hardly imagine anyone less disposed to such purposeless behavior, but then, as is often observed, still waters do run deep.

One might more easily believe such a rumor of her second son, Marlowe Drake, the 3rd Duke of Thornstock, who, it is said, has never danced with a lightskirt he didn't like. His twin sister, Lady Gwyn, newly arrived in London, promises to make such behavior more difficult by forcing him to ride herd on her own suitors. Her first Season should prove most interesting, and yours truly will be observing such with rapt attention.

Finally we come to Sheridan Wolfe, the 4th Duke of Armitage, who has spent most of his life in Prussia, where his late father was ambassador. He's the dark horse of the family, unfamiliar to many in society, though he will probably have no trouble finding an heiress willing to exchange her dowry for the rarified title of duchess. If she does, she'd best bear him an heir and a spare forthwith, since his younger brother Colonel Lord Heywood Wolfe is waiting in the wings for his chance at the title!

Indeed, all the progeny of the dowager duchess Lydia had best bear heirs as soon as they can, given—and one can only shudder to say it—the family propensity to have their dukes perish before their time.

The funeral will take place at Armitage Hall in Lincolnshire.

Chapter One

London, September 1808

One fine autumn afternoon, Fletcher Pryde, 5th Duke of Greycourt, strode up the steps of his Mayfair town house, caught up in thinking through his business affairs. Which was probably why he missed the speaking look on his butler's face as he stalked through the doorway.

"Your Grace, I feel it is my duty to make you aware that—"

"Not now, Johnston. I've got a dinner at eight, and I hope to catch old Brierly at his club before then. He's unloading property near my Devon estate that I must have if I'm to continue my improvements. And I have reports I have to peruse before I can even talk to him."

"More land, Grey?" said a decidedly young, female voice. "Sometimes I think you shop for properties as eagerly as women shop for gowns. Judging from your reputation for shrewd dealing, you probably pay less for them, too."

Grey whirled toward the sound. "Vanessa!" He scowled over at Johnston. "Why didn't you tell me she was here?"

His butler lifted his eyes a fraction, as close as the man ever came to rolling them. "I did try, sir."

"Ah. Right. I suppose you did."

Grey smiled indulgently at Vanessa Pryde. At twenty-four, she was ten years his junior and more like a little sister than a first cousin.

He removed his hat, driving gloves, and great-coat before handing them to the footman. Grey didn't recognize the servant, who was gawking at Vanessa like a pauper at a princess. The footman's fascination was understandable, given her heart-shaped face, perfect proportions, and wealth of jet-black curls, but it was also most inappropriate.

Grey cast the fellow one of the quelling glances at which he excelled.

When the footman colored and hurried off, Johnston stepped up to murmur, "Sorry, Your Grace. He's new. I will be sure to speak to him."

"See that you do." Then he turned his attention to Vanessa, who didn't even seem to have noticed the exchange. "I wasn't expecting you."

"You ought to have been, Cousin." With an elaborate curtsey, Vanessa flashed him a mischievous smile. "Or should I say, 'prospective fiancé'?"

"Don't even joke about that," he grumbled. Every time he tried to think of himself married to Vanessa, he remembered her as a babe in swaddling, being held by her father, his uncle Eustace Pryde, and he knew he couldn't do it. He'd seen her grow up—he couldn't imagine her as his wife.

Fortunately, she had no desire to marry him, either. Which was why whenever her ambitious mother sent her over here with instructions to get him into a compromising position so they could be forced into marriage, they spent most of the time drumming up a plausible reason for why Vanessa had "just missed him."

"Don't worry." Vanessa gave a little laugh. "My maid is with me. As usual, she will swear to whatever excuse we concoct for Mama. So come join us for tea and cakes in the drawing room."

Leave it to Vanessa to take charge of his household. As they strolled down the hall, he said, "You look well."

Preening a bit, she danced ahead and whirled to face him, forcing him to halt as she swished her skirts about her legs. "So you like my new gown? I won't tell Mama. She picked it out herself to tempt you. I told her yellow was your favorite color."

"I hate yellow."

Her blue eyes twinkled at him. "Precisely."

A helpless laugh escaped him. "You, my dear, are a hoyden. If you would put a tenth of the energy you expend in provoking your mother into hunting down a husband, you'd have twenty men begging to marry you."

Her spirits seemed to droop. "I already have that. But you know how Mama is. Until you are off the table, she won't allow me to accept a lesser man's suit." She wagged her finger at him. "So will you please get married? To *anyone* other than me? Or I shall surely die an old maid."

"That will never happen to you, and we both know it." He narrowed his gaze on her. "Wait a minute—is there someone in particular you have your eye on?"

Her blush alarmed him. Vanessa had terrible taste in men.

"Who is he?" he demanded.

She tipped up her chin. "I'm not going to tell you."

"Because you know I'd disapprove, which means he's entirely wrong for you."

"He is *not*. He's a poet."

Damn. Vanessa needed to marry a poet about like he needed to learn to cook. Then again . . . "A *famous* poet?" he asked hopefully. If the fellow had money, it could work. Anyone who married Vanessa would need pots of money, if only to keep up with her gown purchases.

She turned and marched on to the drawing room. "He will be. With my support and encouragement."

"God help us all." He almost felt sorry for this poet, whoever he was. "I suppose your mother disapproves."

"As if I would ever tell her," she scoffed as she entered the drawing room.

Vanessa's lady's maid sat erect on the settee,

her expression bland. No doubt she was used to being the foil to her volatile employer.

"Then things have not progressed to a serious interest," Grey said, relieved not to have to deal with that, too. He was still hoping to get to Brierly's club before the man left.

"How could things progress at *all?*" Vanessa picked up a teacake and devoured it with her usual gusto. "Mama is so focused on my marrying you that I cannot get her to bring me to events my . . . friend might attend." She shot him a dire look. "And thanks to the latest on-dit about you, she's on a tear again. She actually believes all that rot about your running a secret cabal of licentious bachelors."

He snorted. "I'd never run anything so tiresome and predictable. I don't have the time or inclination for it, and that level of discretion requires too much effort to maintain, people being who they are. I hope you told her I'd rather focus my energy on my estates."

"I did. She didn't believe me. She never does."

"Yet she sent you over here to engage the leader of this secret cabal of debauchery. She makes no sense."

"The gossip only made her more eager to marry me off to you. Hmm."

"She's probably afraid I'll spend all my wealth on 'licentious' living before you can grab me and my dukedom for our progeny."

"Or she thinks that a man with such ungoverned desires would be easy to manipulate. She ought to know you better than that. I certainly do. There isn't a single ungoverned thing about you." Vanessa tapped her finger on her chin. "Then again, there's another possibility—that Mama started the rumor about the cabal herself."

"To what end?"

"By making you sound unappealing, she hopes to eliminate my competition."

"I hate to tell you, my dear, but rumors of a man's wickedness rarely seem to eliminate the competition. If that was your mother's plan, it's a foolish one. And it proves my opinion about gossip: Rumors are nothing more than entertainment for the bored. If people in society would put a tenth of the energy they expend in—"

"I know, I know—we're all frivolous, with not a whit of usefulness between us," she said archly. "You're the only one with any sense."

When her maid looked as if she might explode with holding in a laugh, he shot Vanessa a rueful glance. "Do you think me as pompous and arrogant as all that, pet?"

"Worse." Then she softened the accusation with a smile. "And on that note, I shall leave you." Her maid cleared her throat, and Vanessa said, "Oh, I almost forgot! I have this for you."

She fished a sealed letter out of her reticule. "It came to us rather than you. Which is curious. Perhaps your mother heard you hadn't been here in weeks. Though why she thought *we* would see you any more often is anyone's guess."

He ignored the sudden tightness in his chest. "You know perfectly well why."

With a sigh, Vanessa stepped nearer to speak in a low voice meant only for his ears. "Must you still punish your mother?"

"Don't be nonsensical," he said lightly, to hide the guilt that swamped him. "I'm not punishing her. Besides, she has her other children to keep her company. She doesn't need me fawning over her."

Vanessa sniffed. "As if you would ever fawn over anyone. And yes, you are punishing her, whether you admit it or not."

The pity shining in Vanessa's eyes made him regret having said anything about his mother.

He reached for the letter, but Vanessa wouldn't release it. "She does love you, you know."

"I do." What else could he say? He loved her, too, in his own way.

Grey started to shove the letter into his coat pocket, then paused. The missive seemed awfully thin for one of Mother's. With a sense of dread, he opened it to find the briefest of messages:

My dearest Grey,

I regret to inform you that your step-father has passed away. The funeral is at Armitage Hall on Tuesday.

With much love,

Mother

P.S. Please come. I can't do this without you.

Grey stared numbly at the words. Maurice, the only father he'd ever really known, was dead.

Please come. I can't do this without you.

Holy hell, Mother must be devastated.

Apparently, his distress showed in his face, for Vanessa snatched the letter and read it, then lifted a horrified gaze to him. "Oh, Grey, how *awful.* I'm so very sorry."

"Thank you," he muttered, though he felt like a fraud. He'd barely seen Maurice since the family's return from Prussia a few months ago. He had let his bitterness keep him away, and now it was too late.

She was now rereading the letter with a furrowed brow. "Maurice . . . that would be Sheridan's father, right? I suppose he will now become duke."

The odd note in her voice arrested him. "*Sheridan?* Since when are you so chummy with my half brother? You only met him once."

"We've met thrice actually," she murmured. "We even danced together twice."

Uh-oh. Sheridan had best watch himself around Vanessa. When she fixed her affections on a man, she could really dig her teeth in. "Don't tell me he's the 'poet' you have your eye on."

His sharp tone made her glance up. "Don't be ridiculous. Sheridan doesn't have a poetic thought in his head."

She was right, but how had she known that? "You'll have to call him Armitage now that he's duke."

"All the more reason for me not to have an interest in him. I will *never* take a duke for my husband, no matter what Mama wants. You're all too . . . too . . ."

"Pompous and arrogant?"

As if realizing she shouldn't be insulting a man who'd just lost a close relation, she winced. "Something like that." When he said nothing, she added, "You certainly have a number of dukes in *your* family."

"That's what happens when one's mother marries well three times."

"She'll be leaving quite a dynasty behind her. Some would say that's excellent planning."

"She didn't plan on being widowed thrice, I assure you," he said sharply.

Vanessa looked stricken. "Of course not. I'm sorry, Grey, that was most thoughtless of me."

He pinched the bridge of his nose. "No, it's . . . I'm just unsettled by the news."

"I'm sure. If there's anything I can do . . ."

Grey didn't answer, his mind having already seized on the reminder that Sheridan had become Duke of Armitage. Maurice had only been duke a few months, and now Sheridan was being forced to take up the mantle. His head must be reeling. Grey needed to be at Armitage Hall, if only to help Sheridan and Mother with the arrangements for the funeral on Tuesday.

Wait, today was Sunday. But *which* Sunday? Damn it, had he already missed his stepfather's funeral?

"When did this letter arrive?" he asked.

It was the maid who answered. "I believe it was this past Friday, Your Grace."

"That's right," Vanessa said. "Friday."

Armitage Hall was near the town of Sanforth. If he caught the footmen before they unpacked his trunk, Grey could be changed into his mourning clothes and back on the road in an hour. He'd easily reach Lincolnshire by tomorrow. "I must go," he said, turning for the door.

"I'll go with you," Vanessa said.

"Don't be absurd," Grey snapped before her maid could protest. "You will go home as usual and tell your mother I wasn't here. You have the perfect excuse for missing me this time. Just say I'd already been notified of my stepfather's death and had left for Lincolnshire. Understood?"

"But . . . but how could you have been notified if I hadn't yet brought you the letter?"

"Say that the servants told you I'd already received one here." His common sense finally asserted itself. "Indeed, I probably have, since I haven't looked at my mail yet. Mother wouldn't have left anything to chance. She would have sent multiple notices." No matter how distracted by grief she might be.

Vanessa laid her hand upon his arm. "Grey, you need someone with you. You're clearly upset."

"I'll be fine." He would, damn it. "Now go on with you. I have preparations to make before I can leave."

"Of course." She nodded to her lady's maid, who joined her. "I shall tell Mama of your loss. Perhaps that will keep her machinations to a minimum for a while."

"Somehow I doubt it." He leaned close to whisper, "Take care with your poet, my dear. You deserve better."

She made a face. "I don't suppose I'll get a chance at him, anyway, now that you're in mourning. Mama will make me wait to see *anyone* until you're available again."

"Good. I shouldn't like to think of you marrying someone beneath you while I'm not around to prevent it."

Tossing back her head, she walked toward the door. "There's something to be said for marrying for love, you know. I swear, sometimes you remind me of Mama in your opinions about marriage."

With that parting sally, she waltzed out, with her maid trailing behind her.

How ridiculous. He was nothing like Aunt Cora, that grasping harpy. He was merely sensible. Love didn't enter his equations because it had no monetary value. When *he* married, it would be to some sensible woman who'd be content with having a wealthy dukedom at her disposal, who had no dreams of cloud castles and no hope for sentiment or love or any of that romantic nonsense from him.

He had learned the hard way to guard his heart.

Chapter Two

Lincolnshire, England

The Honorable Miss Beatrice Wolfe stood outside Armitage Hall surveying the entryway with a critical eye. The funeral escutcheon had been hung on the door—not crookedly this time—and the arches and windows were draped in black crape. It looked proper, the way it ought for a duke.

She hadn't taken such care with her uncle Armie, as she and her brother Joshua had always called the previous Duke of Armitage. Just the thought of Uncle Armie's last years, of how he'd tried to paw at her or slap her behind every time she'd come to the hall, chilled her.

By contrast, Uncle Maurice, who had inherited the dukedom after Uncle Armie's death, had treated her with respect and kindness. He and her aunt Lydia had brought light and laughter and good times back to the hall.

Now death hung over the place again. Tears welled in her eyes. Why, they'd only a week ago removed the black crape and funeral escutcheon signifying Uncle Armie's death! Two dukes dead in a matter of months. It was a blasted shame. It really was.

Her cousin Sheridan appeared in the doorway, looking like a wraith after the past few days. He'd been close to his father, and was taking his death harder than anyone except Aunt Lydia. No doubt it had hit Sheridan's brother Heywood hard, too, but since Heywood was in the army and probably hadn't even received word yet of his father's demise, she wouldn't know.

Sheridan flashed her a wan smile. "Forgive me, Bea, for troubling you, but Mother asked me to check again to see if Grey has arrived." He surveyed the drive beyond her. "I can see he has not. If he had, there'd be a monstrous grand traveling coach out here."

Beatrice laughed. She liked her cousin. At twenty-eight, he was only two years her senior, so she felt comfortable with him. None of the family stood on ceremony, but Sheridan in particular did not, though that would undoubtedly change. "You'll have a monstrous grand coach yourself now that you're Duke of Armitage."

"Probably not, actually." A bleak sadness crept over his features. "The dukedom is in a bad state, I'm afraid. No money for grand coaches. With any luck, I can improve that, but it will take time. And I wasn't expecting to inherit so soon."

"I know. I'm so sorry. How is Aunt Lydia faring?"

He sighed. "Not well. This has taken us all by

surprise." Shifting his gaze to the wood beyond the expansive lawns, he tensed. "Is . . . um . . . your brother planning on attending the funeral?"

She swallowed. Joshua was difficult, to say the least. "I'm sure he will." That was a lie. She couldn't be sure of anything with him.

But her words seemed to relieve Sheridan. "Good. We don't see as much of him as we'd like."

"*I* wouldn't see him if I didn't live in the same house as he. Joshua isn't fond of people." To put it mildly. Not that she blamed him, given his circumstances, but she'd do her damnedest to convince him that attending the funeral was the least he owed to the new residents of Armitage Hall.

Particularly to Sheridan, his new landlord, who could toss them out of their home, the former dower house, whenever he wished. Especially since Sheridan's mother was now the dowager duchess and might prefer to live in the house that was hers by right.

Beatrice wouldn't think of that. "Is there anything more I can do to help Aunt Lydia?"

"Conjure my half brother Grey up out of thin air?" He shoved a hand through his ash-brown curls. "Sorry."

"I'm sure he'll be here soon."

He uttered a harsh laugh. "I'm not. I can't even be certain that he received Mother's letters.

Sometimes I think my brother has forgotten he even *has* a family. He's too busy being the important Duke of blasted Greycourt."

She didn't know what to say. Though she'd never met the "Duke of blasted Greycourt," she'd read enough in the scandal sheets to know she wouldn't like him. For one thing, he was said to have had several illicit liaisons with women, each more beautiful than the last, and that alone made her wary. It reminded her only too well of Uncle Armie.

"Is it true what they said in the paper?" she asked. "That your brother runs a secret cabal of licentious bachelors?"

"Honestly, I have no idea. Grey tells us nothing of what he's doing. For all I know, he could be running charitable boards in his sleep."

"I doubt that," she muttered, then realizing she was insulting his brother, added hastily, "but the business about the cabal does sound farfetched. Why keep it secret, for one thing? A duke can do whatever he wants with impunity, so why not have a *regular* cabal of debauchery? What's a cabal, anyway? It sounds like a club. Is it a club? I mean—"

It dawned on her that she was babbling as usual. Sheridan was certainly regarding her with amusement.

She should stop. "Anyway, dukes are good at clubs. So it's probably just a club." One that kept the riffraff out. Because dukes were good at that, too.

Especially Greycourt, from what she'd heard. He was richer than God, so he could afford whatever club he wanted. Supposedly, he'd gained his wealth by being ruthless in his business dealings, so he could also destroy whomever he wanted. That might be why society hung on his every word. Or perhaps it was because he rarely spoke without saying something of consequence.

Despite her concern for her aunt, she rather hoped he didn't come. Men like him exasperated her. Not that she met many of them way out here, but the few she'd encountered through Uncle Armie hadn't left a good impression.

Sheridan released a heavy breath. "Anyway, I fear I've dragged you into my annoyance at my brother, which I didn't intend. You've already done so much to help us." He waved vaguely at the windows. "All this. Handling the funeral arrangements. Keeping up with the household ledgers. What would we do without you?"

The praise warmed her. Perhaps Sheridan wouldn't be eager to kick her and Joshua out after all. "Thank you. I like being useful." Especially to her aunt. Aunt Lydia was unlike any woman she'd ever met—full of vim and vigor, with a kind heart and a sharp mind. Rather like Sheridan.

He nodded toward the entryway. "I'd best get

back inside. Mother wanted me to choose the burial suit." His throat moved convulsively. "She says she can't bear to do it."

Poor man. "I can understand that. You're a good son."

"I try to be." He glanced down the drive again, and his face hardened. "Speaking of sons, let me know the moment Grey arrives, will you?"

"Of course."

He started to walk inside, then paused. "One more thing. Mother wanted me to tell you that she intends to continue helping you prepare for your debut. It may just move more slowly."

"Oh!" Beatrice had forgotten about that. "Tell her not to bother with such a thing right now, for pity's sake. I'll be fine."

"Actually, Mother does better when she has a project to throw herself into. And she's appalled that you never had the chance to be brought out properly in society. She intends to remedy that."

"It's very kind of her." Though it was also daunting. Beatrice felt more comfortable roaming the woods with the hunting dogs than roaming a ballroom. She hated having men assess her out-of-season attire, small breasts, and less-than-perfect features before dismissing her as unworthy of their attention.

"Mother is only doing what's right." Sheridan watched her expression with cousinly concern.

"We all know how lax Uncle Armie was in his duty toward you."

"Thank you." If they thought he was only "lax" then it was a good thing they had no idea what her life had truly been like with him.

She held her breath, praying that Sheridan said nothing more about Uncle Armie. When he continued on into the house, she relaxed. Having them all underfoot in the next few weeks might prove more complicated than she'd thought. She hoped that dealing with Uncle Maurice's death kept them too busy to pry into her affairs. And Joshua's. Especially Joshua's, which even she didn't have the courage to examine too closely.

Thrusting that thought to the back of her mind, she took one more look at the exterior of the hall, then went inside. She sent a footman off to cover all the mirrors. That should have been done already, but Armitage Hall was woefully understaffed these days, and it was taking a while to get everything attended to in such a massive house.

Next she turned her attention to the boxes of funeral biscuits delivered by the confectioner that morning. They needed to be laid out on a table in the foyer for the mourners to take as they left to join the funeral procession. She unpacked the boxes and began to arrange the biscuits, each of which was wrapped in white paper printed with images of death and sealed with black wax.

The sight of so many little skulls, coffins, hourglasses, and crossbones arrayed on the table made her shudder . . . and remember. Caught up in memories of being ten years old and devastated at her own father's funeral, she didn't register the sound of footsteps until they were upon her.

"What in God's name are those ghastly things?" thrummed a deep male voice.

She turned to find a stranger standing there, still wearing his greatcoat and hat, with his piercing gaze fixed on the table behind her. This must be the Duke of Greycourt, since his mourning clothes were very fine. She also noticed the family resemblance between him and Sheridan in the aquiline slope of his nose, the color of his eyes—like shattered green bottles—and the height of his brow.

Not to mention his height in general. Although Beatrice was considered tall for a woman, Greycourt must have several inches on her at least. His height and attire and severe features were imposing, and undoubtedly intimidating to most women.

Not her. She was used to dealing with the arrogance of lords.

He shifted his frosty gaze to her. "Well?" he demanded. "What are those?"

"They're funeral biscuits," she said stiffly, put off by his manner. "It's the custom hereabouts to provide them to mourners along with a glass of port."

"Is it, indeed?" he said, removing his costly beaver hat. "Or is it just something the local undertaker uses to plump up his bill for people like my mother? I've never heard of such a custom."

"Oh, well then, if *you've* never heard of the custom, it must not exist," she said, unable to govern her temper. "Anything that doesn't happen in London is insignificant to your sort, isn't it?"

The remark seemed to take him aback, as well it ought, given that she should never have said such a thing to a man who was grieving. Why oh why had she spoken her mind? She usually tried to restrain that impulse, but it was hard when the duke was being such an arse.

Don't use the word "arse," even in your head. Thanks to her brother, that was her other problem: a tendency to curse like a sailor. At least she hadn't cursed aloud.

To her surprise, amusement glinted in his eyes. Which she realized, now that they were fixed on her, weren't green, but a cerulean blue, as if nature had twirled the blue of his mother's eyes with the green of his half brother's to produce an unearthly hue all its own.

It unsettled her. As did the disarming smile Greycourt flashed at her, which softened the

31

sharp angles of his face. "I take it you are not the daughter of the local undertaker that I mistook you for."

This time she *did* resist the urge to rail at him. For pity's sake, an undertaker's daughter? A pox on him! "No, I am not," she said icily.

His smile widened, though it didn't yet reach his eyes. "You're not going to tell me who you are, are you?"

"Clearly you prefer to make your own assumptions." Oh, Lord, there she went again, saying whatever came into her head.

Greycourt chuckled. "So it's to be a guessing game, is it?" His gaze drifted down her in a glance that assessed her attire without making her feel as if he were gawking at her feminine attributes, such as they were. "Well, you're clearly not a servant. No servant would dress so well."

"You're too kind, sir," she said in a voice dripping with sarcasm.

Her tone got a laugh out of him. "Come now, tell me who you are, for I swear I'm at a loss. And I begin to think I'd like to know the answer."

Uh-oh.

At that moment, she was saved by the approach of none other than Sheridan. "Grey!" he cried. "You *did* come! Mother will be so pleased."

Greycourt clapped his half brother on the shoulder with obvious affection. "How is she?"

Sheridan sighed. "She'll be better now that you're here."

Was that guilt that crossed Greycourt's face? If so, it softened her toward him. A little, anyway.

"I would have arrived sooner," he said, "but I was traveling and the letter didn't reach me until yesterday."

Sheridan turned to include Beatrice in the conversation. "You see, Bea? I told you he might have trouble receiving word."

"You did, indeed." That wasn't all Sheridan had told her, but she didn't figure it wise to point it out, even if Greycourt *had* rubbed her wrong.

"I take it you two have met?" Sheridan asked.

"Not formally, no," Greycourt said, shooting her a wry look that flummoxed her.

"Well, then," Sheridan said, "Bea, as you may have deduced, this is my brother Grey."

"Half brother," Greycourt corrected him.

Sheridan scowled. "You just had to make the distinction, didn't you?"

"If I didn't, the lady would be confused. Since you're the heir to the Armitage dukedom, she'd be forced to wonder if I am merely much younger than I look or if I'm illegitimate. I am neither, so I thought it best to clarify."

"Don't worry, sir," Beatrice said with false sweetness. "Not all of us make assumptions without being aware of the facts."

"Really?" Greycourt drawled. "How unusual."

"And if you'd given me time to make the introductions, *Brother*," Sheridan said acidly, "I would have clarified your position to my cousin."

To Beatrice's vast satisfaction, that made Greycourt pale. "Cousin? Child of your uncle Armie?"

"No, his younger brother Lambert. He died years ago."

"I see." Greycourt looked at Beatrice. "Forgive me for my earlier rudeness, Miss Wolfe. I had no idea that Sheridan and Heywood have a cousin."

"Two, actually," Sheridan put in. "Bea's brother is named Joshua." Then he blinked. "Wait, you were rude to Bea?"

"It was nothing," she put in with a forced smile. "His lordship objected to the funeral biscuits, that's all."

Greycourt's eyes gleamed at her. Apparently, it hadn't escaped him that she hadn't actually accepted his apology.

"Ah," Sheridan said, "they're frightful, aren't they? But the undertaker assured us that they're a requirement for any funeral in Sanforth."

"Did he?" Greycourt said, sparing a meaningful glance for her that roused her temper again.

"Trust me," Beatrice said frostily, "if there were no funeral biscuits and port before the procession, the entire county would gossip about the family."

"Yes, all our staff said the same," Sheridan

34

said. "Cook was mortified at the very possibility of our neglecting to offer them. But I still think they're dreadful. Sorry, Bea."

"They *are* dreadful," she conceded, torn between pleasing her cousin and sticking her tongue out at Greycourt. Which would be childish, but enormously satisfying. "We had so many left after Papa's funeral that we and the staff were eating them for months. To this day, I can't abide the taste."

The glint of pity in Greycourt's eyes made her regret having said so much. A decent man might be lurking somewhere deep in there—*very deep*—but she still didn't like his pitying her.

"Speaking of staff," Sheridan said, glancing about the foyer, "where have the footmen gone off to? Poor Grey is still standing here with hat in hand."

"Oh, dear," she said, annoyed with herself for neglecting to call one. No wonder Greycourt thought her a country bumpkin. "I'll take his coat and hat."

Sheridan caught her arm before she could reach for them. "No need. I'll do it." He shot Greycourt a side glance. "Bea has been working dawn to dusk to help us prepare for the funeral. I'm afraid we're rather short-staffed, and she knows more about what's needed than anyone."

"That's very kind of you, Miss Wolfe." Greycourt even sounded as if he meant it.

Perhaps she'd been too hasty to judge him. When he wasn't making assumptions, he wasn't all *that* bad.

A footman rushed into the entry hall. "Forgive me, Your Grace, we were in the back and didn't hear the carriage." He hurried over to take Greycourt's coat and hat. Bobbing his head at Sheridan, he added, "It won't happen again, Your Grace."

"Don't worry about it," Sheridan said genially. "I know everyone has their hands full."

As the footman headed off, Greycourt murmured, "Careful, Sheridan. You're the master here now. You don't want your servants walking all over you. It's important to establish boundaries from the beginning."

And just like that, Beatrice was reminded of why he'd rubbed her wrong. Yes, he was *somewhat* attractive, with his straight white teeth, chiseled features, rumpled black hair, and gorgeous eyes, but he was also a superior arse who thought he owned the world. She was never going to like him.

Never.

Chapter Three

Sheridan said something about going to see their mother, and Grey was willing to follow, especially when Miss Wolfe went along.

Most in society would disapprove of her looks, since she'd clearly never met a ray of sunshine she didn't like, as evidenced by her golden skin and the sprinkle of freckles across her peachy cheeks. The gossips would criticize her bold walk and murmur over her full, sensual lips and coffee-hued eyes, not to mention the thin wisps of straight, nut-brown hair that kept escaping her fat chignon. Straight hair and dark eyes weren't fashionable just now.

But he had never let fashion dictate to him. The idea of trying to unwind that hair to see how far it fell sparked an unwise heat in his blood. Despite himself, her energy did the same, making him wonder how she might use that energy in bed. And when she moved ahead as they headed for the stairs, he didn't mind getting another look at her ample bottom, which would fill a man's hands nicely.

Her turned-up nose just made him want to laugh. She obviously disapproved of him. That wasn't surprising, given his reputation, which wasn't entirely unfounded. He *had* sown his wild oats in his early days of freedom from his aunt and uncle's control.

But that hadn't lasted nearly as long as the reputation he'd gained from it, which was evidenced by Miss Wolfe's reaction. Still, it was usually the matchmaking mamas who despaired of him and not their daughters.

That made him wonder—where was the chit's mother? And why was he not familiar with this branch of the Wolfe family? He supposed that wasn't surprising, given how little he'd seen his family in the past twenty-odd years. Before that, he'd been paying less attention to his stepfather Maurice's relations than to tramping the streets of Berlin with his twin half siblings, Gwyn and the Duke of Thornstock, whom they'd all called Thorn since his birth.

Which reminded him . . . "Where's Gwyn? Has Thorn arrived yet?"

"Last night," Sheridan said. "Fortunately, Thorn was at his London town house when the accident happened, so he was able to get here quickly."

"Accident?" Grey frowned. "Mother only said that Maurice passed away. I assumed it was of some illness."

To his surprise, Sheridan shot Miss Wolfe a veiled glance. "Actually, he drowned, which necessitated the expense of sending to London for an embalmer. But we'll talk more about it later."

Sheridan headed up the stairs behind Miss Wolfe.

After Sheridan's earlier complaint about lack of staff, the remark about the embalmer gave Grey pause. Aware of Miss Wolfe climbing the stairs ahead of them, he lowered his voice. "Are you having a shortage of funds at present?"

"At present?" With a bitter laugh, his brother opened a door and waited for Grey and Miss Wolfe to precede him into the drawing room. "That's something else we'll need to discuss later, too." This time he nodded meaningfully toward the other end of the room.

Grey followed his gaze to find their mother dressed in widow's weeds, with Gwyn sitting beside her in a similar gown of jet bombazine. The two were engrossed in tying black ribbons around sprigs of rosemary. Indeed, the room reeked of rosemary and lavender, both of which were in clear abundance in the vases.

Then Sheridan moved forward, and Grey spotted the coffin. His hands began to tremble, and he shoved them into his coat pockets. Maurice. He couldn't bring himself to approach the body. Not yet.

Instead he turned his attention to his mother and half sister, who were so caught up in their task that they hadn't yet seen him. Mother's eyes looked sunken in her face, her cheeks had a dull cast, and her usual bright smile was absent. He well remembered how Maurice had been able to make her smile even when she was annoyed with him.

Maurice couldn't make her smile today. Grey's throat constricted. Never again.

And yet, when Miss Wolfe went to join the women and asked if they needed help, Mother did smile, though it was a pale imitation of her usual one. "We're almost done," she said, "but thank you. I don't know what we would have done without you, my dear."

That's when she saw Grey. With a choked cry, she jumped up and ran to embrace him. Her familiar smell of starch and lemons made his throat tighten with an emotion he dared not examine too closely. Because behind it lay the pain of his childhood loss, threatening to swamp him.

"I'm so glad you came," she whispered. "I was afraid that—"

"Ah, but I'm here now. You needn't have worried." He brushed a kiss to her red curls before releasing her.

Her *graying* red curls. That reminder of his mother's age hit him hard. Granted, she was only in her early fifties, but how long before they would be here to watch *her* put into the grave? The thought made his heart falter in his chest. He'd had her for so little of his life already.

Then he noticed the tears running down her

40

wan cheeks, and the sight was a punch to his gut. He'd seen his mother cry many times—she was an emotional woman who felt no compunction to hide her feelings, especially if some play or novel moved her. She also laughed, swore, and gushed over her children. It was her way.

But *these* tears didn't stem from her being swept away by a poem. Which was precisely why they twisted his insides. He pressed his handkerchief into her hand. "Mother, I'm so sorry about Maurice."

She bobbed her head, obviously too overcome to answer as she blotted her cheeks with his handkerchief.

"If there's anything I can do—"

"You could call him 'Father' for a change." She fixed him with her misty blue eyes. "It always grieved him that you stopped doing so once you came to England."

Once I was banished *to England, you mean.* No, this wasn't the time for such reminders. And what did it hurt to give her what she asked? It was such a small thing.

Yet it felt huge. "Of course. Whatever you wish."

A sigh escaped her. "Forgive me for being short with you. I am just . . ."

"Grief-stricken. I know." He seized her hand. "You're entitled to be as short as you please."

She raised an eyebrow at him. "I shall throw

41

those words up at you in a week, when you're chafing to be away from me because of my peevishness."

He forced a smile, inwardly groaning at her expectation that he would stay a week. "I've seen you be many things, Mother, but peevish isn't one of them." He spotted his half sister approaching now that she'd finished consulting with Miss Wolfe across the room. "Gwyn is another matter entirely."

Gwyn heard him, as he'd intended. "You'd better not be saying anything bad about me," she chided, "or I will give you grief for taking so long to arrive. I was on the verge of sending Thorn after you, but I feared that the two of you would disappear into the London stews, and we'd never see either of you again."

Ignoring that barb, he bent to press a kiss to her cheek, then scanned the room. "Where *is* Thorn, anyway?"

"There's no telling. You know how he is—good at finding wenches and wine no matter where he travels. No doubt you taught him that skill."

It was a measure of how little time they'd spent together that she still knew naught of his true character. "I did no such thing."

Gwyn surveyed him with a sister's usual skepticism. "Then why did Father always worry that you would lead Thorn astray here in England?"

"I have no idea. Thorn is perfectly capable of leading himself astray, which Mau—*Father* ought to have known. And despite what nonsense you may read in the papers, I'm not Thorn. I don't spend my time in the stews."

"Hmm. Methinks the man doth protest too much."

"Don't quote Shakespeare to him," Mother said plaintively. "Or he'll start mocking me by quoting Fletcher."

"I don't mock you, Mother," he retorted, relieved to change the subject away from his supposed wild nature. "I merely think you're unfairly biased toward our ancestor. Shakespeare is the better playwright, and you know it."

"I know no such thing! Fletcher wrote some of the most engaging, witty plays in the English language. Why, *The Wild Goose Chase* never fails to make me laugh."

"You see what you started, Grey?" Gwyn smiled. "Next thing we know, she'll be acting out the scenes."

"I beg your pardon, Sis," Grey said, "but *you* were the one to start it. I'm just standing here defending myself."

Sheridan came over. "What has Grey done now?"

Mother's irate expression softened. "Nothing. Today he can do no wrong."

A lump stuck in Grey's throat.

"That's good to hear," Sheridan said blandly. "Because I need to steal him for a bit."

Mother tightened her grip on Grey's hand. "Must you? He just arrived."

"I'm afraid I must," Sheridan answered. "But you'll have plenty of time with him later. He's planning on staying at Armitage Hall for a while." He fixed Grey with a hard look. "Aren't you?"

Damn. "I am *now*." Grey narrowed his gaze on his brother. "So tell me, how long am I staying, exactly?"

"We'll discuss that." Sheridan gestured toward the door. "Shall we?"

With a quick squeeze of his mother's hand, Grey said, "I'll be back soon, Mother. Keep a chair warm for me, will you?"

Then he followed his brother out the door and down the hall to what had been Maurice's study when he was alive.

After Grey took a seat, Sheridan went to pour them both some brandy and handed Grey a glass. When Sheridan then stood there staring down into the amber liquor, Grey asked, "Is this about the family finances? Because I'm happy to pay for the funeral and offer you a loan at whatever terms you—"

"It's not about money. Not yet, anyway." Sheridan sipped some brandy, then faced him. "It's about the manner of Father's death."

"By drowning."

Sheridan met his gaze. "Yes. But not an accidental one, I don't think."

"What in God's name do you mean?"

"I believe Father was murdered."

Grey took a healthy swallow of brandy, then another. "And what exactly brought you to *that* conclusion?"

"A few things. First of all, there are the details of his death. He drowned when he apparently fell into the river from the bridge near the dower house—"

"There's a dower house?"

"It's where Bea and her brother Joshua have lived ever since my grandfather died."

Grey had assumed that Miss Wolfe was at the hall only for the funeral, but apparently she was a fixture hereabouts. Odd that he hadn't met her on his two previous visits.

"Where exactly is this dower house?" Grey asked.

"A few miles away, at the other end of the estate. Grandmother and Bea lived there for most of the period when Joshua was serving in the Royal Marines. He's a major, you know. After he was wounded and consequently discharged, Uncle Armie proposed that Joshua reside there and serve as head gamekeeper for the estate. Which he's done for a few years now, since before Grandmother's death."

Grey frowned. "Gamekeeper? A duke's grandson? For God's sake, that is hardly a gentleman's profession."

"I agree, but I gather that his choices were few after his return. It took him some time to recover from his wounds, which left him lame. As a result, he walks with a cane. He has trouble in crowds, and some fear his mind is . . . well . . . disordered. For one thing, he has a vile temper. Indeed, he's prone to violent outbursts."

"War can do that to a man." Then the entirety of Sheridan's remarks registered. "You're not saying you suspect *Joshua Wolfe* of—"

"Yes, I am. I fear that my cousin may have murdered my father."

Chapter Four

The stark words hung in the air, as if the spirit of Maurice himself lingered in the study. Grey shivered before he caught himself. There was no such thing as ghosts, damn it. He set down his brandy glass. "Your *lame* cousin, you mean."

"Hear me out." Grim-faced, Sheridan took the chair next to his. "Father was only on the bridge the night he died because Joshua had summoned him to the dower house. And Father didn't just fall off the bridge; he fell through the railing and into the river. We know this because a large portion of the railing was broken away." He leaned forward. "Now tell me, Grey, what made him fall? It's not as if Father was ever clumsy."

"Well, no, but he *was* getting older, and if it was dark—"

"He was armed with a lantern. And it was a full moon. No reason for him to fall. What's more, the bridge is sturdy, so even if he did somehow stumble into the railing, it should have held under his weight. I believe someone set him up to drown—damaged the bridge before he crossed it and then pushed him through the railing to make it look like an accident. Bad leg or no, Joshua has the muscular arms of a field hand—strong enough to shove an old man into a railing, believe me. Especially if he took that man off guard."

Grey sighed. Clearly, Sheridan's grief had disordered the man's brain. "And why the hell would you suspect Wolfe of such a thing?"

"You're not listening! I told you, Uncle Armie treated Joshua very shabbily—"

"So why didn't Wolfe kill your uncle Armie instead?" Grey pointed out.

With a grimace, Sheridan set down his glass. "That's just it. I think he did that, too."

"For God's sake—"

"Let me finish, blast it!"

Jumping to his feet, Sheridan went to stand behind the desk, its scarred mahogany surface reminding Grey that his half brother had inherited a huge estate with what sounded like a mountain of debt. *That's* what they should be discussing, not this mad idea that Maurice had been murdered.

But Sheridan didn't seem to care about anything else. "Uncle Armie died in an accident that also took place late at night. He was found with a broken neck early in the morning near his precious 'ruins.' Those at the tavern in town said he'd been drinking there the night before and had headed home late. It was the same route he always took and his horse stood grazing nearby. So we assume he somehow tumbled from his horse. It was only a few months ago. Don't you think those two 'accidents' occurred awfully close together?"

That *was* a bit odd, Grey had to admit. Still . . . "Coincidences do happen." After draining the rest of his brandy, he stood and walked over to pour himself more. "Correct me if I'm wrong, but didn't you once tell me that whenever he rode into town he got foxed?"

Just as Grey would have to do to endure this exercise in daft theories. He downed some brandy.

Sheridan shot him a black look. "Yes, Uncle Armie was often drunker than an Etonian after matriculation. But he'd been drinking and riding that road—at night, alone—for twenty years or more. Yet he'd never before fallen off his horse. And even you must admit it wouldn't take much to unseat a drunk man and break his neck."

"So what are you saying?" Grey roamed the study restlessly. "According to you, Wolfe killed your uncle out of resentment for how the family had treated him. Did Maurice also treat him badly?"

"No, of course not."

"Then your suspicions make no sense. Why now? Your uncle Armie treated Wolfe badly for years, so what brought this on?"

"Perhaps Joshua got tired of serving the family like, well, a bloody servant. Perhaps he'd had enough of Uncle Armie's excesses, which were

49

driving the estate into the ground. He figured he could gain the dukedom for himself."

God, but the man *had* lost his mind. "To do that, he'd also have to kill you and Heywood."

"Exactly." Sheridan crossed his arms over his chest. "That's what worries me."

Grey gestured to him with his brandy glass. "What worries *me* is the possibility that you've gone mad."

Sheridan rounded the desk. "You haven't seen how Joshua's behaving. He hasn't once come over here to pay his respects to Mother. And he didn't pay his respects to Father after Uncle Armie died, either."

"Perhaps he doesn't particularly enjoy the company of others," Grey muttered. Especially in such situations.

He thought back to his uncle Eustace's death, and how little he'd wanted to be involved in the arrangements. Grey had been damned glad to see the arse in the grave, where he could no longer torment anyone, could no longer lock a child in a room without food for days to force him to sign—

Grey pushed away the dark memories. "People grieve differently." Particularly when they loath and despise the deceased. "Have you talked to Wolfe about this?"

"No," Sheridan said, a bit sheepishly. "I need evidence. I can't . . . pursue my suspicions without it."

"Exactly." Grey stared his brother down.

"Come now, Grey. Two deaths, so close together? Don't you find that odd?"

When Sheridan set his shoulders, the way he'd done as a boy when he was being stubborn, Grey wished he could pound some sense into him. "And what does Wolfe's sister think of all this? Is Bea complicit in this scheme?"

Sheridan muttered a curse. "Don't be absurd. Of course she's not complicit. Bea would never countenance murder. She's the kindest, most compassionate woman I know."

"We *are* talking about the same woman, right? Because the Miss Wolfe *I* met wasn't kind."

Sheridan scowled. "What exactly occurred between you and Bea while you were alone together?"

"She put me in my place after I . . . um . . . behaved like a pompous arse."

One corner of Sheridan's lips quirked up. "Fancy that—you behaving like a pompous arse."

"At least I'm not seeing murderers at every turn. And if you're so convinced someone murdered Maurice, why didn't you call the constable to investigate his death?"

"I told you. I have no proof. Just my suspicions."

Grey lifted his eyes heavenward. "Which, forgive me, sound daft."

"You might think differently once you've

met Joshua." Sheridan shoved his hands in his pockets. "He's difficult. Angry. Changed, by all accounts, after his experiences in the war. I wouldn't put anything past him, including killing four people to gain the dukedom."

"Well, I'll have to trust you on that," he said dryly, "since I didn't even know of his existence—or his sister's—until today."

Sheridan rubbed the back of his neck. "I should have introduced both of them to you when you visited here before. But we had so little time with you that we wanted to keep you to ourselves. And honestly, that was before Mother decided to take Bea on as one of her projects."

"Oh, God."

Mother was famous for her projects. She liked "helping" young people. Even as a boy, Grey remembered strange youths trooping in and out of their home while Mother tried to figure out how to improve their future prospects.

As if she hadn't had her hands full with her own children. Well, except for the one she sent away. "So what exactly is she trying to do for Miss Wolfe?"

Sheridan shrugged. "Bea has never had a come-out. Grandmother was too sickly to accomplish it, and Uncle Armie too lax. I think the idea was that Bea would eventually become a companion to Uncle Armie's wife, but by the time Bea was the right age, his wife was dead. It's not as if *he* could have brought her out without asking some female relation to do so."

"And why didn't he?"

"God, who knows? He wasn't a nice man, from what I understand. And money was short, so . . ."

"So Miss Wolfe and her prospects got shoved to the side."

"Exactly." Sheridan stared down into his glass. "One more reason for Joshua to hate us."

"Why 'us'? Obviously *you* have no desire to hold her back."

A faint smile crossed his lips. "True."

Something about that smile irked him. "You're not interested in her, are you? Romantically, I mean."

"What? No! Don't be an arse. She's my cousin!"

"Cousins marry in our circles all the time."

His brother went on the defensive. "Are you interested in Vanessa 'romantically'?"

Vanessa? Grey scowled at his brother. "She's Miss Pryde to you, and no, I'm not. She's like a sister to me."

"I feel the same about Bea. We see her as part of the family. That's why Mother is determined to bring her out herself. Even if Bea is a bit . . . shall we say . . . long in the tooth."

"How old is she?"

"Twenty-six."

"She looks younger." Still, Grey didn't mind

her being closer to his age than he'd initially thought, a reaction he refused to examine too closely.

"Nonetheless," Sheridan said, "she's firmly on the shelf."

"What a ridiculous notion. As if a woman were a knickknack to be put away."

Sheridan gaped at him. "I'm surprised you feel that way."

"Don't *you?*"

"Of course, but . . . I just thought . . . that is . . ."

"You believe all the nonsense they publish about me in the gossip rags." He hadn't meant to say the resentful words, but he couldn't help it. "You should know me better by now. You're my brother, for God's sake."

"A fact which you often conveniently forget."

Grey dragged in a heavy breath. "I don't forget it. I just . . ." No, he wouldn't go into that. It wasn't Sheridan's fault that Uncle Eustace had been a greedy bastard. "So Mother means to bring Miss Wolfe out. You know she can't do it while they're in mourning."

"Of course not. But that's one reason she wants to work on preparing her now. They have all this time at the estate when they can't do anything social." Pain flashed over Sheridan's face. "And Mother needs something to keep her mind off losing Father."

"What she needs is time alone to grieve."

Sheridan grimaced. "I've told her that, but you know Mother. She does better when she has something to occupy her time. And she might *need* a whole year to prepare Bea, who hasn't the slightest idea of how to act in social situations. She's a bit of a hoyden, you know. She roams the estate with the hunting dogs and helps Joshua with his accounts, but she rarely attends the local assemblies. Not that it's her fault. She gets invited, but there's no one to take her, and of course, she can't go alone."

"Why doesn't her damned brother take her?"

"You'll have to ask her. But the upshot of it is she barely knows how to dance, has no idea about the many rules of high society, and would rather train a retriever to fetch than embroider a scarf. Mother has her work cut out for her."

"Miss Wolfe seems to have handled the funeral arrangements well enough."

Sheridan snorted. "That's because she's already attended five other funerals in her lifetime, three of which she had a hand in managing. She does know funerals, our Bea."

Poor woman. That sounded dreadful. "No wonder she and Mother get along so well." Grey mused a moment. "So I assume Mother intends for her to be presented at court."

"Probably. You'd know better than I what's involved in bringing a woman out. I gather Bea has to go through a round of social events. Since

Gwyn hasn't had a come-out in England either, Mother plans for them to have their debuts together."

"Makes sense." Grey cocked his head. "How does Gwyn feel about sharing hers with someone not actually related to her?"

"She's relieved to have the company, believe it or not. She'd never admit it, but she's nervous about going into English society. Things weren't the same in Prussia."

"I can only imagine. And I mean that literally, since I was never old enough in Berlin to go into society." When Sheridan shot him an odd look, he pressed on. "How does Wolfe feel about his sister being championed by our mother?"

"I don't know. He's slippery as an eel, that one. He's never around when I go to call on him. Bea keeps saying she'll bring him over, but then that always falls through for some reason." Sheridan drained his glass, then set it on the desk. "That's why I need your help."

Grey tensed. "To do what?"

"Find out what Joshua's been up to, where he goes all the time." Sheridan thrust out his jaw. "Get the evidence I need to prove—or disprove— he was involved in the two deaths. See if you can uncover the truth."

God help him. "Are you asking me to spy on the major?"

"Pretty much."

"Why me?"

Sheridan shrugged. "He doesn't know you, for one thing."

"But it wouldn't take long for him to find out who I am. The minute I start sniffing around, asking questions of people, word will get back to him, and he'll make it his business to learn my identity. If you're trying to keep this secret from him, that's not how to do it."

"So what the devil do *you* suggest? Between helping with Mother's 'project' and trying to get the estate affairs in order, I barely have time to breathe, much less spy on Joshua."

"Ah, but you'd be better at the spying than I," Grey said, "since you could disguise it as getting comfortable with the running of your estate. And the owner asking questions in town about his employees won't seem nearly as odd as some relation of yours doing it." He set down his empty glass. "I can help you with the estate. I can help Mother with preparing Miss Wolfe and Gwyn for a debut. As you said, I know what such things entail. So I'd be better at it, since I've actually been to a few coming-out events. I was very much present at Vanessa's, for example."

"So you're the one responsible for your cousin's impudent manner and sharp tongue, are you?" Sheridan asked.

"Are you responsible for Gwyn's?"

Sheridan glared at him.

"That's what I thought," Grey said calmly. "The point is I don't mind working with you on estate finances and management, and I don't mind giving the young ladies pointers on societal expectations. I don't even mind finding out what I can from Miss Wolfe for you, while helping her prepare for her debut. But I won't spy on her brother. You'll have to tackle that yourself."

Sheridan set his shoulders. "I don't think it's a good idea that you help prepare Bea for her debut. You have a reputation with young women, and she's in a vulnerable situation."

"My reputation is precisely why I should be the one to caution the ladies. I know what men in society expect. And how they should be thwarted. Whereas you—"

"—have barely been to a ball, I know." Sheridan blew out an exasperated breath. "You do have a point."

"Anyway, I'm not giving you a choice. If you want my help, it's going to be in an area where I have expertise."

Honestly, involvement in such a project might make this visit with his family more bearable. Mother wasn't the only one needing something to keep her mind off Maurice's passing.

"So, are we agreed on the division of labor?" Grey asked.

A muscle worked in Sheridan's jaw. But after a moment's hesitation, he nodded.

Then Sheridan went to refill their glasses. "We should seal our bargain with a toast." He returned to hand Grey his glass. "You know, I begin to be glad you'll be helping me with estate matters. Clearly, you're a shrewd negotiator."

"Not for nothing have I tripled my dukedom's income in the past thirteen years."

"Well, if you can help me do that, too, I'd be most grateful." His brother paused to gaze out the window at the dusk graying his land. "But somehow I fear that the Armitage legacy has fallen too far for that."

"You'd be surprised what a bit of judicious investment and wise management can do to one's properties."

"We'll see." With a forced smile, Sheridan raised his glass. "To spying!"

"And to debuts," Grey added.

Before they could drink any, the door opened and Thorn sauntered in.

With his chestnut hair and clear blue eyes, Thorn looked more like Mother than either Grey or Sheridan. But the resemblance stopped there. Thorn was far more of a rebel than Mother had ever been.

Thorn took in the scene, then went over to pour himself a glass. "What are we drinking to?" he drawled.

Grey exchanged a glance with Sheridan and said, "To brothers."

59

"I'll drink to that." Thorn paused. "I forgot, I'm supposed to be corralling everyone for dinner."

"Surely that can wait long enough for you to have a glass," Sheridan said.

"True. And I can use a drink after today." Thorn joined them as they toasted each other. Then he tossed back his brandy in one long gulp.

"Damn it, man, pace yourself," Sheridan said.

Grey laughed. "You probably don't realize this, but Thorn can drink all of us under the table. Eh, Thorn?"

The man winked. "I do my best. Now, bottoms up, lads. If we arrive late to dinner, Mother will blame me, and I refuse to be demoted from my position as favored son."

That devolved into the usual jocular discussion of who was Mother's favorite, a game Grey rarely enjoyed, since he was decidedly *not*. But he played along until the brandy in their glasses was gone, at which time they headed off to dinner.

"Wait," Grey asked Thorn, "who will sit vigil while we're dining?"

"One of the servants." Thorn's expression turned grim. "But I'm sure he won't be there long. Mother has been loath to leave Father's side today. She's determined to be in that bloody room until the funeral procession."

Thorn's reference to Maurice as "Father" jarred Grey, though it was no different from how Thorn

60

usually referred to their stepfather. Thorn and Gwyn's father had died shortly before they were born, so Maurice had been the only father the twins had ever known, too.

"But now that you're here, Grey," Thorn went on, "you can coax Mother into attempting to get some sleep tonight."

"Given that you're the favorite," Grey joked, hollowly, "she's more likely to listen to you."

Thorn laughed outright. "How do you think I *became* the favorite? By indulging her whims. Whereas she sees *you* as the personification of her first husband, who, from what I gather, ordered her about all the time. So she'll listen when *you* order her about."

That made him want to howl. Because he didn't want to be that man. But it was too late to change anyone's perception of him, so he'd play the role as usual.

After all, *someone* had to take charge of his unruly family. It might as well be him.

Chapter Five

Dinner at Armitage Hall was more informal than it had been under Uncle Armie. Not that Beatrice had dined here that often when he was in charge. Even when she and her brother had been invited, Joshua had refused to attend, and she hadn't been about to have any tête-à-têtes with Uncle Armie.

But dining with Aunt Lydia's family reminded her of the time years ago when her grandparents had both been alive and she'd lived at the hall, after Papa's death. At ten, she'd been too young to live alone, especially with Joshua in the Royal Marines abroad. So she had lived here with her grandparents.

For a child, the dining room had been a magical place of glittering chandeliers, gleaming silver, and snowy tablecloths. Every time Grandmama had brought her down from the nursery to practice her dinner etiquette, she'd felt like a princess sitting at this table.

Unfortunately, teaching her the rudiments of polite dining had been about all Grandmama had managed before Grandpapa had died and Grandmama had fallen ill. But at least Beatrice knew precisely what fork to use for the cucumber salad and how to dip one's spoon in the turtle soup properly. Thank heaven. Because given how Greycourt kept staring at her, he was just waiting for her to fail at it, the arrogant devil.

Tipping up her chin, she met his gaze and dipped her spoon with perfect form. As if he'd guessed precisely what she was up to, a knowing smile crept over his face.

Blast. That was an unexpected effect of challenging him. Best not to look at him at all, because every time she did, she got this odd sinking in her belly. It was the way she felt when bolting down a hill with the dogs—terrified and exhilarated at the same time.

She didn't need to feel that with *him,* of all people. With any luck, he would leave the day after the funeral, and she'd never have to see him again.

So she turned her attention to the humorous story the Duke of Thornstock was telling. It seemed a bit salacious for mixed company, but since Aunt Lydia didn't seem to mind, it was fine with Beatrice.

Although not quite as tall as Greycourt, Thornstock was the more conventionally handsome. His features were more symmetrical, his smile more polished, and his nose more perfect. His straight locks were reddish-brown rather than the inky hue of Greycourt's wavy hair, and his eyes were a pure, crystalline blue.

Worse yet, he turned on the charm all too easily.

After Uncle Armie, men like that always put her on her guard.

"So, Miss Wolfe," Thornstock said amiably, "I assume we'll see you at the funeral tomorrow."

"Of course not. It isn't allowed."

Both Thornstock and Lady Gwyn were surprised. "What do you mean?" Lady Gwyn asked. "This is your uncle's funeral!"

Aunt Lydia put down her spoon to regard her daughter with a steady gaze. "Women here do not attend funerals *or* join the procession, my dear."

"Since when?" Thornstock asked.

Beatrice cleared her throat. "Since forever. It's always been frowned upon."

"How absurd! And hardly fair." Lady Gwyn shifted her gaze to her mother. "But you're going anyway, aren't you?"

Aunt Lydia sighed. "I see no point in giving rise to gossip locally. England is now our home, and we have to adapt to its customs."

"Well, *I'm* going," Lady Gwyn announced. "They can't stop me."

"Good for you," Thornstock said. "Sounds like a stupid custom to me."

"Every English custom sounds stupid to you, Thorn." Greycourt looked at Gwyn. "Do you promise not to cry at the funeral?"

She blinked. "What do you mean?"

"That's why women aren't allowed. Because

it's believed that they show too much emotion in public, when they ought to be stoic."

"Then Mother definitely mustn't go," Sheridan muttered into his soup, having wisely stayed out of the conversation until now.

"Sheridan!" Aunt Lydia said.

"Well, it's true. You haven't been stoic a day in your life. Indeed, you have a tendency to be rather . . . dramatic at times."

His mother glared at him. "I can't help it. My ancestor was a playwright."

"And you never let us forget it," Thornstock said, though with unmistakable fondness. He grinned slyly at Beatrice. "You may have noticed, Miss Wolfe, that all of us are named after dramatists."

Beatrice hadn't noticed, actually. She ran through their Christian names in her head: Thornstock's was Marlowe, Greycourt's was Fletcher, and then there were Sheridan and Heywood. All playwrights, yes. How odd.

Then something occurred to her. "But not Lady Gwyn, right?"

"I am named after an actress," Lady Gwyn said in an arch tone. "There aren't enough female playwrights of renown, and Mother could hardly name me Inchbald or Behn, so she chose to name me after Nell Gwyn. Thankfully, everyone assumes that Gwyn was taken from some Welsh ancestor of ours."

"Nell Gwyn was one of the most famous

actresses of her age," her mother said with a sniff. "It's nothing to be embarrassed about."

"Poor Nelly was also a 'famous' mistress of Charles II, Mother," Greycourt said dryly. "The Prince of Wales even owns a portrait of her in which she is wholly nude."

His mother eyed him suspiciously. "How do *you* know?"

He shrugged. "I've seen it." When she gasped, he added, "At a royal function. And my point is, I don't blame our Gwyn for wanting to hide who her namesake is."

Neither did Beatrice. She couldn't imagine having the origins of such a name become known. And here she'd always thought Papa mad for naming her after Dante's one true love. At least her namesake had been virtuous. Only imagine what sly jokes Uncle Armie would have made if she'd actually been named after a loose-living actress.

Greycourt turned to his sister. "If Mother isn't going to the funeral, Gwyn, then you're certainly not going. She needs someone with her."

Lady Gwyn frowned at him. "Bea will be here."

"That's not the same, and you know it."

"Don't insult Bea," Lady Gwyn protested.

"I'm not insulting anyone," Greycourt said. "But Miss Wolfe hasn't spent the years with Mother that you have. Mother would benefit from having you *both* here."

"Listen to your brother." Aunt Lydia reached over to grab her daughter's hand. "I'd like to have you with me." She shot Beatrice a fond glance. "And Bea, of course."

Lady Gwyn huffed out a breath. "If I must. But I still think it's wrong that I can't attend Father's funeral just because I'm a woman. For all intents and purposes, he *was* my father. So I have the right to grieve as much as Thorn or Grey or even Sheridan does."

"I agree," Greycourt said, to Beatrice's surprise. "There are any number of society's rules I find wrong. But if you are to have a successful debut, you'll have to follow some of them. At least until you can catch a husband." He smiled at Beatrice. "You too, Miss Wolfe."

While she was wondering at that odd remark, Sheridan said, "This is probably as good a time as any to announce that Grey will be staying a few weeks so he can help Mother prepare Gwyn and Bea for their debuts."

"The devil he will!" Lady Gwyn cried.

She'd taken the words out of Beatrice's mouth. The very thought of the lofty Duke of Greycourt advising her on such matters made her heart falter.

"What? Don't you want me around, Gwyn?" Greycourt asked with an odd note in his voice.

"Why would I?" Lady Gwyn shot back. "You can be very dictatorial. Mother will tell us everything we need to know."

"My dear," Aunt Lydia said, "I haven't been in English society in nearly thirty years. Things change. And I didn't actually ever have a debut." Her face clouded over. "Grey's father and I met through family."

Bea looked at Greycourt, whose expression turned suddenly grim.

"In any case," the duchess went on, "men know things that it would behoove a woman to know, too. I refuse to see my daughter and niece head into society without a full awareness of its workings. And it wouldn't hurt to have a man around who can stand in for dances."

Beatrice swallowed as an image of her stumbling through a dance with Greycourt leapt into her mind.

"Why can't Sheridan do it?" Lady Gwyn asked.

With a glance at Greycourt, Sheridan said, "First of all, Sis, I need to focus on learning how to manage the estate. Second, I don't know enough about debuts to instruct anyone, whereas Grey has been moving in society for years and was even involved in his cousin Vanessa's coming out. Between him and Mother, you and Bea should have no trouble making a splash in society."

"I don't want to make a splash in society," Beatrice blurted out. When everyone's gazes shot to her, she blushed. Still, she soldiered on. "I merely want to find a suitable husband."

So she could secure her future, and in the

process, perhaps secure Joshua's. Clearly, *he* wasn't going to make any attempt in that direction.

"I'm afraid those two go hand in hand these days, Miss Wolfe," Greycourt said softly.

"Even for a woman with no dowry and a father who died in a duel?" she snapped. "I daresay I'd be better off playing by the rules in hopes that some vicar or physician in need of a circumspect wife notices me. At least *that* sort of husband probably won't die scandalously and leave me destitute the way Papa did."

Everyone gaped at her. Then they swiveled to look at Greycourt to see what he would say. Blast it, why did he bring out the worst in her? She'd spent years teaching herself *not* to speak her mind, yet when she was around him, things just came out.

She dropped her gaze to the table. "Forgive me, Your Grace. I didn't mean to—"

"First rule," he said, a thread of amusement in his tone, "don't apologize. For *anything*. You're a duke's granddaughter. You must walk into every room as if that duel was a single faux pas in a line of virtuous deeds. And why was it scandalous, anyway? If it was a matter of honor—"

"I think it was more a matter of *dis*honor," she said dryly, "although Grandmama wouldn't confirm that." Beatrice had heard it was fought over a mistress, but she wasn't about to tell the lofty Greycourt *that*. "No one liked to talk about it."

"So it happened years ago, right?"

"Sixteen years, actually," Beatrice said.

"Perfect. No one will remember. Hell, I had no idea of it."

"Fletcher Pryde!" his mother exclaimed. "You won't be of any use to Gwyn and Bea if you use profanity in social situations."

Rather than murmuring his apologies the way Bea would, Greycourt laughed. "Mother, you haven't been in society much in the past few years, have you? We're at war. Gentlemen are scarce, and officers aren't always nice with their language."

Aunt Lydia turned to Thornstock. "Is that true?"

Thornstock snorted. "I wouldn't know. To be honest, I avoid good society as if my life depended on it. Which it often does."

Alarm filled his mother's face. "What does *that* mean?"

"You don't want to know, trust me," Greycourt said, casting his half brother a quelling glance.

But Beatrice wanted to know. She found everything about Aunt Lydia and her children fascinating. They were all so . . . so *blunt* and unapologetic. She'd never met anyone like them.

Well, except Joshua. But he didn't speak his mind in *their* entertaining fashion. For that matter, neither did she.

"It will all be fine, Mother," Greycourt went on. "You'll see. And Sheridan has his hands full right now. As for Thorn—"

"There is no way in bloody hell I'll be teaching anyone about how society works," the man cut in. "And yes, Mother, 'bloody hell' is definitely unacceptable language for society."

"Or for anywhere," Lady Gwyn chided her brother. "Even *I* know that."

Thornstock shrugged. "All the more reason for Grey to take charge of this nonsense."

Aunt Lydia sighed. "I shall leave it to you boys to sort things out as to who does what. I'm sure you know what you're doing." She looked at Beatrice. "That reminds me, my dear—you *have* spoken to Joshua about approving our scheme, have you not?"

Caught off guard, Beatrice said, "Of course."

Liar. She needed to do so, although she dreaded it, not knowing how he might react. Still, she would give him the rough side of her tongue if he refused to allow it. She might struggle not to speak her mind around other people, but she never fought her impulses around Joshua. If ever a man required frank speech, it was her brother.

Aunt Lydia smiled. "Because I wouldn't wish to do anything without his say-so. We're still mostly strangers to him, and I don't want him thinking we've overstepped our bounds."

"I understand," Beatrice said.

Oh, yes, she understood only too well. Women never got to make these decisions for themselves. They were at the mercy of their brothers, fathers, and husbands.

It wasn't *fair*. She and Lady Gwyn were certainly in agreement on *that*.

Her aunt rose. "Now, if you don't mind, I must return to the drawing room."

The men stood, too, and Sheridan rounded the table to his mother's side. "I'll go with you."

But before they could leave, Greycourt spoke to his mother. "Promise me you'll get a good night's sleep. Even if you're not attending the funeral, tomorrow will be taxing, and you need your rest."

"If you wish it, Grey." Aunt Lydia gave him a melting smile. "Thank you for coming, my son."

Some unreadable emotion flickered in his eyes. "Of course. Where else would I be?"

That broadened her smile.

"I'll join you in a moment," he added. "As soon as I finish dessert."

"That would be lovely, thank you," she said.

The moment Aunt Lydia and Sheridan left, Greycourt sat down to fix his gaze on Beatrice. "I have a favor to ask of you. I know your brother didn't attend your other uncle's funeral. So please make sure he attends my stepfather's tomorrow."

The urgency in his voice startled her. As did his use of the word "please." "O-of course he will attend."

"Good. Because it's important that he do so."

There was something he wasn't saying. She desperately wished she knew what it was. But the twins were exchanging bewildered glances, and his enigmatic expression gave no indication of what it might be.

"I will do my best to make sure that Joshua shows up here promptly for the funeral procession," Beatrice said.

"Excellent." Grey finished his wine. "Thank you."

Somehow that roused her suspicions even more. "May I ask *why* it's so important?"

He rubbed his finger along the rim of his glass. "Mother will be hurt if he doesn't attend. And I don't wish to add more sorrow to her present situation."

Her heart twisted in her chest. "Of course not," she said hastily. "Neither do I."

Lord, she hoped that was Grey's only motivation. The last thing she and Joshua needed was a duke breathing down their necks to learn all their secrets, a duke who clearly was very good at sifting out truth from lies.

She could only hope she was reading too much into his reactions. Otherwise, she and her brother were, at best, about to end up cast into the street, with no one around to help them.

And she'd do anything to prevent that.

Chapter Six

The day after the funeral, Beatrice hurried up the hill to the kennels where she hoped to find Joshua. Unfortunately, she could no longer put off discussing her impending debut with him.

Fortunately, the funeral had gone according to plan yesterday. Judging from the compliments Beatrice had received from the male servants in attendance, everything had met with the family's approval. Not to mention, the townsfolk's. The liberal pouring of port for the mourners hadn't gone unnoticed. The Wolfe family's generosity had mightily impressed the locals who hadn't been fond of Uncle Armie and his skinflint lack of support for the town.

That might also ease how Sanforth's citizens regarded her and Joshua, who were both presently seen as somewhat freakish—her because of her tomboy ways and Joshua because of his erratic behavior and his bad leg. If the town accepted their relatives, and their relatives accepted her and Joshua, then the town might actually change its opinion about her and Joshua, too.

She could only hope so, since she feared that despite her aunt's efforts, she was well on her way to becoming a spinster. Especially if Joshua refused to allow her aunt to give her a come-out.

Oh, but she would give him what for if he balked. Just see if she didn't.

Emboldened by that thought, she entered the empty yard that adjoined the kennels, a limestone structure at the other end. The yard, too, was surrounded by limestone—high walls meant to keep the hounds in when they were dashing about.

At once she spotted her brother leaning on his cane and speaking to the Master of the Hounds, Mr. MacTilly. She closed the gate behind her, so no dogs could escape.

When Mr. MacTilly saw her coming, he halted his conversation to tip his hat to her. "A good day to ye, miss. Come to take some of the wee beasties for a walk, are you?"

"That . . . and to speak to my brother."

Joshua swiveled to face her, his weathered face wrought in a frown. "What about?"

"And a cheery good morning to *you,* too," she said acidly. "You must have risen quite early. *If* you came home last night at all." When Joshua's frown deepened, she cast Mr. MacTilly a meaningful glance, who hastily said, "I'll go gather the hounds most in need of exercise," before hurrying off into the building itself.

"What do you want, Beatrice?" Joshua asked.

"Aside from desiring to know where you were last night that had you coming in so late I never saw you?"

His face closed up. "I had things to attend to in Leicester."

Leicester was three hours away by post. He'd been making frequent trips there in the past few months, for no reason she could see. "Oh, and what might those things be?"

"None of your concern."

"Joshua—"

"I don't have time for one of your inquisitions!" When she stiffened, he rubbed his hand over his face. "Just tell me what you need, all right? So I can get on with my work."

What she needed was to hear why he'd been disappearing to Leicester for several nights in the past year, but she'd asked before, and "none of your concern" or something of that ilk was all he ever said. She would worry he spent the time drinking in one of the taverns, except that he never smelled of spirits and there were taverns in Sanforth he could go to more easily. So what was he up to that required such secrecy?

It didn't matter. That wasn't why she was here, anyway. Let him keep his secrets, as long as they didn't involve her. "I need to talk to you about something concerning our aunt and cousins."

He muttered an oath. "I went to the funeral as you demanded, even though you know I'd rather bite off my tongue than go to such an affair. So, in my estimation, I've more than met my obligations to our relations."

Egad, sometimes the man was so testy it made her insane. "Well, just barely, since you didn't even come back to the house after the funeral to speak to my aunt or the other ladies." When he bristled, she added hastily, "But don't get your dander up. I'm not asking you to do anything more for *them*." She thrust her hands behind her back to hide how her fingers were already forming fists. "I merely need to inform you of something they're planning to do for *me*. Unless the gentlemen already mentioned it yesterday?"

His frown vanished. "No, no one mentioned anything. Thankfully, they spoke to me very little."

"I can't imagine why," she said dryly. "You're always so amiable in company."

To her surprise, he laughed, which was rare enough that it heartened her. Perhaps this would go better than she'd feared.

"Anyway," she went on, forcing some softness into her voice, "Aunt Lydia wishes to help me have a come-out. Along with Lady Gwyn."

His amusement vanished as myriad other emotions washed his face, none of them readable, even to her. "A come-out," he said dully. "In London society."

"Of course, 'in London society.' Where else would it be? It's hardly considered a come-out if I show up at an assembly in Sanforth, not that I ever could, since you won't accompany me."

"Your precious aunt Lydia could accompany you," he said snidely. "Or even that Lady Gwyn woman, now that they both live at Armitage Hall."

She stepped close to hiss, "Before long, they may be living in *our* house, and we may be living in the street. Once Sheridan takes a wife, he might wish to move Aunt Lydia into the dower house. And then where will we be?"

Looking away, he rubbed his hand over his stubbled chin.

"At least *I* am trying to endear myself to them," she went on. "Not that it's any great trial. They're nice people. They treat me like family. And they don't go hieing off to places at any hour of the night to do Lord knows what without a word to anyone. Nor do they expect their sisters to hang about for years, futilely hoping for some . . . some future beyond—"

"Enough, Beatrice." A muscle flexed in his jaw. "If you want a come-out, have one. I'll see if I can't . . . scrape together some funds."

"You don't need to. My aunt says she can afford to pay for mine since Thornstock is paying for his twin's. Indeed, both Aunt Lydia and Lady Gwyn seem eager to help me gain a husband."

"Which is all you want, isn't it?" he said bitterly. "To get away from me."

Of *course* he would see it like that. "I want to have a *life,* blast it! Yes, I want a husband and children to love and a home of my own that I can be sure won't be pulled out from under me! Is that so unreasonable?"

He gaped at her, clearly thrown off by her fervent expression of her true desires, which she did try to hide around him, because she never knew what might set him off.

"It's not unreasonable," he finally said, tightening his hand on the head of his cane. "I just wish you would find a husband *here,* in town."

"Yes, because there are so many young men around with a war on."

The minute he went rigid she regretted mentioning the war. "Right," he snapped. "All those men off serving their country while I hobble around here—" He caught himself. "Forgive me. I'm merely . . . annoyed that I can't be the one to help you gain what you want. To ensure you have a proper debut."

That stuck a pin in the balloon of her anger. "Oh, Joshua. I know where your heart is. I do." She couldn't resist lifting a hand to stroke his cheek. When he shied away from the affectionate gesture, she stifled a sigh and dropped her hand. "And it's not as if you could do it on your own, anyway. I must have a woman present me. It's really very kind of our aunt to offer."

"Very kind, indeed," he bit out. "That lot is nothing if not 'kind.' "

The way he said it gave her pause. "What is *that* supposed to mean? You've barely spent time with our aunt, you ignore Sheridan, and you haven't even met Lady Gwyn."

"None of them has ever given a . . . bloody damn about what happens to you until now, and suddenly they show up offering you a debut in good society? Mark my words, they have some ulterior motive."

"I'll take that chance."

Somehow she had to get her and Joshua out of this place, find somewhere more secure, where he could flourish . . . where *she* could flourish. Because right now they were dying a slow, miserable death amid the debris of Papa's scandalous actions and Joshua's deep wounds.

She was so sick of it. "Are you saying you won't approve the scheme?"

The bleak anger in his hazel eyes made her want to cry. To her surprise, he said, "Of course I'll approve it."

She threw her arms about his neck, unable to keep from touching him. "Oh, thank you, thank you! You're the best brother ever!"

Though he stiffened a bit, he didn't push her away as he usually did. But he did say gruffly, "It isn't as if you're giving me much of a choice."

She hugged him close. "I always give you a choice, Brother. As long as you make the right one."

When she drew back, he was actually smiling. "I swear, duckie, you are growing up too fast."

He hadn't called her "duckie" in an age. "In case you hadn't noticed, I'm not only fully grown but rapidly approaching spinsterhood."

"Nonsense. Any man with eyes can see you're a diamond of the first water."

"A diamond in the rough, perhaps," she quipped. "And apparently, only blind men live around here."

"Except our cousins, right?" Before she could answer, he added, "Very well, go on out into the great, wide world. I shan't stop you."

"You could accompany us to London," she said on a breath. "I'm sure our aunt wouldn't mind. And you deserve to be out in society, too."

He scowled. "There is no way in hell I'm going near that cesspool. And trust me, no one wants me there, poking at all their pretensions." He shoved his free hand in his coat pocket. "You go and enjoy yourself. You'll have more fun without me. Just . . . well, I hope you'll return here occasionally once you've taken some fine fellow for a husband."

"I'll be here so often you'll be sick of me," she said.

Still, she earnestly hoped that her "fine fellow" of a husband could help her discover a better post for her brother. One that made use of his education and experience and banished the sorrow in his eyes.

Because he deserved better. And by God, so did she.

Grey stood outside the gate to the kennel, noting the sounds of dogs barking as Miss Wolfe greeted each by name. He hadn't meant to eavesdrop on her and her brother. He'd come looking for her partly out of restlessness and partly out of a desire to get started on Sheridan's damned assignment.

But then he'd overheard them arguing and had figured he might as well find out what he could, if only to pacify Sheridan. Grey had met Wolfe at the funeral, but he'd only had the chance to notice a few things. Wolfe was better-looking and more gentlemanly in appearance than Grey had expected, given his profession. Sheridan hadn't been wrong about Wolfe's arms, either—the major was built like a wrestler. He might walk with a cane, but it clearly didn't keep him from working with his hands. And he was tall, too, though Grey had anticipated that since Beatrice wasn't exactly short.

Still, other than noting aspects of Wolfe's appearance, Grey had gleaned little, since he and the major had scarcely spoken two words to each other.

At least eavesdropping had elicited a bit more information. Grey hadn't been able to make out the entire conversation, but he'd heard enough to determine that Miss Wolfe was concerned for her future. And rightfully so, since Wolfe was apparently going out at night to places he wouldn't speak of to his sister.

But despite that and the major's general crankiness, Wolfe didn't seem the sort to fight for the dukedom. Nor did he sound like the reckless, half-mad fellow Sheridan had described. Wolfe certainly didn't seem interested in murdering four men to inherit.

Miss Wolfe spoke from inside the kennel yard, "All right, lads, time for our walk."

Holy hell. They were coming out. Grey didn't want her to catch him lurking about like a servant listening at doors.

Feeling like an idiot, he retreated a short way down the hill, then waited until the kennel door opened before he retraced his steps up the hill toward her.

She emerged with three leashed pointers and shut the door behind them. Then she bent to say, in a girlish voice, "Now don't tell Mr. MacTilly, but we're going to have a fine run without these leashes, aren't we?"

Caught off guard by her tone, Grey paused to watch as she continued to speak sweet nothings to the dogs while she unfastened the first leash.

He'd seen her shrewish and he'd seen her subservient, but he hadn't yet seen her gentle. It twisted something inside his chest, making him uneasy.

When she went on to the next dog, she put her back to him and bent in a way that showcased her lovely bottom. Damn it all to hell. Her simple gown of black wool skimmed it provocatively. Ah, how he would love to put his hands on that luscious, full derriere.

To the last dog, she said, "None of that misbehavior you showed last time, do you hear me, Hercules? You'll be a good boy for Beatrice, won't you? I know you will, you darling rascal."

As Grey's loins clenched, he had the errant thought, *Ah, yes, Miss Wolfe, I will be a very good boy for you. Just try me.*

He wondered what she'd be like in bed, with her soft hands and full mouth caressing him. Or perhaps she'd turn fiery as she had the day they'd met, and she'd rise to meet his every thrust, wrapping those long legs about his hips as they—

God help him, what was he thinking?

Fortunately, just then the dogs rushed off down the hill and she turned to see him approaching.

She blushed deeply. "Your Grace." Nervously she glanced back at the closed door, and lowered her voice. "What are you doing here?"

"Looking for you," he said as he reached her. "Sheridan told me you would most likely be at the kennels, and someone directed me to them."

To you. And your very fetching behind.

Good God, he must get that image of her bottom out of his head. He felt as off-kilter as the hounds, who dashed madly down the hill, then back up, trying to coax her into following.

"Is something wrong?" she asked. One of the hounds came up to nuzzle her hand, and she scratched his head idly. "Does Aunt Lydia need me?"

Her mention of his mother dampened his desire at once. "No. She's taking today to rest, thank God."

An instant wariness darkened her features, which her short-brimmed bonnet didn't shield in the least. "So why are *you* here?"

"Before I begin advising you and Gwyn on society's rules, I thought you and I should get to know each other better. It might make things easier."

"Then why isn't Lady Gwyn joining us?" she asked, now clearly on her guard.

"Because I already know my sister quite well, Miss Wolfe," he joked.

She didn't so much as crack a smile. "I-I meant . . . That is . . ."

"I know what you meant," he said, taking pity on her. He wished he could make her feel as easy around him as she clearly did around Sheridan. "And besides, Gwyn is keeping Mother company."

"Oh. Right. Of course." Refusing to look at

him, she smoothed down her rumpled skirts. "I have to walk the dogs. Pointers need lots of exercise or they—"

"—become restless and unmanageable. Yes, I know. Why don't we walk them together? I promise I don't bite, Miss Wolfe. No pun intended."

Her lips twitched as if she fought a smile. "In my experience, sir, any man can bite if provoked."

"Then don't provoke me, and I won't show my teeth." When she bristled, he flashed her a grin meant to soothe. "You may have noticed I'm not easy to provoke. I'm like your pointers—ready to come to heel at a command."

She snorted. "I rather doubt that, Your Grace."

The use of the honorific irritated him. "Call me Grey, if you please, like the others do. Or even Greycourt, if you prefer. You're not a servant, and I'm not your master."

"All right. But then you must call me Beatrice like the rest of the family."

"Not Bea?" he asked.

A sigh escaped her. "Don't say anything to the others, but I can't stand 'Bea.' It makes me think of old ladies."

"Thank you for telling me. Though you ought to tell them, too."

"I can't. They've been so kind to me."

"Ah. And no one could ever accuse *me* of that."

Her cheeks reddened. "I didn't mean—"

"I'm teasing you," he said with a laugh. "I told you, I'm not easy to provoke. All appearances to the contrary."

"If you say so . . . Grey." But her tone showed she was still wary.

Not waiting for him to lead the way, she headed down the hill with the dogs dancing ahead of her. Grey followed, noting how she seemed to control the hounds with an invisible leash. They never got too far ahead of her nor dashed off into the woods. And when one of them looked as if he might do so, she merely murmured a word, and he came to heel instantly.

"Your pointers are very well trained," he observed.

"If you can tell that, you must be quite the hunter."

"Actually, hunting isn't my favorite pastime, but I do know dogs. I used to have two setters as pets. They were *not* well trained or even well behaved, for that matter. You've never seen a more rambunctious pair of rascals. No one could control them, including me." He shot her a sideways glance. "Though I daresay *you* could have."

"I should hope so. Setters aren't so hard to train." She fixed her gaze on the dogs gamboling ahead of them. "You said you 'used to.' What happened to your pets?"

After a moment, he said, "I had to leave them behind in Prussia when I came back to England to attend Eton."

"Oh, how *awful*." Sympathy flooded her face. "You must have missed them terribly."

Not as much as I missed my family. "They were dogs, Miss Wolfe. Not children."

He'd meant to put her off. Instead, she eyed him closely. "That doesn't mean you wouldn't miss them just the same."

"I didn't have time to miss them," he said, then changed the subject. "So, I understand that you and your brother live in the dower house on the estate."

For some reason, that turned her prickly once more. "We do, yes. At least as long as your mother prefers to live in the hall."

"Trust me, my mother will always live as close to her children as is possible, so unless Sheridan kicks her out—"

"Or his new wife does," she said tartly. Then she caught herself. "Forgive me, Your Grace. That was too blunt."

"Would you please *stop* that?"

"I'm sorry," she mumbled. "I meant to say 'Grey.' "

"That's not what I'm talking about. Stop apologizing for saying what you think. It's what I do every day of my life."

That made her stiffen. "Because you *can.*

You're a duke, and a wealthy one at that. No one is going to stand up to you, and if I had any sense, I wouldn't, either."

Her forthright retort made him chuckle. "That's more like it." When she blanched and opened her mouth, he added, "Don't you *dare* apologize for that."

Her eyes glittered at him. "I wasn't going to."

"The hell you weren't." When she glanced pointedly down to where his hand still gripped her arm, he released her. "Looks like it's my turn to apologize. Forgive me for manhandling you. Though I get the impression that *everything* I do annoys you."

With a furtive look down the hill to make sure the dogs were still in her line of sight, she said, "That's not true. You were kind enough not to tell my cousin about our . . . heated exchange when we first met."

"Was it heated?" he quipped. "I hadn't noticed."

That brought a small smile to her lips. "Liar."

"I tell you what. How about if we pretend that I am not a duke and you are not my mother's latest pro—" He caught himself before he could say, "project." "My mother's protégée. Let's pretend, for the moment, that we are merely two people with no ulterior motives. I will say what I think, and you will say what you think, and neither of us will apologize."

"Why?"

"Because your stopping to apologize is taking up far too much of my valuable time," he said with a smile. "You see? That's how it's done. I will be my usual arrogant self, and you will be your usual forthright self, and we will get through this together with a minimum of fuss."

And perhaps she would reveal some useful secret about her brother. Not to mention that he would get to see the real her more often.

She eyed him askance. "I thought you were supposed to be preparing me for moving in high society. I doubt that in such a case I should be saying whatever comes into my mind."

"I agree—you should not. Unless it's to me alone. As long as no one else hears, as long as it's between us, it will be perfectly acceptable. And it might actually keep you from blurting out the wrong thing elsewhere."

Coloring very prettily, she said, "So you've noticed my tendency to . . . er . . ."

"Blurt? How could I not? It's the thing I find most refreshing about you."

"Truly?"

"I swear." He thrust out his hand. "So, what do you think? Do we have a bargain?"

She hesitated before taking his hand. "I suppose. As long as what we say goes no further."

"I can't promise that." The words were out of his mouth before he could stop them, making her slip her hand from his and her brow cloud over.

Hastily he recouped. "Mother is going to want to know everything we said to each other, and I'll have to tell her something."

Her face cleared. "Oh. I'm sure that's true." She touched one gloved finger to her chin and shot him a mischievous glance. "Very well. You may tell her that my come-out lessons are progressing wonderfully."

He laughed. "Come-out lessons?"

"That's how I've been thinking of them." She lifted one eyebrow. "It's better than thinking of myself as your mother's latest project."

He winced. "You caught that."

"It's all right," she said lightly. "Sheridan called me her 'project' first."

"I would apologize, but it would go against our new rules."

She smirked at him. "Indeed, it would . . . Grey."

Now *that* was more like it. When she was like this, teasing him, with her eyes dancing, he could easily imagine her in an evening gown, flirting with some fellow at a ball. Preferably him.

Damn it to hell. *Not* him.

She turned to look down the hill, and her smirk vanished. "Oh no, the dogs are into the gorse again. I should have been paying better attention. If I don't keep my eye on them, they get bored. A pox on them!"

The lady cursed, too? Sheridan hadn't been lying when he'd called her a hoyden. Though when she picked up her skirts and bolted down the hill, it was a woman's stockinged calves Grey saw flashing white above her half-boots.

And quite a trim pair of calves they were, too, momentarily distracting him from the interesting sight of her trying to coax the dogs out of the gorse bushes. Perhaps he should help.

He strode down the hill. "I'll get them out."

"Don't you dare go in there!" Planting her hands on her hips, she glared at him. "They'll come out eventually. But the last time they got into the gorse, Mr. MacTilly went in after them and got stuck fast. If you do the same, at the very least you'll destroy your fancy clothes."

"Which is precisely why I'm not going in after them." He pulled a funeral biscuit out of his greatcoat pocket, opened the wrapping, and broke a piece off. Tossing it to the closest dog, he watched as the hound scarfed it up and then barked at him for more.

When he held another piece up, the dog came running out after it. That was all it took for the others to come trotting out, too, and he rewarded them by giving each a piece.

Squatting down, he petted the one whose name he remembered. "There's a good lad, Hercules." He looked up at Miss Wolfe, who was gaping at him. "What?"

"How did you . . . Why on earth would you have funeral biscuits in your pocket?"

Because I never want to be trapped without something to eat ever again.

No, that would require revealing too much. So instead he shrugged. "I'd been told you were at the kennels. Since that meant I was about to be around dogs, I figured it was best if I brought treats."

In other words, he'd come prepared to win her over by winning over her dogs. Was it working?

Perhaps. Because a helpless laugh escaped her. "You're as much a rascal as they."

"Probably." He grinned at her. "What are the names of the other two?"

With a shake of her head, she came up to seize one by the collar. "This is Hero. And the one with the spots is Hector."

"Whoever named them certainly has a fondness for Greek mythology."

"It wasn't me," she said. "I prefer a good novel, myself."

"I prefer the *Times*." He scratched Hector behind the ears. "What about you, lad? Do you enjoy being saddled with a fancy name like Hector?"

Hector's answer was to lick his face. Though Grey chuckled, Miss Wolfe frowned.

"Stop that, Hector!" she ordered, and the dog instantly obeyed, though he then licked Grey's gloved hand. She sighed. "We'll have to put you lot back on the leashes, if only to keep you from slobbering all over His Grace."

"Don't do it on *my* account," Grey said as he stood and dusted off his trousers. "A little dog slobber never hurt anyone."

"Uh-huh," she said skeptically. "All the same, I don't want to risk them bolting into the gorse again, either. You'll run out of those biscuits eventually."

"True."

She put their leashes on, though Grey noticed that she knelt to do it this time, more's the pity. Then she tugged at the dogs' leashes. "Come on, lads, let's go to the woods."

But they were hoping for more treats and stood about Grey, sniffing at his greatcoat. Apparently, his presence had thrown their good behavior into disarray.

She scowled at them. "Come along now. You know you like tramping through the woods, you scoundrels."

"I'm flattered that you noticed, Beatrice," Grey joked.

Clearly fighting a smile, she said, "Watch it, sir, or I'll make *you* take them walking."

"As long as you lead the way, I wouldn't mind that a bit," he countered, and held out his hand for the leashes. "We scoundrels will follow you anywhere."

She swallowed, her throat undulating in a fashion that made him want to put his lips just there, in the hollow. Now where had that thought come from?

Then she seemed to catch herself, for she went rigid as she held out the leashes. "All right. Then *you* can walk them. If you think you can keep up."

When he took the leashes from her, her fingers brushed his accidentally, and an alarming current snapped between them.

But if she felt the same, she showed no sign of it. As she pivoted on her heel and marched off along the edge of the gorse toward what looked like a forest of elms, he hurried after her with the dogs.

"You see, lads," he drawled, "the way to turn a lady up sweet is to acquiesce to whatever she wants. That's how you get exactly what *you* want."

Her sniff made it clear she'd heard him. So did the very feminine toss of her head and the subtle swing of her hips as if she were aware of him watching her from behind.

Satisfaction coursed through him. Clearly, a day with Beatrice was going to be far more interesting than spending his time cooped up in the study with Sheridan and going over estate documents, as they'd done last evening after the funeral.

And who knew? It might even give him a chance to look at the infamous bridge where Maurice had died, so he could report to Sheridan on that as well. All he had to do was coax her into showing him the dower house.

He began to think that might not be as difficult as he'd feared.

Chapter Seven

Beatrice stalked down the path, all too aware of His Grace coming along behind her. He was probably laughing at his clever bon mots and what he surely saw as his winning ways. Not to mention his ability to get on the good side of her dogs.

The blasted traitorous curs. Of *course* they would like him. He was as bad as they. "Turn a lady up sweet," indeed. He thought he could wrap her about his finger just by charming her pointers, did he? It wouldn't work.

But she grudgingly admitted that few dukes would accept a tongue-lashing from a dog without blinking an eye. Well, other than Sheridan, who was newly minted and unfamiliar with the rules of being a duke.

Why, she doubted even Thornstock would carry treats for the lads in his greatcoat pocket. Or, for that matter, take the time to help his mother with her "latest project," even if he *were* inclined to do so, which, Thornstock had made clear last night, he was not.

Grey's interest in her as a "project" didn't make any sense, although she finally began to understand why people gossiped about Grey in London. His seductive glances alone could start rumors swirling.

Suddenly, she realized there was silence behind her. She turned to see the duke some distance back, waiting patiently as Hero relieved himself in the leaves.

Speaking of luring a woman, now she had Greycourt's bargain to entice her. The very idea of always saying what she thought without apology was invigorating. No rules when she was around him. No chiding looks. It sent a thrill down her spine to think of just . . . being herself with such a man. She wasn't even herself with his mother or Sheridan.

He caught her looking at him and smiled. Lord, he was handsome in his many-caped greatcoat left casually open to reveal a stark black mourning suit, white shirt, and black cravat. Not to mention his hat trimmed with grosgrain ribbon and his shiny black hessians that showed him to be the height of fashion, especially for Sanforth. Why must he be so very attractive? It simply wasn't fair.

"Where do these woods lead?" he asked.

"Down to the river that skirts the property."

"Ah yes." He shifted his gaze to the dogs. "The river where Maurice drowned."

There it was again: the odd way he had of addressing his stepfather by his Christian name.

"Why don't you call Uncle Maurice 'Father' like the others do?" she asked.

His jaw tautened. "Because he's not my father."

"He's not the twins' father, either, but *they* call him 'Father.' "

"They weren't sent away by him at the age of ten." He ground out a curse. "Forgive me, I didn't intend to malign the memory of—"

"I thought we weren't going to apologize for saying what we meant."

He smiled thinly. "Right. I forgot."

"And your rule was that we wouldn't reveal to anyone else what was said in these conversations. So feel free to malign the memory of my uncle if it makes you feel better." Especially if it helped her to understand the undercurrents that eddied between him and his half siblings.

"That would never make me feel better. I admired my stepfather." He returned his gaze to the dogs. "But I only knew him as that for a few years. I was five when he married my mother, and ten when I left home."

"I thought boys didn't go to Eton until thirteen."

"I . . . er . . . didn't go to Eton right away. I went to live with my aunt and uncle."

"And why is that?"

He shrugged as if it didn't matter to him. But his hand gripping the leash said otherwise.

"So it's to be a guessing game, is it?" she teased, remembering their first meeting.

His baleful gaze shot to her. "It's a boring tale."

"Why don't you let *me* be the judge of that?

You did say you wanted us to get to know each other."

Calculation flashed in his eyes. "Fine. I'll tell you. *If* you show me the bridge where my stepfather died."

She ventured a soft smile. "I understand. Gravesites themselves mean nothing to me, either. *I* wanted to be at the last place my father was on earth. I couldn't, of course, since no one would tell me where the duel occurred, but I used to imagine that if I could go there, I might find his spirit lurking about, waiting to impart some last profound message." She looked down at her hands. "It's silly, I know."

"Not the least silly." He came toward her, the dogs finally having finished their business. " 'There are more things in heaven and earth than are dreamt of in your philosophy.' "

She fell into step beside him. "You're a lover of Shakespeare?"

"More of a connoisseur. I like the major works and, within those, the best lines." He smiled faintly at her. "Not that I had a choice. The whole playwright thing, remember? Mother does love her plays. We often acted out scenes in my youth." His gaze turned searching. "And speaking of mothers, you never mention yours. Dare I ask why?"

"My mother died bearing me, I'm afraid."

Pity flashed in his eyes. "I'm sorry."

"Don't be. I never knew her, so I never realized what I was missing. And I had my grandmother to look after me until Joshua returned from the war."

"Then you started looking after *him*."

"Yes, I . . ." It suddenly dawned on her what Grey was doing. She stared him down. "You're very adept, sir, at shifting the conversation away from yourself. We were supposed to be talking about *you* and why you returned to England at ten."

He shot her a rueful glance. "You noticed that maneuver, did you?"

"My brother used to be a master at it. Now he doesn't even bother to use a strategy—he just grunts and growls and expects me to leave him be. You're more polite at it while essentially doing the same thing. So let's return to the subject of how you ended up back in England so young."

Reining Hector in before the pointer could dart after a hare, Grey released a long breath. "My father died when I was a babe. He left behind a will that named his only brother, Eustace, as my guardian. Fortunately for me, my uncle preferred to leave me with my mother. For a while, anyway."

"Oh? What changed all that?"

His mood darkened so dramatically that even the dogs noticed and came up to nuzzle his hand.

He rubbed their heads idly to reassure them before going on.

"After my cousin Vanessa was born, my aunt was told she could have no more children. Which meant that my uncle had no heir to his estate or even to mine, if something happened to me. So he exercised his guardianship rights, went to Berlin to fetch me, and brought me back to England to be taught by him to run the dukedom."

The hard tone of his voice whenever he mentioned his uncle told her there was more to the story. She tested out that theory. "How selfless of your uncle to take that on when he wouldn't benefit from it."

"Selfless," he said in an acid tone. "Right."

"Did you not think him selfless?"

He shot her a cold glance. "I answered your question, Beatrice. That should suffice."

Hardly. But she let it go, and instead focused on another aspect of his tale. "Did you ever go back to Berlin to visit your family?"

"No. Either I was too young or the Revolution prevented me from traveling through France to get there or I was in school or . . . There was always some reason I couldn't go, some reason they couldn't come here."

Oh, the poor boy. "So essentially you were orphaned at ten, as surely as if they'd died."

His gaze sharpened on her. "You're the first person to see it like that. Everyone else outside my family considers me lucky to have been allowed to return to almighty England before Napoleon came to power."

Her heart ached for him. She couldn't imagine being uprooted from her home and forced to live with people she barely knew. "When you came here, did you have memories of your uncle and aunt to reassure you? Or of being in England before?"

"Not really." He mused a moment. "I barely remember my mother's second husband, who was Thorn's father. I do recall making a fuss about my naptime the day of Mother's wedding to Maurice. And I remember my grandmother a bit, since she took charge of me at the wedding reception. I have a few vague memories of playing in the garden at Thornstock Castle. I fell and split my chin open on a paving stone." He lifted his chin to show her. "There's a scar that's too faint to see. But you can feel it. Here, I'll show you."

He halted so he could tuck the leashes under his arm and take her hand to draw off her glove. Then he pressed her fingers to his chin in an act so intimate that she caught her breath.

But it wasn't a trick or a sneaky way to catch a look down her gown or press against her chest. Grey was a gentleman. Nothing like her sly uncle.

She could tell because he kept his eyes, now

green in the muted forest light, on her. "I do . . . feel a bit of a scar." She also felt the faint roughness of his shaved whiskers and the tautening of his jaw at her touch.

Oh, Lord. This was unwise.

Hastily she dropped her hand, retrieved her glove, and donned it once more. Then she walked on, her pulse doing a mad dance.

When he followed her and began to speak again, his voice sounded ragged. "Anyway, I guess my nursemaid was woolgathering that day."

"She must have been, to allow the little duke to hurt himself."

He continued beside her a few moments in a silence only punctured by the crackle of leaves beneath their feet and the snuffling of the dogs as they examined every inch of the trail.

"It's odd, but I don't remember the nursemaid at all." Then he lightened his tone. "Though I do remember our nanny in Berlin. She was a stout German widow who enjoyed sweets . . . and loved sharing them with us. We adored her."

She matched his light tone. "Who wouldn't adore a steady supply of sweets?"

He snorted. "When Mother found out, she was apoplectic and made Father admonish Nanny to not give us so many."

She pounced on that. "So you do call Uncle Maurice 'Father' sometimes."

"I suppose I do," he said ruefully. "I always did

when I was a boy. I just . . . After they sent me away, I . . ."

"Resented them for doing so. I can only imagine. Berlin was your home."

A soft smile crossed his lips. "Exactly."

"And I take it you didn't like your aunt and uncle here very much?"

The smile faded. "No."

When he offered nothing else, she took pity on him and picked up the thread of conversation. "I understand. As I'm sure you deduced from the other night, I was the same age as you when my father died. It's a difficult age to lose a parent. Or both parents, in your case."

Still, he said nothing. Apparently, his tales of being a child in Berlin were over.

"But I did have my grandparents," she went on, "whom I adored every bit as much as you did your nanny. Although sadly they weren't as generous with the sweets."

That seemed to crack his reserve. "A grievous fault in any guardian of children, to be sure." He slanted a glance at her. "What about your brother? How did *he* feel about your grandparents?"

She shrugged. "He liked them well enough, I suppose. But he never really lived with them. Joshua is five years older than I, so Grandfather bought him a commission in the Royal Marines after he turned sixteen, then packed him off to the Continent."

"You lost your brother and father in one fell swoop?" he asked, sympathy in his voice.

"Pretty much." She searched his face. "Rather like your losing your entire family in one fell swoop, only to have them supplanted by strangers."

He merely nodded, then quickened his pace. "So, how far *is* this bridge, anyway?"

The man could be decidedly uncommunicative. Perhaps it was a characteristic of dukes. Uncle Armie had never spoken to her of anything except how he liked her gown, how it made her breasts look bigger and her behind smaller . . . intimate statements that had invariably embarrassed her.

Somehow she couldn't imagine Greycourt saying such rude things. Though he *could* be officious, that was a different sort of rude. It wasn't vulgar.

They'd walked a few more steps in silence when she felt something give way in her half-boot. One of her laces had broken.

"Blast it all!" she cried. Recently she'd noticed it was fraying and had been meaning to replace it, but not soon enough.

Then she realized she'd cursed aloud. In front of the duke.

But instead of disapproving, he burst into laughter. "You have a very colorful vocabulary, madam."

She blushed to the roots of her hair. "That's

what happens when one spends all one's time around men who don't govern their language."

"Not my stepfather, I hope."

"No. Just Joshua and Uncle Armie." She sighed. "When I said bad words as a child, Grandmama used to frown and say I was as naughty a saucebox as Papa had been. I do *try* to watch my language. I just don't always succeed."

He chuckled. "What made you fail this time?"

She pointed to her boot. "I've broken a lace."

"Ah." He followed the direction of her finger. "So you have."

She gazed up at him hopefully. "I don't suppose you have any extra laces or even string in those capacious pockets of yours?"

"Sadly, no. But I do have a cravat."

"What good will that do?"

"I'll show you."

He led her to a fallen oak trunk, tugging the dogs along with him. Handing her the leashes, he removed his greatcoat and spread it over the massive log with the outside down. Then he began to unknot his cravat. "Sit here and remove your shoe with the broken lace."

"I can walk with it like this. I'll merely have to go more slowly."

"Nonsense. You could easily turn your ankle if your boot is ill-laced, especially on this uneven ground."

She was used to always having to look after

her own needs, to manage under difficult circumstances. It felt odd to have a gentleman being so solicitous of her. "Truly, there's no need for you to sully your—"

"Sit!" he said firmly.

All three dogs dropped onto their haunches. The startled look on the duke's face tickled her so much that she burst into laughter. After a second, Grey joined in, while the dogs sat patiently, waiting for the next command.

"As I said," Grey remarked once he stopped laughing, "the hounds are very well trained."

"They ought to be. I trained them." When he blinked, she said, "Don't look so astonished. We don't have the luxury of hiring a man to do it. As it is, MacTilly's hands are full with the feeding and breeding, and Joshua's hands are full with managing the rest of the gamekeeper's duties. So I help where I can." She scratched Hector's head. "I trained these three fellows myself."

"I see." Grey waved his hand at the log. "If you would please take a seat . . ."

"What, have you given up on commanding me like the dogs?" she quipped.

"Beatrice, I beg of you to sit down," he said, his tone a bit testy.

That only made her want to tease him more, though she did at least perch on his coat before saying, "Whatever Your Grace wishes."

"Watch it, minx, or I will hold you to that one

day. And given your recalcitrant nature, that won't end well."

"Me! I'm no more recalcitrant than you."

"True." He knelt on one knee to remove her boot, then took her stockinged foot and set it on his other knee.

His hand lingered on her ankle, the warmth of his fingers practically searing her through the stockinet. Yet it could not have been more than a second before he moved his hand away to focus on unlacing the half-boot he now held in both hands.

By propping her foot up, he was merely behaving as a gentleman who didn't wish her to ruin her stockings on the leaf-littered ground. She was certain of *that*. Still, there was something very intimate about having her heel resting on his thigh. His very muscular thigh.

But he didn't seem to notice the impropriety of it, even when the dogs began whining, as if to chide him. He merely knelt there and worked on her boot without appearing to be remotely concerned that his cravat hung loose, exposing part of his neck and throat.

Both of which fascinated her. She wished she could reach out and touch his prominent Adam's apple. Or perhaps the hollow below it, which seemed wonderfully formed for placing one's lips—

She dragged her gaze away. Lord, but it was

suddenly warm in the woods. She forced herself to focus on how he was now re-lacing her boot with the shortened lace.

"That's not going to work," she said. "The lace broke too low."

"I know."

He pulled his cravat from about his neck, drawing her attention back to that lovely expanse of bared male flesh. Then he slid her boot on and began to wrap his cravat tightly—but not too tightly—about her ankle, starting at the bottom near her foot and working his way up to beneath the leather cuff, where he tied it off.

Dear Lord. Lifting her gaze to his face, she colored as she saw him watching her.

"See something you like?" he asked in a low rumble.

And as usual when she was taken off guard, she blurted out the first thing that came to her mind. "Why? Do you?"

She'd intended it to come out as cold and sarcastic, but instead it sounded like a throaty invitation, even to *her* ears.

And she knew he'd heard it when his eyes darkened, then dropped to fix on her lips. "Yes. Definitely yes."

Devil take it, she should never have said such a thing. What must he think of her? What would he—

Her thoughts shattered as he leaned forward and pressed his lips to hers.

Lord save her, he was kissing her. The Duke of blasted Greycourt himself was *kissing* her! And it wasn't like anything she'd have expected. His kiss was light, tentative, as if he waited for her to push him away.

But she was incapable of that. Oh, heavens, the feel of his mouth covering hers, tasting and testing as if to determine how soft were her lips, was a heady sensation unlike any other.

And who could have known that a kiss one actually desired could be so . . . intoxicating? That smelling his spicy cologne would make her heart flip over? That feeling his hand slide behind her neck to hold her still would not only *not* alarm her but spur a wild need to rise through her body and clamor for more?

Half in a trance, she let the dogs' leashes slip from her fingers so she could place her hand on Grey's shoulder, accidentally knocking off his hat. He didn't seem to notice. With a guttural moan, he pulled her forward a little, forcing her foot to fall off his knee. Then his lips were coaxing hers open, and his tongue was sliding into her mouth.

This joining of lips and mouths and tongues was *amazing*—unfamiliar and a bit unusual, but enjoyable nonetheless. Her hand slipped down to his chest, and the feel of his heart pounding through the fabric beneath her fingers incited her to be bold, to twirl her tongue with his and throw herself into the conflagration he'd ignited in her body.

So *this* was what it was like to be kissed, truly kissed.

Suddenly, she felt something tugging her arm away. At first, she thought it was Grey, but when she then felt another something snuffling her hand, she realized what it was.

The dogs. They were jealous or bored or wanted attention.

Whatever the case, it meant this delicious interval was over. And judging from how the duke pulled away and muttered a curse under his breath, it was over for good.

He rose and took a step back, raking his fingers through his hair. "Forgive me, Miss Wolfe. That was most rude of me, and I swear it will never happen again."

The way he loomed over her made her self-conscious—that, and the fact that he was calling her Miss Wolfe again and behaving as if the kiss was a mistake. It hadn't felt like a mistake. Perhaps if she'd thought of it as a prelude to something else, she would realize how unwise it had been, but she'd been thinking of it more as a delightful experiment. One she wouldn't mind repeating.

Which apparently was never going to happen.

With a word to the dogs to stop their grousing, she grabbed their leashes and stood, smoothing her skirts as she struggled to keep her thoughts to herself. "I thought you and I agreed never to apologize to each other, Your Grace."

"For what we say, not what we do," he bit out. "I'm not the sort of man to kiss a woman I've only known for two days."

"I understand," she said, desperate to halt the insulting flow of his words before the wounds he was casually inflicting succeeded in reaching her heart.

"No, I don't think you do. I'd *never* intentionally take advantage of—"

"Was it that awful?" she snapped, unable to contain herself any longer. "Am I *that* incapable of pleasing a man like you?"

He blinked at her, then swore under his breath. "It wasn't remotely awful. You far exceeded my expectations in that respect, trust me."

Well. *That* eased the pressure in her chest. A little.

"Then why are you apologizing?" she asked, though she wasn't sure she wanted to know. "I don't regret it. Why should you?"

He blew out a breath. "Because I had no right."

A sudden thought came into her head that was so awful she of course blurted it right out. "You're engaged to another."

"No! No, I'm not betrothed to anyone."

She stared at him, trying to make sense of his behavior. Then she forced a light smile to her lips. "It was merely a kiss, not a profession of undying love. Rest assured I would never expect a man of your wealth and rank to consider marrying the orphaned daughter of a scandalous scapegrace— the impoverished sister of a gamekeeper—merely because we have relations in common."

"We are not remotely related," he growled.

He *would* point that out, if only to torment her further. "Not by blood, no. But we have mutual connections who might wish . . . who would prefer . . ." Lord, she was babbling. "My point is, I'm not *that* much of a fool. It's as I told you at dinner two nights ago: I'm not looking to make a splash in society. I merely hope to find some vicar or physician in need of a circumspect wife."

His features darkened. "Because you are nothing if not 'circumspect,' " he said acidly.

Her blood ran cold. How dared the man get angry at *her? He* was the one who'd just fallen all over himself trying to explain why he hadn't meant anything by their kiss.

She was gearing up to give him a piece of her mind when the dogs fortunately began tugging on the leashes.

"You're welcome to think what you want," she said, tossing off the words with what she thought was admirable nonchalance, "but do it while we walk. The rascals are growing restless, and I assume you still wish to see the bridge. So unless you want Mr. MacTilly wondering what the devil has happened to me, we should go on."

He caught her by the arm before she could leave. "Beatrice, I didn't mean to insult you."

Oh, Lord, if he kept talking one more minute she was going to cry, and she *never* cried. "There was no insult, Grey. Honestly, you're placing far more significance on one kiss than is warranted."

He searched her face as if trying to ascertain her true feelings. And that would not do. Pasting a falsely pleasant smile to her lips, she tugged her arm from his grip so she could gesture toward the path. "Shall we?"

After picking up his hat and dusting it off, he murmured, "Ladies—and dogs—first."

Great. *Now,* he wanted to play the gentleman.

Holding her head high, she stalked up the trail ahead of him. Let him play the gentleman if he pleased. But next time he gave her his melting look and lowered his mouth to hers, she wouldn't be so complacent. Clearly, he wasn't a gentleman, but another version of her uncle, or for that matter, her dogs. Grey might be more polite and his attentions might be more subtle and inviting, but in the end, she was still just the object of his illicit desires and naught else.

She'd had enough of *that* to last her a lifetime.

Chapter Eight

Grey followed Beatrice with his blood in high riot. Holy hell, he'd made a hash of that. What had he been thinking, to kiss a woman like her? He'd let his worst impulses get the best of him.

Now, instead of coaxing her into feeling easy with him so he could learn enough to show Sheridan how mad his suspicions were, Grey had put her on her guard. But he hadn't planned to find her so refreshing. Entertaining. Damn-it-to-hell desirable. His good intentions had flown out the window the minute his mouth had met hers.

It was merely a kiss.

God help him, not a mere kiss. What they'd done had been dancing and delight, fireworks and fantasy. Yet even as he'd plundered her mouth, he'd felt a perverse pain running through his pleasure.

Because he'd known she wasn't for him. He'd heard her tell her brother she wanted a love match, which Grey wouldn't give her. Not for nothing had he stood up to his uncle's bullying year after year to save what was rightfully his. Years of schooling himself to nonchalance had instilled in him an inability to care.

But a woman like Beatrice would never allow him to keep his feelings private. She'd dig until she knew all his secrets and emotions, until she left him no choice but to split himself open to let her inside.

The hell she would.

It was just as well she assumed he wouldn't marry her because she was penniless and beneath him. Better that than for her to guess the truth—that his heart had atrophied. If he could keep her regarding him as a pompous, arrogant arse, he'd be safe from her probing.

Unfortunately, his damned cock ignored his sound arguments. It followed after her like those bloody mindless dogs. Even now, the sight of her hips swaying down the path ahead of him made him harden in his drawers.

Clearly, he'd been too long without a woman in his bed.

She halted on the path to look back at him. "We're almost there," she said, pointing ahead to where the woods opened out into a field. "It's not far now."

The sound of rushing water reached his ears. He was about to see the place where Maurice had died. The thought sent the same chill through him that witnessing Maurice's body had done.

But as they reached the riverbank and Grey viewed the infamous spot, he felt nothing. No ghostly presence. Not even a sense of Maurice. Some part of him had almost hoped he might. Instead, it was just an old wooden bridge with a section of missing rails where his stepfather had fallen through.

Yes, an *old* bridge. That gave him pause. When Sheridan had said the bridge was sturdy, he'd exaggerated. From where Grey stood on the bank, the planks looked rough and worn, and the railings seemed flimsy.

And there was one other curious feature. "Where does that lead?" He pointed to where their path merged into a dirt track coming in from beyond the woods.

"It's the carriage road to Armitage Hall. It's more circuitous than the shortcut through the woods, and joins up with the drive leading out to the main road."

"So someone could drive to the bridge without ever being seen."

"Yes, but they couldn't cross it."

"Ah. Not sturdy enough for that, I suppose."

"Actually," Beatrice said, "the bridge is plenty sturdy. It's just not wide enough for any equipage to pass comfortably. But if you want to go out on it, you can. It's only the railing that's gone in that one spot."

Thankfully, she had misinterpreted his interest in the soundness of the bridge.

She went on. "And I need to cross and walk up to my house anyway so I can change my boot lace and return your cravat to you. If you'd like to wait here—"

"I would, thank you."

She nodded. "I'll take the dogs with me."

No doubt she wanted to give him privacy and quiet for communing with his late stepfather. That was just as well. It would allow him to examine the site of the accident without her prying eyes.

Her behavior did tell him one thing—Sheridan had been right about Beatrice not being complicit in anything. Because if she had been part of some scheme, she wouldn't have wanted to bring Grey here, and she certainly wouldn't have suggested leaving him alone.

He walked with her and the dogs onto the bridge, then waited until they'd disappeared up the bank on the other side before he started poking about. As she'd said, the bridge seemed perfectly capable of holding a man's weight, despite its ragged appearance. The railings, however, were questionable. When he pulled on one, he felt a bit of give. So Maurice *could* have fallen through into the river.

Grey would have preferred to examine the broken rails themselves, but they'd apparently gone into the water with Maurice, leaving only a gaping hole. He did examine the posts, but saw no evidence of cuts. The rails were broken off on either end. Strange that such a sizeable section had gone into the river. But then, Maurice had been a large fellow.

Next, Grey went down to the water. It looked

deep enough to drown in, especially at night, with the current rushing. The rivers had supposedly been swollen from recent rains, and sadly Maurice had never learned to swim.

Grey gazed up at the bridge from underneath, but could see no obvious structural problems—no holes, no missing planks. So what would make Maurice trip while walking along a perfectly level bridge with a lantern?

Perhaps something had startled him. There were wild boars hereabouts. If one had run onto the bridge, Maurice might have backed into the rails or even fallen against them. Unlikely, but possible.

Grey ought to walk the banks of the river to see if and where the broken rails had washed up.

"Your Grace?" called a voice above him.

Holy hell, she was back. "Down here!" he cried, but doubted she could hear him above the roar of the water. He hurried up the muddy bank.

After he reached the top, he heard her grumble to the dogs, "Leave it to a blasted duke to do as he pleases without telling anyone." As he approached her from behind, she glanced in the opposite direction. "I only hope he didn't try going up to my house. I might have missed him on the way back. Then what would I do with this?"

Pulling his cravat out of her pocket, she stared down at it. "I can't go into the hall and give it to him, or people will get ideas about us. His Blasted Grace would be appalled. But if he wanted to be discreet, he ought to have stayed where I left him so I—"

"Beatrice," he said, though he was loath to stop the entertaining flow of her words.

She jumped, then whirled to see him standing there. "Your Grace! I-I mean, Grey. That is . . . Where the devil did you come from?"

He nodded toward the broken railing. "I went down to the river."

"Oh. Right. Because that's where Uncle Maurice—" She halted, a pretty blush spreading over her cheeks. "You . . . um . . . didn't hear what I was saying, did you?"

Much as he would like to tell her the truth, he figured there was no point in embarrassing her further. "I thought I heard you call me, but it was hard to tell down there by the water. It's very loud."

Her face cleared. "Of course. Yes. It generally is. Very loud, I mean." She halted, as if aware she was babbling. "So, did you wish to stay longer? Or are you ready to leave?"

"We can go. I know this is probably a long walk, even for your pointers."

"Not really. We do a lot of roaming. Nothing much else to do around here. And I like to walk."

"So do I." He gestured to the edge of the bridge. "Shall we?"

With a bob of her head, she came toward him, then seemed to realize she still held his cravat in her fist. "Oh! This is yours."

She thrust it at him, and he took it, careful not to touch her hand.

They walked awhile in a silence that grew heavier by the moment. Then she cleared her throat. "Were you close to your stepfather? I know you didn't get to see him, but surely you wrote letters home."

Damn. He'd prefer silence to her probing. "I did. But letters aren't the same, as I'm sure you know."

"I do. I liked your stepfather. He always treated me kindly, and he never behaved as if he were better than I."

"Maurice was the sort of man who treated people as equals when other members of society might not."

"Precisely. Sheridan is like him."

"And I am not."

She dropped her gaze to the path. "You are . . . not like anyone I know."

"I suppose you consider me more like your uncle Armie." He glanced over in time to see her blanch.

"Why on earth would you think such a thing?" she asked, sounding alarmed.

"I don't know. I gather that your uncle Armitage lorded it over you and your brother."

"Oh. Right." A long breath slipped from her. "Yes, he was a bit . . ."

"Full of himself?"

"You could say that."

She'd grown stiff and reserved. Mentioning her uncle seemed to have set her off.

How curious. Sheridan had been sure his uncle had been murdered as well. And something was making her reluctant to speak of the man.

"Fortunately," Grey said, "living over here at the dower house, you probably didn't see him that much."

"We saw him more than enough."

"So you didn't like him."

"As you say, he lorded it over us."

Grey was certain there was more to it. "I understand your uncle died here on the estate."

If he hadn't been watching for her reaction, he wouldn't have seen the expression of utter panic on her face.

"Yes." She wouldn't meet his eyes. "It was tragic."

Her reluctance to speak of it sent ice through his veins. What if Sheridan had been wrong about his father's death, but right about his uncle Armie's? Did that mean she knew something about it? He couldn't see *her* riding out at night to murder her uncle, but her brother? Perhaps.

She halted. "Forgive me, sir, I forgot something I must do at my house before I return. But you needn't wait. I'm sure you can find your way back to Armitage Hall on your own."

"I'm happy to come along, Beatrice. I could hold the dogs for you."

"No reason for that, truly. I have no idea how long it might take, and I'm sure your mother is pining for you already."

Her tone brooked no argument. His interlude with Miss Wolfe was clearly over.

"Very well. I'll see you tonight then. At dinner."

She bobbed her head and hurried off with the dogs.

He waited until she was out of sight before walking into the woods and looking for a place off the path where he could watch for her. He didn't have to stand there long before she passed him.

Just as he'd suspected. Her needing to go home had been a ruse to avoid his questions. Holy hell. What if Sheridan *had* been right about *some* of his suspicions?

If so, then Beatrice knew something. Now Grey would have to figure out exactly what she was covering up.

Chapter Nine

Beatrice had avoided dinner last night, but she couldn't avoid going to Armitage Hall today for her come-out lessons. Which meant she would see Grey.

She stifled a sigh. A part of her—a very small part—wouldn't mind taking him as a lover. If ever there was a fellow she would want to initiate her into the pleasures of the bedchamber, it was him. Because every time Grey had touched or kissed her, it had been a mutual enjoyment, utterly different from the years she'd spent fending off her uncle's slaps on the behind or hugs that smashed her breasts against him or slobbery busses to her lips in the guise of greetings.

Grey's kiss yesterday had made her think it was possible to enjoy a man's kisses. Unfortunately, she knew what happened to women who took lovers, and she refused to let that happen to her. Even for the thrill of having Grey in her bed.

Her cheeks heated. *In her bed?* What nonsense! How could she even entertain such a notion? She knew from the gossip rags what sort of women Grey preferred, and she wasn't that sort—beautiful and immoral and willing to risk everything to be the mistress of a duke.

As she approached Armitage Hall, she steeled

herself. She must keep her distance from him. Even if she *were* curious about his past. Because something had happened to make the duke reluctant to speak of it or let anyone close. Not that it mattered—not to her. None of her business.

She would let him keep his secrets. That way perhaps he would let her keep hers, and stop asking about Uncle Armie. Clearly, he was suspicious about how her uncle had died. And she couldn't let that continue, couldn't let him guess what she feared—that Uncle Armie's death had been no accident.

Fluffing up the gauze fichu that hid the way her repurposed gown showed too much of her bosom, she walked into Armitage Hall. She halted when she spotted Lady Gwyn talking to the butler and gesturing wildly about some matter that had her agitated.

A sigh escaped Beatrice at the sight of Lady Gwyn's custom-tailored crape mourning gown with its glorious black trim and collar of scalloped lace. How was Beatrice to become part of that world? Granted, by the time she was ready for her come-out, she would be out of mourning, but even if she *had* a dress as pretty as Lady Gwyn's, she could never wear it with the woman's elegant air. She would feel like a hound wearing a petticoat—utterly out of place.

Uncle Armie's nasty words leapt to mind: *Be happy I want you at all, girl. Most men wouldn't*

give the time of day to such a mannish creature.
You're no beauty.

A pox on her uncle. She had new relations who were kind to her, and she would cling to that.

Lady Gwyn accepted her as an equal as always, for when she saw Beatrice, she brightened. "There you are. Mother has been asking for you. She's eager to begin our training for our London debuts."

Beatrice handed her bonnet and gloves to the butler, then managed a smile as she fell into her usual role. "It's very kind of my aunt."

"Enough of that." Lady Gwyn planted her hands on her hips. "We're not doing this because of some notion about duty. We adore you. And this is the least we can do to make up for your uncle Armie's neglect."

The words were so sweet that a lump formed in Beatrice's throat. "That is lovely of you to say, Lady Gwyn."

"Call me Gwyn, I beg you. We are both pupils in this odd new world." Lady Gwyn—Gwyn—smiled. "And I could use an ally in keeping Mother from going too far." Gwyn approached to loop her arm through Beatrice's before breathing a long sigh. "She has a tendency to overshoot her mark, if you know what I mean. And I confess I'm so weary of fighting it I'm liable to go along."

Beatrice chuckled. "I can understand that. Aunt Lydia can be very persuasive."

"Indeed she can." Gwyn looked glum. "Between my mother and my brothers, I don't know how you and I shall survive."

With a laugh, Beatrice said, "We'll be fine," though the idea of Grey being part of her come-out lessons still sent her senses flailing. How could she be around him without remembering their searing kiss? Not to mention the alarming questions he'd asked about Uncle Armie.

"In any case," Gwyn went on, "we're supposed to work on dancing today."

Oh, Lord. Dancing with Grey. How would she get through *that?* "Surely you know how to dance already."

"Not English country dances. In Berlin, we danced other steps. And the waltz, which is only two people. I can manage that. Anything else . . ."

"I've never even heard of the waltz. But give me a good Scotch reel or Irish jig, and I can perform as well as any dancing master."

"Then I'll teach you the waltz and you'll teach me the reel, and we'll impress everyone at the balls."

Beatrice laughed, unable to resist Gwyn's amiable approach. She'd nearly even convinced herself that Gwyn's presence could make dancing with Grey tolerable when they entered the ballroom to find him absent. Thornstock was the one speaking to his mother about the dancing.

Disappointment sliced through her before she

caught herself. She refused to feel such a foolish emotion over the thought of losing the chance to dance with Grey. No doubt Grey had asked to be relieved of his duties with her after what had happened yesterday. One more sign he hadn't felt half of what she had when they'd kissed.

"Ah," Thornstock said. "The ladies have arrived, Mother. So let's get this over with, shall we?"

Just then, Sheridan entered the ballroom, obviously cutting through from the garden to the hall at the end opposite them that led to Uncle Armie's stu—

Not Uncle Armie's, but *Sheridan's* study, now. It gave her a little burst of satisfaction to think of her cousin there instead of her wretched uncle.

"Thank God you're here," Thornstock told Sheridan. "We need all the help we can get with the dancing lessons."

"I can't," Sheridan said, with a trace of irritation. "I've got more than enough to handle right now." Then he looked beyond Beatrice to a spot behind her. "Ask Grey—he'll tell you. Why don't you get him to do it?"

Beatrice turned to find him lounging against the wall in the large, rounded alcove behind her, which was custom-built to hold a small orchestra, but at present only held the pianoforte.

Grey fixed his eyes on her. "I'm happy to partner Miss Wolfe if she needs it."

Was he willing to dance with her because of their kiss yesterday? Or was he merely hoping to interrogate her about Uncle Armie's death? Either possibility was worrisome.

Though Grey was dressed in another black mourning suit, he'd changed out his hessians today for shoes more fitting to a ballroom. But even without the fancy boots, he was as incredibly attractive—and terrifying—as she remembered.

And when he pushed away from the wall and straightened to his full height, she was hard-pressed not to swoon, though whether in awe or alarm, she wasn't sure. Only the fact that she'd never swooned a day in her life kept her from it.

Meanwhile Thornstock kept trying to fob his female relations off on Sheridan. "Grey is already helping. But if you stay, they won't need me. I was hoping to go for a ride on one of your hunters."

"Sorry, you'll have to delay that." Sheridan continued on through the room. "I have important matters to attend to."

"So do I! Like riding!" Thornstock cried after him.

But it was too late. Sheridan vanished from view through the other door.

Gwyn gave her twin a look of mock sympathy. "Aw, poor Thorn, having to dance with respectable ladies for a change. Such a trial for you, I'm sure."

"Don't start with me," Thornstock grumbled. "Or I'll take you over my knee."

"I should like to see you try!" Gwyn planted her hands on her hips. "Because I can still box your ears. Just give me a chance to—"

"Hush, you two." Aunt Lydia headed for the pianoforte in the alcove with determined steps. Her usual creamy skin was the color of ash, and she looked as if she might crumble any moment. "I would think that after so many years apart, you'd have learned to appreciate each other."

Grey went to stand next to his mother. "Surely you're joking. Gwyn always needs someone to sharpen her tongue on, and Thorn is her favorite choice of strop."

Gwyn raised an eyebrow at him. "Watch it or I'll box your ears, too."

As Beatrice smothered a laugh, Aunt Lydia cried, "Enough, all of you!" Rounding the end of the pianoforte, she plopped down on the bench and started flipping through sheet music with a scowl. "I swear, sometimes I wonder why I ever married and had children in the first place."

That pronouncement gave them all pause.

Thornstock was the first to rally. "I understand why you wouldn't want to be stuck with Grey, your ill-favored firstborn. But surely the devastatingly handsome fellow you bore next makes up for your having *him*."

Grey snorted. "She didn't bear you next, you

lummox. Gwyn is fifteen minutes older. *You* were just an afterthought."

"Quite so," Gwyn put in with a sniff. "And the only reason Thorn doesn't want to help with the dancing is he has two left feet."

"I beg your pardon." Thorn stared her down. "I'll have you know I can caper as well as any man on the floor."

Gwyn looked down at her fingernails as if studying their shape. "There's no question you can caper, dear Brother. The issue is, can you dance? Frankly, I don't think you have it in you. Not that *I've* ever seen, anyway."

Thornstock stalked up to his twin. "Mother, play something. Let's *see* if I have it in me, damn it."

Beatrice fought back a smile. Amazing how Gwyn could outmaneuver Thornstock without his even realizing it.

Gwyn lifted an eyebrow as she faced Thornstock. "Mama, why don't you play a minuet?"

Aunt Lydia looked at her twins warily. "Do you really think we should start with something so intricate?"

"All the better to prove my abilities," Thornstock said.

"I'm not thinking of *your* abilities, Son. Or even Gwyn's. She knows the minuet." Aunt Lydia looked over at Beatrice. "Do you know the steps for that one, Bea?"

Beatrice tensed at the very thought of having to stumble through a new dance. "I'm afraid not, Aunt."

"We'll sit it out, Mother." Grey left the alcove and headed for Beatrice. "She and I will watch, and then she'll get a feel for it so she'll be ready when we teach it to her later."

"Very well then." Aunt Lydia thumbed through pages of music, searching for a tune suitable for dancing a minuet to. "But I shall choose something more appropriate for the occasion. Something stately and mournful. Your father *is* fresh in the grave, you know."

That sobered Gwyn. "Mama, perhaps we should wait—"

"No, indeed," her mother said fiercely, brushing tears from her cheeks. "I want to play. Dance, you two." As she launched into a dignified piece, the twins began the minuet.

Beatrice looked over to where her aunt was playing determinedly, her eyes still bright with tears. "Is this wise?" Beatrice murmured to Grey, who was now standing next to her.

"Mother handles things better if she feels needed and useful," he said softly.

Hoping to regain yesterday's comfortable rapport, she asked Grey, "Is it part of the dance for them to hold their arms out like that? They look like marionettes whose strings are stuck."

"Sadly, it's considered graceful," he replied.

"Anyone who thinks a marionette is graceful has never seen a Punch and Judy show." She focused on other aspects of the dance. "It's like a slower jig, isn't it?"

"Not quite. It's a different step entirely." Grey gestured to a settee against the wall opposite where the twins were dancing. "Let's sit down, Miss Wolfe." His tone brooked no argument. "You can see their feet better this way."

It reminded her of yesterday, when he'd commanded her—and thus, the dogs. She glanced at him to see if he remembered, but he gave no indication he did. Instead, his expression showed only a polite disinterest.

She followed him to the settee, then perched on the edge. Grey took a seat beside her, his hand casually drumming the beat on his thigh inches from her own.

Pay attention! she told herself. They all expect you to remember how to do this.

So she focused on observing their feet. Her aunt was right—the steps *were* intricate. "I'll *never* master that," she murmured, half to herself.

"Of course you will." Grey raised his voice to be heard over the music. "It merely requires practice. Personally, I dislike the minuet. All that mincing looks silly, even if you do consider the 'marionette' look of the arms to be graceful. But alas, every society ball has a minuet or two, so you must learn to dance it."

"Clearly it requires a certain lightness of foot that I lack."

He eyed her skeptically. "Somehow I can't believe that. Any woman who can trip down a hill in skirts without falling, as you did yesterday in pursuit of your dogs, possesses all the lightness of foot necessary to dance a minuet."

She did not want to remember what happened yesterday. "Well, your brother and sister clearly possess it. They're doing the steps without even a stumble—and still managing to argue."

"You must forgive the twins for their rudeness—they barely tolerate each other at the best of times."

"That surprises me. I would have expected twins to be more easy together. You know, feel more of a connection."

"At one time, they did."

Noticing the edge in his voice, she slanted a glance at him. "What changed between them?"

He shrugged. "From what Mother has said, I gather that things changed after Thorn returned to England when he came of age. He wanted Gwyn to come with him, but she refused."

"Why?" Beatrice asked.

He shifted to look at her, searching her face as if trying to decide how much to say. "Gwyn had a beau, some officer, whom she was sure would marry her eventually. Then something happened between them. The end result was she jilted him, apparently because of something Thorn said." He observed her a bit too closely. "You know how brothers are."

Oh, dear, this was probably Grey's oblique way of trying to get her to speak about Joshua. "I do, indeed."

When she said no more, Grey went on with a frown. "After that, she couldn't forgive Thorn for meddling in her affairs. She won't say exactly what happened, Thorn won't even acknowledge his part in it, and Mother doesn't know. So, here they stand, always at odds."

"I sympathize," she muttered, thinking of Joshua.

"How so? Do you and your brother not get along?"

"Not since Joshua returned from the war," she admitted reluctantly. "We . . . don't know how to be around each other anymore."

"Ah. I can understand that." He watched the twins. "I feel much the same about *my* siblings. When you're apart for a long time, you—" A thin smile crossed his lips. "Discover that you've found different interests and formed independent opinions, and now you're practically strangers."

She shot him a smile of pure relief. Grey understood exactly what she was feeling. How lovely to find someone who did. "He's not even the same person anymore. The Joshua I knew before the war was quiet and contemplative. He liked nothing so much as a good book and a glass of wine . . . or a long walk in the woods. Then Grandpapa bought him a commission, he was wounded on the Continent, and—"

"He changed."

She nodded. "Dramatically. He became temperamental—melancholy one moment, angry the next. It's hard to explain. I so want him to be how he used to be."

A bitter laugh escaped Grey. "Battle alters people, and such a change is generally permanent."

"How would *you* know?" Beatrice cast him a hard stare. "You've never been to war."

He gazed blindly ahead. "There are more kinds of battle than those fought in wars."

She opened her mouth to ask what he meant, but at that moment, the music ended.

Her aunt burst into applause, forcing Beatrice and Grey to do the same.

"Well, Miss Wolfe?" Thornstock said, coming to stand in front of Beatrice. "Who's the better dancer? Me or Gwyn?"

"You are both very accomplished, truly. I couldn't possibly—I mean—"

"Ignore my idiot brother," Grey said. "He's just being an arse. Thorn has never worried about anyone else's opinion of him. None of us do, I'm afraid. It's a family trait." He arched an eyebrow at his half brother. "And Thorn is the worst."

As if to prove Grey's point, Thornstock burst into laughter. "Grey is right—I don't need a judge of my abilities to know that I proved Gwyn wrong." With a taunting glance back to where Gwyn was rolling her eyes, he held out his hand to Beatrice. "And I'll prove it again. Come dance with me."

"Forgive me, Your Grace," Beatrice responded, "I don't know the steps. I've never even seen a minuet danced until just now."

"Then you must learn," Thornstock said.

A muscle worked in Grey's jaw. "I'll teach her."

"You will not," Thornstock replied. "I've already danced once with Gwyn. She's your problem now." Then the man waggled his fingers at Beatrice. "Come, Miss Wolfe. We'll start with my showing you the steps, and then Mother will play the slowest minuet over and over until you can master it."

Grey crossed his arms over his chest. "I thought you didn't even want to be doing this. Go have your ride. I'll take care of teaching Beatr— Miss Wolfe."

Mischief gleamed in Thornstock's eyes as he apparently caught the slip. "I've changed my mind. I'd be delighted to instruct Miss Wolfe in . . . all sorts of things."

Grey began to look as if he might throttle the man when Gwyn breezed over to take Beatrice's arm. "Good Lord, *I* will teach her the steps, thank you very much. Why don't you two go call for some tea to be brought? I daresay we'll need it if you intend to keep snarling at each other."

"The only thing I'm calling for, Sis," Thornstock muttered, "is brandy."

Gwyn drew Beatrice closer to the piano. "If you want to be foxed by noon, go ahead. *I* would like some tea, and I'm sure Mama and Bea could use some, too." She made a shooing motion. "Go, both of you. Give us a while to ourselves. No woman wants a male audience when she's just learning a dance step."

Grey glanced at Beatrice, then grabbing his brother forcefully by the arm, he led him out the door. Beatrice released a long breath.

With a rueful smile, Gwyn patted her hand. "How does it feel to have two dukes fighting over you, my dear?"

"If they weren't using me merely to provoke each other, I might enjoy it."

Gwyn shot her a considering look. "I'm not entirely sure that's the motivation of *both* of them." Her expression turned enigmatic. "But we'll see." She turned to her mother. "Mama, can you play the first bars of that piece very slowly?"

Nodding her approval, Aunt Lydia did so. And thus began Beatrice's first minuet lesson.

Chapter Ten

As soon as Grey left the ballroom, he released his idiot brother and gave instructions to a footman to have refreshments brought for the ladies. Then he headed for the study to see what Sheridan was up to.

Thorn followed him. "Sheridan mentioned that you might have an interest in Miss Wolfe, and I didn't believe him. Apparently, I was wrong."

"You're both wrong." Grey fought to keep his temper in check. "My interest in Miss Wolfe is the same as I'd have for any relation of Maurice's."

He only wanted to make sure she wasn't hiding something concerning her uncles' deaths and thus determine if her brother was the murderous fellow Sheridan had made him out to be. It was purely a matter of doing what Sheridan had asked him to. Nothing more.

"Then why are you so eager to dance with her? And to keep *me* from dancing with her?"

Grey lifted an eyebrow. "I merely wish to make sure you don't toy with her. She's not your mouse to bat around like a tomcat before he goes in for the kill."

Thorn cocked his head. "Has it occurred to you I might actually be looking for a wife?"

"No, it has not." Grey faced his brother. "You

see women merely as conquests to add to your score. You ought to respect the fact that she's Sheridan's cousin and stay away from her, if only for his sake."

"For *Sheridan's* sake?" Thorn laughed. "That's not why you want me staying away from her. Actually, I see *Miss Wolfe* as an entertaining way to drive you mad. Admit it, you fancy her."

"Don't be absurd." The last person to whom Grey would admit his fascination with Beatrice was Thorn, who would try to seduce her just to get Grey to acknowledge that he wanted her. And while the woman was obviously hiding something concerning her uncle, she was doing it poorly enough to convince Grey that she wouldn't know the first thing about fending off a determined philanderer like Thorn.

Best to ignore Thorn's remark and proceed with caution by appealing to the man's reason. "You must understand—Miss Wolfe isn't worldly wise, and your tactics aren't in her limited experience of men. I'm merely doing what any true gentleman would—protecting an innocent and respectable woman from a blackguard like you."

All Thorn's amusement vanished. "A 'blackguard' like me." He advanced on Grey. " 'Let he who is without sin cast the first stone.' *I* am not the one with a reputation for dissolute cabals."

"You can't be serious." Grey snorted.

"Dissolute cabals, indeed. You know damned well that the gossips will say anything to get a rise out of me."

"You don't see that they do the same to me?" Thorn bit out. "I swear, you're such a bloody arrogant prick sometimes. You think you're the only man in this family with any decency."

"That's not true—I think Sheridan has plenty of decency," Grey said, deliberately taunting Thorn out of some perverse urge to punish him for daring to toy with Beatrice.

Thorn's hands tightened into fists before he caught himself. "You almost had me there, Brother. But I will not engage in this tug-of-war with you, especially when it's merely your attempt to distract me from the real issue— that you desire Miss Wolfe and won't admit it." He started to march off, then paused. "And incidentally, I would *never* ruin a woman, no matter who her relations were."

Belatedly, Grey realized he'd stepped over some invisible line with Thorn. "Glad to hear it."

"One more thing." Thorn regarded him with a steady stare. "I suspect that Miss Wolfe is more worldly wise than you think."

Grey found it suddenly difficult to breathe. He'd spent enough time with "worldly wise" women to know that they tended to be schemers, at least around a duke. And he hated schemers more than anything.

Though he would never admit that to his brother. Forcing nonchalance into his voice, he said, "You'd best not speculate on Miss Wolfe's character around our mother, since Mother seems to think the young woman hung the moon."

Thorn let out an exasperated breath. "I'm not casting aspersions on Miss Wolfe's character. I'm saying she's not the starry-eyed fool you assume. For one thing, she's intelligent enough to tell the difference between a man who's merely flirting and one who actually has designs on her virtue."

Like me? God, he did *not* have designs on her virtue. "I never thought her a fool. She's an innocent." As long as Grey kept telling himself that, perhaps he'd keep his mind on his task for Sheridan instead of wanting to touch her, taste her mouth, take her to—

Damn it all. Grey stared his brother down. "A fool and an innocent aren't the same thing."

"You barely know her. It's far too soon for you to be pursuing her."

"Pursuing her! I'm doing no such thing."

"Right." Thorn rolled his eyes. "But while you're busy *not* pursuing her, you might consider learning a bit more about her. From someone other than our mother and sister and possibly our brother, I mean."

Grey blinked at him. "Who else is there?"

"The servants, for one." Thorn's tone turned sarcastic. "You might lower your bloody self to talk to them for a change. See what *they* have to say about her."

Having often been the subject of rumor-mongering, Grey found servant gossip to be as unreliable as the society kind. He didn't like to encourage it. And Thorn knew that.

"Why are you prodding me to talk to the servants about her? What have you heard?"

"Just that some of the maids—" Thorn ran his fingers through his hair. "Never mind. It was probably groundless, anyway. My point is, you seem to desire Miss Wolfe. She's not my cup of tea, mind you—I prefer blondes myself—but she's clearly yours. Which means you should take care how you behave around her."

Grey bristled. "I don't see *you* being careful."

"That's because Miss Wolfe knows I'm not serious. And you obviously are."

"I am not pursuing her."

"You're such a liar. Though I can't tell if you're just lying to me, or if you're lying to yourself as well." With a sigh, Thorn headed down the hall for the drawing room. "Now, I'm going to have myself a decent glass of brandy before I tackle the minuet again. I suggest you do the same."

"Not at this early hour."

"Suit yourself."

Grey waited until Thorn disappeared through a door before he returned to the ballroom. But he didn't enter. He just stood in the doorway watching Gwyn work with Beatrice on the minuet steps and fuming at what Thorn had said. Damned arse, with his sly insinuations concerning Beatrice's experience with men. From what Grey could tell, she'd had little. But Thorn seemed to regard her as some budding enchantress.

Looking at her now, Grey was reminded of how guileless she seemed when she was with him.

Grey huffed out a breath. No doubt she *was* guileless. Thorn was probably merely goading him as usual. Typical Thorn behavior. Or, just as likely, Thorn was expressing his usual cynicism about women. He'd certainly withdrawn his remarks about Beatrice's experience with men quickly enough.

A maid came down the hall with a tea tray, headed for the ballroom. Grey stood aside to let her enter, his mind racing. Perhaps he *should* speak to the servants, if only to confirm that Thorn was full of shite. After all, what damning information could the staff possibly have about Beatrice? Yes, she'd become evasive when Grey had brought up her uncle Armie's death. But there might be a hundred innocent reasons for that.

As the maid set out the tea, Beatrice went over to pour and nearly got some on her weepers, those white lace cuffs added to mourning attire so women could use them to wipe their tears. The old design of her gown—along with the muslin fabric and the white filmy fichu she'd tucked into her obviously snug bodice—hinted that this was an old day dress she'd dyed black. Which spoke to how poor she and her brother were.

Damn her selfish uncle Armie to hell. And her brother, too, for that matter. Had neither of them any sense of their responsibilities? Their duty to their relations? Beatrice should have been given a come-out long ago.

When the maid came back out into the hall, Grey fell into step beside her. "Pardon me, but I'd like to ask you a few questions, if I may."

Bobbing her head, she crossed her arms over her chest as if preparing for anything.

You might lower yourself to talk to the servants for a change.

His brother's words made him wince. Grey was fully aware that his reserved manner could be off-putting to staff.

Perhaps a more oblique approach was warranted. "It's about Miss Wolfe. I merely want to know what I can do to help her, since Mother seems to rely so much on the lady."

The servant relaxed her stance. "Oh, sir, whatever you could do for her would be very kind. We should all like to see Miss Wolfe better looked after. She's such a fine woman, always considering the needs of others without any reward. Even the servants."

"I gathered as much. Miss Wolfe seems to know everything that goes on in this house."

"Indeed she does, Your Grace. She helped run the household for her uncle Armitage and even served as his hostess after the duchess died."

"Right. I gather that the duchess was supposed to take Miss Wolfe on as a companion, but her death cut that short."

"Exactly. She died long afore I came here, and that's already been ten years. Though I did hear that he and his duchess was always at odds, on account of his—" As if realizing she was saying too much, she pressed her lips together.

"His what?"

"Don't wish to speak ill of the dead, sir."

He smiled. "Trust me, I've already figured out that her uncle Armie wasn't a very nice man."

She let out a breath. "Well, then, you probably heard about him and his dalliances."

"Of course," he lied.

"He wasn't even circumspect about them, neither. I hear it fairly drove his duchess mad."

"I'm sure it did."

"Though they claim you wouldn't have knowed it to watch her. Like stone, that lady was. Or so I'm told. She let him visit his tarts without saying a word."

"She didn't have much choice, I would imagine. But surely he hid his dalliances from Miss Wolfe. She was his niece, after all, and a maiden as well."

She sniffed. "A man like that don't hide his

true character from nobody, sir." Then something seemed to dawn on her, and she dropped her gaze. "Not that I was implying anything about *you*. I didn't mean . . ." She cast a panicked look behind her toward the kitchens and mumbled, "If that's all, Your Grace, Cook will surely be needing me."

Grey stared at her blankly as he tried to figure out what she was hinting at and why she'd turned odd all of a sudden.

Then it dawned on him. Oh, for God's sake. If she'd heard the gossip about him and his "dissolute cabals," then in her eyes he was as bad as her former employer. He would undoubtedly have trouble getting anything more out of her. But he'd learned enough for the moment.

"I understand." He forced a smile. "I don't want to keep you from your duties."

Relief crossed her face. "Thank you, Your Grace. And I didn't mean—"

"I took no offense, I assure you. Now go on with you."

With a bob of her head, she practically raced in the direction of the kitchen.

Sighing, Grey walked back to the ballroom. What the maid had told him was enlightening. It might explain Thorn's claim that Beatrice was more worldly wise than Grey thought. She'd have to be in order to deal with her uncle's peccadilloes.

And it might explain why she became so closed-mouthed whenever he brought up her uncle Armie.

Could she be protecting her brother? Come to think of it, she'd grown nervous again today when the subject of Wolfe had come up. This might all be about her brother. She might actually know what Sheridan already suspected—that Wolfe had murdered her uncle. She might even be complicit in it.

The possibility chilled Grey. Could she really be such a schemer? Could he be so mistaken in her character?

She *had* managed to charm the entire family in a matter of weeks. Look at how easily Gwyn had accepted her. And Mother, too. Even Sheridan. Could she have a reason for ingratiating herself with the family?

With *him?*

Grey scowled. If that was her motive, she would be disappointed. She was wrong for him for so many reasons. She wore her heart on her sleeve; he had none. She blurted out her every thought; he held his closer to his chest than his shirt. She was eager to please everyone in her orbit; he was eager to avoid everyone in his.

Yet he couldn't look away from her as she danced, her movements graceful and her face flushing with enjoyment as she nimbly—

His eyes narrowed. She'd picked up the steps

of the minuet with surprising ease for a woman who'd protested she could never learn the steps. She was a puzzle, to be sure, one that he meant to untangle.

And he must do it carefully. Thorn was right about one thing: Unless Grey meant to pursue her, his behavior toward her must be above reproach.

Never again did Grey intend to be that ten-year-old boy who craved love and attention, only to discover that the people who should have offered it—his aunt and uncle—were incapable of anything but using him to advance their own situation. Never again would he give anyone else the power to hurt him.

All the same, when he heard a door open and shut somewhere and realized it could be Thorn coming to join the ladies, he walked swiftly into the ballroom. No way in hell was he going to let his brother be the one to dance with her.

He told himself it was because he needed more of a chance to find out what had her so agitated about her uncle Armie's death. Needed to be certain she wasn't nurturing any secret hopes of becoming his duchess.

But the truth was, Grey simply wanted to dance with her.

So dance with her he would. He would just have to make sure to keep his wits about him as he did.

Beatrice was concentrating so hard on dancing the minuet that she didn't notice Grey had returned until he spoke in that seductive voice of his.

"If you're ready to dance with a partner, Miss Wolfe, I'm at your disposal."

Gwyn greeted this announcement with a clap of her hands. "Wonderful! Beatrice really needs a man to practice with because when I take the lead, I forget what I'm doing and fall into the woman's part. Much more of that and she'll never get the way of it."

Beatrice wiped her clammy hands on her skirt. What if she made a fool of herself in front of him? "The one to blame for my not having the way of it is *me*."

"Nonsense." Gwyn smiled. "You're better than you think. And Grey will help you perfect your dancing, I'm sure." She glanced to the door. "Or Thorn, if he's the one to dance with you. Where *is* Thorn, anyway?"

When she looked to Grey for an answer, he shrugged. "Last I saw him, he was heading off to find brandy."

"Lord help me," Gwyn muttered. "You two start while I fetch him. But I'm not letting him dance if he's foxed. That won't help anyone."

"It certainly won't help Bea," Gwyn's mother remarked from the pianoforte, although Gwyn was already gone. Aunt Lydia shot Grey a defeated look. "Can't you get Thorn to stop drinking so much, dearest?"

Grey walked into the alcove and around the pianoforte to lay a hand on her shoulder. "Everyone grieves in their own way. *You* try to stay busy to keep your mind off missing Maur— missing Father. Thorn drinks. You must give him time to mourn."

His mother patted his hand. "And how do *you* grieve, Grey?"

He bent to kiss her head. "By teaching Miss Wolfe to dance the minuet, of course. Play some music so we can try to forget our loss. Then when Gwyn arrives with Thorn, they can join in."

His mother's gaze darkened. "It will be a slow and somber minuet. I can't bear a happy tune just now."

"All the better to help Miss Wolfe learn," he said, his voice noticeably softer. He squeezed his mother's shoulder, then returned to Beatrice and held out his hand. "Shall we?"

As she let him lead her to the floor, Beatrice was all too aware that the duke was holding her hand. And neither of them wore gloves, as they normally would in a ballroom. Granted, he didn't hold her hand long, since the dance didn't allow for it, but still, every brush of his fingers against hers drove the air right out of her lungs.

After a few steps, which she thought she'd

executed fairly well, he caught her hand for a turn, his gaze intent upon her face. "You dance better than you led me to believe."

"Your sister is an excellent teacher."

"And you're a quick study," he said blandly.

"Thank God!" she blurted out. "I-I mean, thank heaven. I was sure I'd bumble through it once I was dancing with an actual man."

Amusement glinted in his eyes. "An *actual* man? As opposed to what? A painting of one? An effigy? A statue, perhaps."

Against her better judgment, she laughed. "As opposed to your sister. I haven't managed to master the French version, though. I can only do the English one."

"Not too many people do the French step in London anyway. But if you really want to learn, it's not so difficult. Just let me lead you."

"I will do whatever you wish, Your Grace."

Something dangerously enticing flickered in his gaze. "Every time you offer to do whatever I wish, you tempt me, Beatrice," he murmured. "So don't offer unless you mean it."

Blast, she was in trouble. If he kept saying things like that, she'd melt into a puddle. The duke could seduce a saint, and she was no saint, just a woman caught in circumstances beyond her control, with a man who turned her knees wobbly.

Now he was looking at her as he had in the

woods yesterday—with hunger in his eyes. As the music continued, she forgot about counting the beats or feeling clumsy. She matched his motions, relishing the masterful way he led her, his hands clasping hers as they circled each other. His eyes flashed green or blue depending on whether he faced the windows as they turned, and the effect was hypnotic.

Dancing with him was hypnotic. Every clasp of his hand as they came together was a pleasurable agony, every dark smile an invitation to debauchery. She could hardly catch her breath, her heart was pounding so. Surely he must hear it and think her the veriest peagoose he'd ever met, to be so flustered by a mere dance.

Suddenly, Gwyn burst into the room. "Mama, Thorn is leaving for London!"

The music ended abruptly. "What?" Aunt Lydia rose. "But why?"

Grey and Beatrice moved a respectable distance apart as Gwyn stalked to the pianoforte. "My stupid brother says he has important things to do in town. That he shan't waste any more time around here. He's packing up right this minute!"

"The devil he is!" Aunt Lydia cried. "That boy will be the death of me yet." She caught Gwyn by the arm. "Come with me. He's leaving because of *you,* you know. And I've had enough of you two squabbling. We're going to settle this right now."

Halfway out the door, Aunt Lydia paused to

say to Beatrice and Grey, "Keep practicing! The three of us will be back in a moment."

"Somehow I doubt that," Grey muttered. "Not even Mother can undo years of disagreement in a single moment." He cast Beatrice a wry smile. "And I'm not sure how she expects us to dance with no music." Calculation gleamed in his eyes. "You and I should just talk until they return."

So he could ask more questions about Joshua and Uncle Armie to coax her into babbling her foolish fears? No, thank you. "If I hum the music, we could continue to practice the steps."

"I'm not sure you need more practice." He eyed her uncertainly, as if trying to figure out her game. "You seem to have mastered the minuet well enough to pass muster."

"Then perhaps you could teach me another dance."

"What do you have in mind?"

"Let me think." She ran through all the dances she'd heard of until she hit on one. "How about 'Jenny's Market'?"

An odd look crossed his face. "'Jenny's Market'? Are you certain that's one you wish to learn?"

"I've heard the dance is quite popular in high society. Do you know it?"

"I do indeed. Very well."

Thank *God.* Now she wouldn't have to talk about Uncle Armie with him.

Although the way he'd said, *I do indeed,* with a hint of suspicion, gave her pause. Because now he was gazing at her with a heat in his eyes that made her heart drop into her stomach.

Uh-oh. She might have jumped from the frying pan into the fire. And she really wasn't sure how.

Chapter Eleven

Grey had begun to think that Beatrice was as guileless as she had seemed until she'd mentioned wanting to learn "Jenny's Market."

Unless . . . "How do you know about 'Jenny's Market'? Have you ever seen it danced?"

She sighed. "I'm afraid not."

That explained a great deal. He walked over to close the door leading to the hall. When he caught her gaping at him, he said, "Someone seeing us dance 'Jenny's Market' without music could misinterpret what we're doing, so it's best to keep the servants from chattering. If we were wise, we'd also practice over by the pianoforte, since we'd hear anyone enter before they turned around to spot us in the musicians' alcove."

"Oh, dear." Her face fell. "Then it must be quite a scandalous dance."

"Without music, yes, it might be seen as something scandalous. In a ballroom with other couples, it's perfectly acceptable."

"Can I admit something to you?" she asked.

Absolutely. "We do have a bargain about saying what we think."

"Well then, learning that the dance is scandalous sort of . . ." She leaned close and lowered her tone to a confidential murmur. "It makes me even more eager to learn it. Though I suppose it's wicked of me to think such a thing, let alone speak it."

His pulse beat a rapid tattoo. "Wicked? No. Let's just say that your grandmother was right—you *are* a naughty saucebox. But it happens to be something I like about you."

Her gaze sharpened on him. "Because you want to take advantage of it."

"I'm a man." He shrugged. "We take advantage whenever we get the chance. Remember that, when you're in society and some fellow who's less of a gentleman than I tries to get you alone. But scandalous or not, 'Jenny's Market' is still merely a dance. If you want to learn it, I'm happy to teach it to you."

She seemed to consider the matter. Then she squared her shoulders and met his gaze with a certain impudence. "All right. Why not?"

His pulse did an impudent dance of its own.

Down, boy. She merely wants to dabble in the scandalous. So let her. God knows you want her to.

He led her into the musicians' alcove. "To begin, we stand opposite each other at about arms' length."

With a nod, she took that position. Then she muttered a curse that sounded distinctly unladylike. "I just realized—I have no idea what tune to hum."

"Do you know 'Lucy May'?"

Her face lit up. "I do!"

"That will work. But hum it at a slower pace than usual, so I can instruct and you can follow without too much trouble."

"All right." She began to hum in a deep, throaty voice so thrilling that fire rose in him anew.

He fought to tamp it down. "First, we bow. Then we take one step toward each other . . . and one step away. Right, like that." He held out his hands. "Next we clasp hands in a wide arc and circle around until we're back to where we were."

She stopped humming just long enough to say, "I'm not sure why you considered this dance so shocking."

"We're coming to that." He tugged her close, apparently taking her by surprise, for her color heightened. "You lift your left hand over your head to touch your fingertips to *my* left hand as you align your right shoulder with my right shoulder. At the same time you place your right hand on the left side of my waist and I place my right hand in the same spot on yours."

As the position entwined them so that their right forearms lay across each other's stomachs and their left hands met overhead, forcing them to gaze into each other's eyes, she stopped humming. "Oh my," she said breathlessly.

He didn't move, though he relished the feel of

her slender belly against his arm and the widening of her eyes as her lips formed a surprised O. "Now you understand why the servants might misinterpret our . . . lesson."

"Indeed." With her color deepening to scarlet, she dropped her gaze from his.

God help him. That blush made everything harder. Including certain parts of his body. He would need an ice bath after this was done.

"Wh-what comes next?" she asked.

"We make two turns in this position." But he didn't move. When she glanced up to find him regarding her steadily, he murmured, "Are you going to hum the tune? Or shall I count it off?"

She groaned. "Of course I'll hum. Forgive me for stopping."

A choked laugh escaped him. "No man alive would complain about being locked in this pose with you."

At once she started humming.

That was a different sort of torture, since he now had to move. He led them into the turn while staring into the warmth of her pretty eyes, which he wished weren't gazing at him so greedily. If she was even aware of that.

He couldn't *stop* being aware of it. Or of the sensuality of the dance. The slow swivel they made was all the more erotic because her fingers dug into his waist, probably so she could keep her balance. But he indulged in a wild fantasy that those questing fingers were sliding inside his coat . . . waistcoat . . . *shirt,* so he could feel them exploring every inch of his chest.

And lower.

Holy hell. It was all he could do to keep his touch steady when he really wanted to smooth his hand up her ribs and over her bodice to cover one—

"Keep turning," he said in a guttural voice as they finished the first circuit, though his breath felt scratchy in his throat and he could hardly get the words out.

As if recognizing his difficulty, she hummed louder. Which only made him want to halt the humming with his mouth.

"Now we bring our left hands down," he said, "clasping them together while both of us pivot to face forward, and we slide our right hands over until they meet between us where we can join them together, too. In other words, our arms should form a cross in front between us."

It was comical to watch her expression as she tried to make sense of his instructions. After getting everything mixed up, she stopped in mid-step. "I'm sorry, you'll have to show me that one again."

"Of course." He faced her once more. "Let's return to our former position." *The one where I caress your waist and stare into your lovely face.*

"Lord save me," she muttered.

He agreed, though he doubted anything would save them from the conflagration this dance sparked between them.

As he laid his arm over the front of her waist again, her breathing grew ragged and her stomach trembled, making other parts of him catch fire . . . especially the parts that craved the touch of her hand. Which was pretty much all of them.

Best to finish the lesson quickly. So as soon as they were situated properly, he moved them into the next step by essentially forcing her hands into the position while saying, "Then slowly we turn to face forward as we slide our hands across—"

"Oh, yes!" she cried with relief in her voice. "I've got it now."

"Good. Let's start it once more from where we were, but with the music."

She nodded as he shifted them backward into their former provocative position. Then she began to hum.

It was all he could do to take up his instructions at the next part. "We walk forward together one step and back one step, before we separate to circle around behind the couples and go to the end of the line."

Stupid as it seemed, when they parted, he felt keenly the loss of her . . . though they'd only moved a few feet due to being in the alcove, and no one stood between them as would happen if other people were dancing, too.

As if drawn by an invisible thread, he approached her once more. "After we're at the end of the line, we face each other and start the steps again in our new place. Bow, join hands, et cetera. That's the dance in a nutshell."

She stopped humming, looking reluctant to have reached the end. "I see."

"Let's go back to the beginning. This time we can practice it with the music uninterrupted, to make sure you have the steps down. What do you think, sweetheart?"

When her gaze warmed on him, he cursed himself for letting the endearment slip. Fortunately, she merely said, "Why not?"

His blood roared through his veins. They both knew this wasn't about practicing. It was about wanting more stolen, reckless moments alone together. Even though nothing could come of it. Even though Grey knew it was insanity.

So much for keeping his wits about him. That was difficult when she was so refreshingly genuine. Truthful.

Intoxicating.

Yet he took the appropriate position once more, fully determined to make hay while the sun shone in her face.

He counted, and they bowed in time before clasping hands. The next few steps went well. She was following his lead perfectly without him having to utter a single instruction.

When they reached those turns where they were intimately entwined, he forgot everything except the lilting sound of her humming and the feel of her waist going taut beneath his arm. As they twirled slowly, one pair of hands touching in the air, the other pair half caressing each other's waists, he saw only her face and the sensual awareness pooling in her big brown eyes, threatening to drown all his resolutions.

After a moment, she murmured, "I've lost count of how many turns we've made."

The words only half broke the spell she'd cast over him. "So have I."

Yet they kept turning.

"Are we still even dancing 'Jenny's Market'?" Her voice was breathy, her eyes wide with arousal.

It mirrored his own. "Not quite." Lowering his mouth to within a hairbreadth of hers, he said, "I believe musicians would call this a variation upon the dance."

He hovered there a moment to give her a chance to protest what they both knew he meant to do. Then he covered her mouth with his, exulting in how she rose to his kiss with all the eagerness of a woman newly discovering her power over a man. Which was obviously considerable, since he couldn't seem to stop tasting her lips, despite the warnings his conscience screamed at him.

And once she opened her mouth to let him

plunge his tongue inside, even his conscience fell silent. Waves of hunger swamping him, he brought one hand up and the other down so he could clasp her head and kiss her deeply, thoroughly. She tasted of oranges and smelled of rosewater, a heady mixture surprisingly feminine for a woman said to be a hoyden. Willingly he sank into its dangerous depths.

And every time he came up for air, he had to go back in, over and over until he thought he might explode if he couldn't touch her more intimately. So he staved off that urge by kissing her closed eyelids, the curve of her cheek, the sweet shell of her ear.

But kisses weren't enough. He wanted to fondle her, entice her as she was enticing him. Even as he pressed his lips to her temple, he slipped his hands to her shoulders and kneaded them through her flimsy gown in an attempt to resist doing what he mustn't—tracing a path down to her breasts so he could caress the forbidden parts of her.

"I rather . . . like this variation on the dance," she said.

So did he, God save him. Before he could stop himself, he muttered, "Shall I improve upon it?"

The pulse in her temple quickened beneath his lips. "I don't see how you can."

"I can do whatever you wish," he rasped, in a deliberate echo of her words earlier.

To his surprise, she stretched up to whisper in his ear, "Then by all means, Grey, improve upon the variation . . . if you can."

Giving in to his craving, he took her mouth once more and slipped his hand over her breast.

Chapter Twelve

Beatrice froze. Grey's *hand* was on her breast. She ought to push it away. No, she *ought* to wrench her mouth from his and give him a piece of her mind. That much she'd learned from managing Uncle Armie. Not that it had ever worked. The only thing that had worked with *him* was her leaving or threatening to tell her brother.

But Grey wasn't Uncle Armie. His kisses were a delight and his blatant and wicked caress an invitation to adventure she badly wanted to accept.

She broke the kiss to whisper, "This is an interesting variation."

He stared at her with eyes like blue flames in the shelter of the alcove. When she boldly returned his stare, he growled low in his throat before backing her up against the wall behind the pianoforte to kiss her.

Unlike his other kisses, this was a marauding one, fierce and hot and savage. It should frighten her, make her want to fight him off. It didn't. How could it when every thrust of his tongue, every motion of his hand on her breast, made her come alive?

She slid her hands up to clasp him about the neck, which only freed him to fondle her other breast. Her nipples ached beneath her shift, especially when he tore his lips from hers to say in a voice rough with need, "You're driving me mad. You know that, don't you."

"Should I be sorry?" she managed, though her breath seemed lost in the recesses of her throat.

"I hope you aren't. Because I damned well am not, sweetheart."

Sweetheart. There was that lovely word again, piercing her as surely as if he'd driven a stake through her. Did he mean it? Did it even matter if he did?

She had no time to dwell on that before his mouth covered hers again and he kneaded her breasts so softly and sweetly that she wanted to stay against the wall forever.

Dear Lord. This was . . . *heaven*. It made her go all melty inside, like Cook's delicious Welsh rarebit. She would never have expected that a man could rouse such tumultuous feelings in her. And when her fingers flexed in his unruly hair, mussing it even more, he dropped onto the piano bench, hauling her down with him and onto his lap.

"Grey!" she squeaked. "Someone will see!"

"No one will see." He wrapped one arm about her back so he could better settle her on his lap. "They'd have to come into the room and turn around. We'd hear them before then."

"Someone could come in from the garden."

"No one's in the garden." He kissed a path from her temple to her ear. "Shall I stop? I'd rather not. I'd prefer to do *this*." He tugged her gauzy fichu out of her gown, then slipped his hand inside the layers of bodice, corset cup, and chemise to seize one breast and thumb the nipple over and over, seeming to relish its hardening point. "But I can stop. If that's what you want."

He was caressing her bosom so deliciously, she could hardly think. "I want . . . I want . . ." *For you to do that some more.*

Eyes gleaming, he bent her back so he could pull her clothes down just enough to bare one breast.

"What are you doing?" she rasped.

"I'm indulging in another variation. So I can taste you." The fire in his face seared her.

Taste her? He'd already tasted her. She laughed shakily. "How many variations to this dance are there, anyway?"

"You have no idea," he muttered, and bent his head to her bosom.

Daringly, he licked her naked nipple as his gaze burned into hers. It sent her quite out of her mind. And when she moaned and thrust her breast up toward his mouth, he proceeded to devour it, using teeth and tongue to suck and torment her so gloriously that she could think only of having more.

This luxurious passion was unlike anything

she'd ever felt. She wanted to savor it. To revel in being able to tempt a man like him. Given how he'd reacted after their last kiss, she hadn't been sure she could.

But when his eyes drifted closed and his hands wandered down her skirts, she was sure of one thing. He desired her. And she, God help her, desired him.

Oh, dear. That was where the trouble usually started. She should end this before they got too carried away. No matter how lovely it felt.

"And you?" She caught his head in her hands, still unsure whether to push him away or pull him closer. "What about *your* pleasure?"

"I want only to keep tasting you." He sucked her nipple just enough to tantalize. "That's plenty of pleasure for me."

"Liar." With her heart hammering in her chest, she drew his head back up so she could meet his gaze. "As you said, you're a man. You take advantage when you get the chance."

He flinched. "Whatever you may have heard of me, I am not Thorn. I don't . . . behave like this with every woman I meet."

"Just with women you mean to bed," she said, fighting to hide her hurt.

His eyes glittered at her. "I don't try to *bed* every woman I meet, either."

"Then what are we doing, exactly? Remember that we swore to be honest."

The question seemed to flummox him. That was her answer. She slipped from his lap and feverishly worked to restore her clothing before anyone saw her.

He remained seated on the pianoforte bench, his fingers flexing on his knees and his breath coming in hard gasps. "Beatrice," he finally said, "I honestly don't know what we're doing. But I swear I don't generally behave so . . . recklessly. And I certainly have no intention of taking advantage of you."

Unsure whether to be pleased or alarmed that he claimed to act differently with her than with other women, she rounded on him. "So you mean to marry me."

His lips opened and closed repeatedly as if he were seeking words to set her at ease. Apparently, he didn't find them.

"That's what I thought." She buried her disappointment. He must never see it. "A duke can only *dally* with a woman like me, not marry one."

He jumped up, anger sparking in his features. "I was *not* dallying with you, damn it! We were both . . . caught up in the moment, and it got away from us."

"It certainly did," she said, trying and failing to tuck her fichu in properly.

"I wish you'd stop referring to yourself as a pariah. You're the granddaughter of a duke, for

God's sake, and certainly worthy of any duke's attention."

"Just not yours." Lord save her, but she sounded far too needy. She must watch that. She would not have him pitying her.

He blanched. "That's not what I said."

"It's what you meant." And she was fighting hard not to let him see how much it wounded her.

"My reluctance to marry has naught to do with you personally. You're a lovely woman, and if not for . . ."

When he seemed to catch himself, she said, "I wasn't asking you to marry me." She attempted to sound unconcerned as she struggled with her fichu. "Dear Lord, for a man of your reputation, you certainly take these things seriously."

"You obviously do as well. Or we wouldn't be having this discussion. I did not force anything on you, and you know it."

She pulled her fichu free so she could do it properly from the beginning, then looped it about her neck. "You're right." She swallowed her temper. "It was a delightful private interlude, one I freely embraced. But if you don't mind, Your Grace, I'd prefer to forgo any such future private interludes." *They're too hard on my heart.*

No, saying that would be unwise. She must appear nonchalant.

Grey touched her arm. "This isn't how I would

have things between us. I'd prefer we be friends at least."

I cannot! she wanted to scream. But she dared not do that, either. As an enemy, he was far more dangerous, since he clearly suspected her brother of *something*.

She forced a smile. "Of course. I bear you no ill will, sir. I merely think it wise we do no more dancing in private, if you take my meaning."

For a moment, she thought he might protest. His gaze dropped to her mouth and she feared—hoped?—he was on the verge of kissing her again.

Then he seemed to catch himself, for he straightened into the very picture of the self-important duke she'd first met in the foyer. "That is probably best," he clipped out.

Their gazes locked and held. Unable to bear the sudden coolness in his eyes, she was about to flee when a male voice intruded into their intimate corner.

"What the devil is going on here?"

She nearly jumped out of her skin. It was Sheridan. Of all people, why must her cousin be the one to find them back here?

Grey must have felt the same for he swore under his breath as he released her arm. "Miss Wolfe and I have been practicing some dances."

Wrestling her expression into a semblance of calm, she faced Sheridan. "Your brother and I . . .

that is, he's been showing me a few . . . a variety of dance steps, since I'm badly prepared for balls and such. To *dance* at balls and such, I mean." Lord, she sounded like a fool.

Sheridan's lips tightened into a line as he seemed to assess her agitated state. "And that's why you're dancing back here out of sight."

Grey shrugged. "I played a few bars on the pianoforte so we'd know what tune to dance to."

"Then I hummed the music," Beatrice blurted out. "So we could dance. That's why Grey had to start it on the pianoforte."

Sheridan frowned. "Is that why your fichu is hanging out of your gown?"

Beatrice's hands grew clammy. Lord help her, she'd forgotten to finish fixing her fichu! "I got hot." What other excuse could she give?

"I'm sure my brother had something to do with that," Sheridan said.

"Now see here—" Grey began.

"I took it off while we were dancing." Beatrice struggled to gather her composure. "I was about to restore it when you came in." She drew in a few deep breaths to steady herself. Then deliberately leaving her fichu hanging down, she approached Sheridan. "If you have something to accuse me of, Cousin, I suggest you do so."

Sheridan shot her a remorseful look. "It's not *you* I wish to accuse." He glared at Grey.

"Don't be silly," she broke in. The last thing

she needed was Sheridan trying to force Grey to marry her when the man clearly couldn't stand the idea. "Grey is merely doing what you asked, and quite capably, too."

Out of the corner of her eye, she saw Grey shoot her a sardonic look, which told her she was doing it up brown, but she pressed on. "So I'm not sure why you must subject us to an inquisition." She crossed her arms over her bosom . . . and the nipples still hard beneath her bodice. "What business is it of yours how I learn to dance? I'm a grown woman of some years. I can take care of myself." She tipped up her chin. "And now, if you gentlemen will excuse me, I shall go to the retiring room to repair my fichu."

"You might wish to go through the garden," Sheridan said blandly. "Mother and Gwyn are returning, and I'll be partnering one of you ladies, since Thorn is definitely heading back to town. But you mustn't let them see you as you look right now, or they'll make the same assumptions as I."

She gulped down her mortification. "True. Thank you for the warning." As she marched off to a garden door, she prayed she didn't look as guilty as she felt.

Chapter Thirteen

Still aching to bed her, Grey watched Beatrice march off.

"What just happened?" Sheridan asked.

"Hell if I know." Grey's blood pounded in his veins . . . and his cock. "I have yet to figure out your cousin. She blows hot and cold."

That was his own damned fault. His body wanted her in his bed; his mind warned him to be a gentleman. He couldn't blame her for not knowing which one governed his true intention. Half the time *he* wasn't sure.

"You shouldn't have maneuvered her into being alone with you," Sheridan said. "It's not right."

Taking a leaf from Thorn's book, Grey said, "Has it occurred to you I might actually be looking for a wife?"

Sheridan irritated Grey by bursting into laughter. "That's rich." The man could hardly choke out the words for laughing so hard. "*You* . . . looking for a wife in the wilds of Lincolnshire . . . Don't even try to convince me . . . of such a mad thing."

"I do intend to marry one day, you know," Grey grumbled.

His brother sobered. "When you do, it will be to some elegant lady as haughty and sure of her place as you. Not to the likes of my self-conscious, awkward cousin."

Grey bit back the urge to tell Sheridan that Beatrice wasn't awkward and self-conscious when she was in her element . . . or in his arms. But telling his brother that would only make matters worse.

That was proven when Sheridan glowered at him. "Which is precisely why I don't like you being alone with her."

Belatedly Grey remembered how he'd ended up here in the first place. Damn it, he would wipe that scowl off Sheridan's face if it was the last thing he did. "How the devil do you expect me to find out about Wolfe's involvement with the deaths if I can't speak to Beatrice alone? It's not as if she'll confide in me in front of the entire family."

His brother shoved his hands in his trouser pockets. "I told you, she doesn't know anything."

"She knows more than you think, at least about her uncle Armie's demise." Grey drummed his fingers on the top of the pianoforte. "Every time I bring it up, she gets nervous. She wouldn't even show me the site of the accident when I asked her to. And what have *you* done to investigate Wolfe?"

Just as he'd hoped, Sheridan got defensive. "I've scarcely had time to breathe, much less investigate my cousin. You have no idea how bad

Uncle Armie left things. He was in debt up to his roving eyes when he died."

"Roving eyes? So you know about his dalliances."

"Everyone knows, at least around here. How do *you* know?"

"As you said, everyone around here knows."

Fortunately, his mother and sister arrived at that moment. But he couldn't pay attention to their complaints about Thorn. He was still rattled by what he and Beatrice had just done.

Why was it that when he was alone with her, he behaved differently, even recklessly? She eroded his reserve so he acted more himself and not the haughty fellow he displayed in society to put people off.

What's more, he liked it. Being allowed to say what he really felt was a heady intoxication that he craved as desperately as any drunkard.

Clearly, she wasn't angling to marry a duke at any cost, as Thorn had seemed to imply. Otherwise, when Sheridan had come in on them she wouldn't have fought so hard to hide what they'd been doing.

Devil take her for that. It made him feel like the worthless debaucher everyone thought him. He almost wished he were. Then he'd have no compunction about seducing her. Then he'd finally gain satisfaction for the yawning abyss of need he felt around her.

But no, he was a gentleman and didn't believe in deflowering innocents he never intended to marry, even ones equally attracted to him. So somehow he must endure the next few days, perhaps weeks, of trying to elicit the truth about her brother from her without giving in to his urges.

Without showing her all the many ways they could reach ecstasy together.

The thought made his blood rise again, so fiercely he gritted his teeth. He must gain control over these impulses, damn it! Otherwise, he would find himself leg-shackled, at the mercy of a woman who couldn't even keep from blurting out her true opinions.

And that would never do.

Beatrice sank against the wall, her heart pounding. She had to go in, but she had to compose herself first. That was no easy task, considering what she'd just overheard Sheridan and Grey discussing.

Not only had they both thought Joshua might have killed Uncle Armie, Sheridan had put Grey up to trying to learn the truth about Joshua's actions! She fought down a wave of nausea. All this time Grey had probably only cozied up to her to find out about Joshua's involvement in Uncle Armie's death. What sort of fellow used a woman like that?

A heartless scoundrel, that's who. It made his smoldering glances, forbidden kisses, and wanton caresses feel like even more of a betrayal than Uncle Armie's. Fool that she was, she'd actually believed Grey desired her. She'd probably imagined his arousal, too caught up in the thrill of it.

What had she been thinking? A handsome man of his broad experience with women—a blasted duke as rich as Croesus—didn't crave being with some . . . some country girl with no social graces and no knowledge of how to tempt a fellow like him. Why, Grey probably *did* have a cabal of lying devils like himself somewhere in London. No doubt that was where he'd learned how to make a woman's blood sing.

Well, he'd no longer be affecting *this* woman's blood, if she could help it.

Uncle Armie's vile words wriggled their way into her thoughts once more: *Most men wouldn't give the time of day to such a mannish creature. You're no beauty.*

Tears clogged her throat. She'd assumed that Uncle Armie's insults had just been his nasty reaction to her refusal to do as he wished. But what if he was right?

The voices inside the ballroom grew louder. She'd best go in, if only to keep Sheridan and Grey from suspecting that she'd overheard them earlier. After making sure her fichu was properly

180

tied, she fixed a smile to her face and breezed in. Fortunately, Gwyn didn't even break in her conversation.

Unfortunately, Sheridan noticed Beatrice and came right up to her. "Are you all right?" he whispered. "You look pale."

"I'm fine," she lied. "A bit tired is all."

He grimaced. "I'm so sorry. Do you wish to postpone the lessons until tomorrow? I don't mind accompanying you to the dower house."

The thought of trying to dissemble while alone with Sheridan made her ill. "I don't need you to chaperone me. I've been roaming this estate by myself for years."

She regretted the sharp words the moment her cousin frowned. "Of course," he said stiffly. "Forgive me for presuming."

Now she felt awful. In truth, Sheridan had said nothing to alarm her. It was *Grey* who suspected her of knowing more than she was letting on.

She didn't, but not for want of trying to find out. She'd searched the spot where Uncle Armie had died without finding anything to implicate Joshua. She'd parsed every word her brother said, but couldn't tell if he knew of Uncle Armie's obnoxious overtures to her.

She'd even considered asking Joshua point-blank if he'd had anything to do with Uncle Armie's death. But even if he *had* been involved, he would never tell her. He wouldn't want to put that burden on her. So he'd either lie or not answer. And if he *hadn't* killed Uncle Armie, then Joshua would be wounded beyond repair to hear that she thought so ill of him.

That kept her quiet. He'd suffered so much already that she hated herself for even considering he might be guilty.

In any case, none of this mess was Sheridan's fault. "I'm sorry, Sheridan. I'm a bit cross, that's all." Fumbling for a plausible reason, she added, "I fear I'll never be as accomplished a debutante as your mother and sister wish me to be."

"Nonsense. It merely takes practice. You can't go out into society for months, anyway. So you have plenty of time."

"I keep telling her that." Grey approached to stand on her other side. "But she still worries."

Beatrice felt trapped between the two brothers, neither of whom she could trust anymore. "I merely don't want to disappoint my benefactors, Your Grace," she said in a cool voice, trying to hide how much Grey's presence agitated her.

Grey flashed her an exasperated look that she ignored.

The next few hours were taken up with learning the cotillion and quadrille . . . and choking down her anger at Grey. Fortunately, the dancing lessons finally ended for the day when dinner was announced. Although Aunt Lydia asked her to join them, Beatrice got out of it by protesting she didn't want to leave her brother to dine alone. That enabled her to flee before it got dark, so that neither of the men felt obliged to accompany her.

For once, when she got home to find Joshua gone, she was relieved because it meant she didn't have to keep pretending another minute. Somehow she must get through the next few weeks—or however long Grey was here—without giving anything away. If she could keep from rousing his suspicions, all would be well.

Then she'd just have to pray she never saw his face again.

Chapter Fourteen

To Beatrice's vast relief, the next two days fell into a comfortable pattern—dancing at the hall during the day and dining at the dower house with her brother at night. Since Sheridan was too busy to help instruct them, they could dance no more cotillions and quadrilles. Instead, Grey took turns partnering her or Gwyn as his mother played a succession of tunes for jigs, reels, and other country dances. Since Beatrice knew those figures, she ended up being the one to teach Gwyn.

It became clear that Grey, while capable of performing any dance, wasn't fond of the entertainment. It required going into society, and, as he repeatedly stated, he'd rather "live out his days as a hermit than endure an hour with those self-important dullards." Sometimes he sounded exactly like her brother. How odd was that?

At least she was evading his questions. She made sure they were never alone, even when he tried to maneuver it otherwise. After dealing with Uncle Armie, she was good at that. And when they danced, she kept up a steady stream of queries about London society and the behavior expected of her.

That was how she learned how intensely Grey

disliked the *ton*. His feelings emerged in snide asides about the rules and cutting remarks about the people. Beatrice might not trust him with her own secrets, but he did always seem to speak the truth about society. So by the end of their third day of lessons, she'd begun to wonder if the glittering mass of accomplished lords and ladies she feared meeting in London might not prove to be merely a larger group of the people she'd already been dealing with in Sanforth, with the same petty vanities, prejudices, and propensity to gossip. If so, then she might manage this debut nonsense perfectly well after all.

On Sunday, their fourth day, there were no lessons since they went to services. Afterward, while everyone else was chatting, she let herself feast her eyes on Grey.

Why must he look so *delicious* today? He always dressed casually at the house, but for church he'd donned a suit of black superfine wool that set off his ebony hair most attractively, and a waistcoat of figured white silk that made her think of the frothing waters of the river running past the dower house. Even the folds of his cravat evoked rolling clouds on a windy day.

Unfortunately, he caught her staring and broke away from the others to come toward her. She should head somewhere else, but her guard was down. Otherwise, why was she standing here like a ninny, watching him approach?

"Why isn't your brother here?" he asked.

Her heart sank. "Why don't you ask him yourself? I'm not my brother's keeper."

She regretted the blunt words when he searched her face, then drawled, "I would if I could. But he avoids me almost as much as you do."

"I don't avoid you. I've danced with you nearly every day."

His gaze heated as it skimmed her. "That's not what I mean, and you know it."

She nearly bit off her tongue to keep from throwing his perfidy at him. Instead, she focused on his question, which oddly seemed safer right now. "Joshua never comes to services. He says he can't stand to attend anymore. I assume it has to do with the war and the men he saw die when he was fighting for God and country."

"Perhaps." He stared her down. "Or perhaps there's another reason. Church often holds a mirror up to one's actions."

Lord save her, Grey was saying what she dared not—that perhaps Joshua felt too guilty to attend. She nearly protested that Joshua hadn't attended services since long before Uncle Armie died, but she caught herself before she revealed that she knew what Grey was up to.

Even as her chest tightened and her hands shook, she fought to seem nonchalant. "Or perhaps Joshua doesn't like the music." Then she forced herself to walk away.

Let Grey have his suspicions. She wouldn't be the one to betray her brother—especially since she didn't know his secrets.

The next day, when she arrived at the hall, she was surprised to find that they were to be taking a break from dancing for the day. Instead, they were to receive instruction on etiquette rules for the ballroom, provided jointly by Grey and Aunt Lydia.

It went on for *hours*. Sheridan, who'd joined them at his mother's insistence, and Gwyn periodically chimed in to either voice their opinions . . . or mock what Grey and Aunt Lydia said, depending on the rule.

Beatrice couldn't blame them. There were so *many* rules, like how and when a lady was to curtsey upon meeting a gentleman, which involved keeping one's head in line with the upper part of the body and not flexing one's limbs too much. They actually made her and Gwyn practice it!

She and Gwyn were also instructed in who could dance with whom, though that seemed to depend upon whether the ball was private, public, or impromptu. One rule was sacrosanct, apparently—brothers and sisters weren't allowed to dance together. Which meant poor Gwyn couldn't fall back on her brothers as partners at a ball.

"But Mama," Gwyn said, "what if none of these

toplofty gentlemen asks me? How am I to show off my ability on the dance floor if I'm forced to stand on the sidelines because of some silly rule about not dancing with my brothers?"

"You're sister to three dukes," Sheridan said dryly. "Trust me, you'll have partners aplenty." When Aunt Lydia cleared her throat, he blinked, then shot Beatrice an apologetic glance. "You too, Cousin—partners to spare, no doubt."

She swallowed her sigh at his feeble attempt to reassure her. "I should hope so," she said with forced gaiety. "I'll have all of *you* to dance with, since none of you is my brother . . . and since my real brother will never darken the door of a London ballroom unless one of you holds a pistol to his head."

Instantly she regretted her unfortunate reference to violence, but before she could amend her statement, Grey said, "That won't be necessary. He can trust us to take care of you in any ballroom."

His speaking look turned her blood molten in her veins.

Curse him for that. His tactics were *so* unfair.

With a stern glance in his direction, Aunt Lydia stood. "We should also go over how one behaves when accepting a man's request to dance. For example, the gentleman will offer his right hand, and you will take it with your left."

"What happens if he's left-handed?" Beatrice

asked. That had happened to her at a harvest dance, leading to a good deal of embarrassing fumbling.

"Then he won't be allowed to dance," Grey said in apparent seriousness.

"Grey, don't tease her like that," Aunt Lydia chided.

He burst into laughter. "Every gentleman at a marriage mart knows these rules, Miss Wolfe. No matter which hand the man generally uses, he must always offer his right to a lady at a dance. And you must take it in your left."

"Because it would be quite a mess if you tried to take his right hand with your right," Sheridan said from the settee.

Just like that she remembered the figure she and Grey had danced, with their left hands joined and their right hands, too, so that they were scandalously close for several steps. Her gaze flew to Grey, and for a second something dark, knowing, and intimate passed between them, sending a delicious shiver down her spine and making *his* gaze slide to her mouth.

She pulled hers away, before she turned into a blithering idiot under his practiced stare. "How do we behave if we wish to *refuse* the gentleman's request to dance?"

"You can't," Gwyn grumbled. "They had this rule at the embassy in Berlin, too. Tell her what happens, Mama, if you *do* refuse the fellow."

"You have to sit out the rest of the evening's dances," Aunt Lydia said. "You can say you don't intend to dance anymore, but that's your only recourse."

Beatrice blinked. "Even if I don't like him? Even if he, say, insulted my brother or . . . or, I don't know, tried to kiss me when he shouldn't have? Even if he's a scoundrel?"

Grey stared hard at her. "*Thorn* is a scoundrel. But trust me, if a young woman like you gave him the cut direct on the dance floor, it wouldn't be *his* reputation that suffered. He's a duke. You're expected to accept his invitation . . . unless he's breaking other rules of the ballroom, like trying to have you partner him for a third set when you've already partnered him for two others."

Annoyed now, Beatrice huffed out a breath. "And what blasted rule is *that?*"

As Grey, Sheridan, and Gwyn burst into laughter, Aunt Lydia clearly fought a smile. "You can't say 'blasted,' dear. Not anywhere."

"However much you might wish to," Gwyn muttered under her breath.

"What was that?" her mother asked with an eyebrow raised.

Gwyn sighed. Loudly. "Nothing, Mama."

"That's what I thought." Still, Aunt Lydia's eyes twinkled as she turned to Beatrice. "You can't dance a third set with the same gentleman because showing such preference for one man gives people the impression that you're engaged. Then *everyone* in the ballroom will be gossiping about you."

Beatrice sifted through the madness of what they'd said. "So, even though generally I'm supposed to accept every man's invitation to dance, if a gentleman wishes to dance a *third* set with me, I am to turn him down."

"He won't ask because he knows better," Grey said. "But if he does, then yes, turn him down. Unless you want the rumormongering populace to pronounce you betrothed."

"The truth is," Gwyn said, "it's better if you can avoid being put in that situation in the first place. Nothing is worse than having to dance a full set with some beady-eyed fellow with roaming hands."

Sheridan scowled. "Who *is* this 'beady-eyed fellow with roaming hands'?"

"It's hypothetical," Gwyn said. "Don't be an arse."

"Gwyn, you know better than to speak that word," her mother said.

Gwyn thrust out her chin. "Forgive me for my coarse language, Sheridan. I *meant* to say, 'don't be an *utter* arse.'"

As her brothers howled with laughter, Aunt Lydia lifted her eyes to heaven. "I can see we're going to *need* three months to get you two ready for a debut." She frowned at her sons. "Especially with those two rascals encouraging you."

"It's hard not to encourage them when the ladies are making valid points," Grey said. "Some of these rules are outdated and idiotic."

"Exactly." Gwyn turned to Beatrice. "Which is why you have to develop tactics to combat them. Trust me, there's a way to reject a beady-eyed gentleman with roaming hands before he even gets the chance to ask for your hand in a dance."

Grey cocked his head. "Don't be absurd."

"I'm not," Gwyn said. "The only way a sensible woman can get through the nonsense of a ball—in any country—is to make certain only to dance with those gentlemen who suit her best."

"You mean, the rich and handsome ones," Sheridan teased her.

"I'm more concerned with avoiding the top-lofty, arrogant ones like my brothers," she quipped.

"Hey!" Sheridan protested. "Since when am I arrogant?"

"Can we get on with this?" Grey said impatiently. "I want to hear whatever nonsense Gwyn proposes."

"You see?" Gwyn said. "Arrogant."

"Bored, more like." Grey pulled out his pocket watch. "We don't have all day, you know."

Gwyn stuck her tongue out at him. "Feel free to leave anytime. We don't really need either of you for this part. Why don't you and Sheridan go . . . brush up on your lordly manners or crush a peasant under your boot or something?"

"Sorry, Sis, I don't know any peasants." With a wink at their mother, Grey added, "And we have no intention of missing this."

Sheridan laid his arms across the back of the settee. "Not when we're about to hear the age-old secrets of womankind."

Gwyn glared at him. "Now you're being an utter *bloody* arse."

"Gwyn!" her mother cried, truly shocked this time.

"Sorry, Mama," Gwyn mumbled. "But honestly, Bea, you need to ignore my brothers."

"I always ignore insolence," Beatrice said tartly, garnering a smile from Gwyn. "You were saying?"

"The key is to manage things so the gentleman never guesses that you maneuvered him into not dancing with you. Now, let's pretend that I am a gentleman approaching you on the dance floor." Pitching her voice lower, Gwyn walked up to Beatrice and said, "I hope you're having a lovely evening, madam."

Before Beatrice could even answer, Grey cut in. "Good God, if that's how you think men *sound,* I'm afraid to hear what you think we'd say." He came over to stand between his sister and Beatrice. "You do it like this." He bowed politely. "Miss Wolfe, would you do me the honor of standing up with me for this set?"

"No, no, you're missing the point!" Gwyn cried. "Once you say the words, she can't refuse you. She has to make it so you don't get the chance to ask."

"Oh, right." Grey shook his head. "What a stupid exercise."

"Says the duke who can't be refused," Beatrice put in.

As he raised an eyebrow, Gwyn said, "If you think it's stupid, Grey, go away and let me handle it." She made a shooing motion at him before turning back to Beatrice. "There are plenty of things you can do to stave a man off. As soon as he comes toward you, you can erupt into a coughing fit that will surely make him change direction. No man wants to risk catching a cold from you."

"Exactly," Sheridan said, "so the coughing fit will also make all the other gentlemen avoid you."

"If they're so easily turned away," Gwyn said, "then we don't want *them*."

"I agree," Beatrice said, determined to show solidarity with Gwyn.

Gwyn went on. "You can also ask him to fetch you a glass of punch in hopes that someone else asks you to dance while he's gone."

"That seems mean," Beatrice said.

"Oh, trust me," Grey said, "once he realizes you're dancing with another, he'll leave the punch for you and go off to seek better prey. I've seen Vanessa pull that maneuver on any number of gentlemen."

"Vanessa is an heiress, Grey," Sheridan called out from the settee. "She can get away with far more than Bea can."

Gwyn ignored him. "You can send the fellow on other errands: Ask him to fetch your chaperone if she's out of sight or fetch a shawl you left across the room earlier for that purpose. Sending him on errands makes him feel like a knight helping his lady. But if you happen to get asked to dance while he's away, it's not *your* fault, right?"

"If I were that fellow," Grey said, leveling his gaze on Beatrice, "I wouldn't be put off so easily."

Beatrice tamped down the thrill his words gave her. She couldn't imagine trying most of Gwyn's tactics, anyway. "Perhaps I should simply hide under the furniture if I see an unsuitable fellow approaching," she said glumly.

A new voice came from the doorway. "That tactic doesn't even work with the dogs, duckie."

Beatrice whirled to find her brother standing there. "Joshua! What are you doing here?"

With a pained smile, he ignored the others to limp toward her, leaning on his cane. "I thought I should see what these lessons in preparing you for society entailed. And if you're contemplating hiding under furniture to avoid men, I came in the nick of time."

Sheridan rose from the settee. "Good afternoon, Cousin. It's good to see you."

His stiff manner belied the welcome in his words. All at once, their merry camaraderie disappeared, reminding Beatrice with a horrible lurch that Sheridan and Grey suspected her brother of murdering Uncle Armie.

Aunt Lydia went to kiss Joshua's cheek without any indication that she felt the tension between the men. "We're so glad you came over, Nephew. I do hope you'll stay for dinner."

"I'm afraid I can't," Joshua said, flashing her a genuine smile. "I came to fetch Beatrice since we have to discuss the needs of the kennel before I go over to Leicester to look at a couple of hunters tomorrow."

"Oh, dear," Aunt Lydia said. "I do wish you could stay."

Gwyn cleared her throat.

Aunt Lydia glanced over and colored. "I'm forgetting my manners. Joshua, please let me introduce you to another of my sons and to my daughter."

"Actually, I met Greycourt at the funeral." Joshua shot Gwyn a furtive glance. "But I haven't yet had the privilege of meeting Lady Gwyn, though I've heard a great deal about her."

"That certainly sounds intriguing." Gwyn smiled as she stepped forward. She swept her gaze down him in a quick assessment. "You're Major Wolfe, I presume?"

He bowed his head. "At your service, madam."

Unlike most women Beatrice and Joshua encountered these days, Gwyn showed no trace of disgust or coolness toward him for his damaged leg. Nor pity, either, which was equally unusual.

To Beatrice's surprise—and delight—Gwyn gazed at Joshua with more curiosity than anything else. And perhaps a little attraction? Beatrice had always considered her brother relatively handsome, despite his limp and the straight black hair he kept unfashionably long. Gwyn's reaction to him proved her right.

Nor was there any mistaking the blatant survey he made of Gwyn's figure. Her brother never looked at any woman that way . . . or at least he hadn't since before the war.

How very interesting.

"I've been telling my brother about all of you," Beatrice put in, not wanting Gwyn to wonder where Joshua had heard of her.

"Yes, my sister sings the praises of our new relations . . . and *their* relations," Joshua said caustically, though he kept his eyes fixed on Gwyn.

Far from being put off by his tone—or his bold

stare—Gwyn flashed him what could only be called a coquettish smile. "Well, your wonderful sister has hardly said a word about *you,* sir. I began to think you a hermit in a cave somewhere. How delightful to learn I was wrong."

Clearly unused to having a woman flirt with him these days, Joshua gaped at Gwyn as if she were an odd new creature in a menagerie.

Beatrice stifled a laugh and walked over to stand next to him. "My brother isn't one for company, I'm afraid. He buries himself in his work."

Grey spoke up then. "I understand, Major Wolfe, that you're the head gamekeeper for the estate."

"I am indeed," Joshua said testily.

"I'm sure my brother is delighted to have you handling that position so admirably," Grey said, "since he's had to spend so much time untangling your uncle Armitage's financial affairs."

Devil take the man for his deliberate mention of Uncle Armie!

"Good luck," Joshua told Sheridan amiably. "As you've probably noticed, our uncle was terrible at managing money. Your father despaired at having to figure out where his brother had spent it all."

"And now *I* am despairing, though it does seem Uncle Armie wasted a great deal of blunt on new landscaping," Sheridan said, more warmly than before.

"Ah, yes," Joshua said. "Several ha-has were built, and Uncle Armie became obsessed with creating a 'wilderness' area that everyone in town calls 'Armie's Folly.' Not to mention the fortune he spent on the various garden buildings."

"Am I right that there's even a ruins on the estate?" Grey persisted, sending a chill through her.

Blast it, did he know that Uncle Armie had died near the ruins? Because if so, she must change the subject. "There's a ruins and a Chinese gazebo and the prettiest little hermitage—"

"A ruins!" Gwyn exclaimed, unaware of how she thwarted Beatrice by seizing on that particular building. "Why am I only now hearing of this?"

"Because we've all been rather busy," Sheridan told her, shooting Grey a veiled glance she couldn't interpret.

"And because it's not a real ruins." Joshua's voice was surprisingly courtly. "Uncle Armie had them constructed. You'd be shocked how much blunt it takes to create a ruined abbey with a fully functional bell tower."

Beatrice relaxed. Either Joshua was dissembling very well, or he had no idea that Grey had been trying to trip him up.

"I wouldn't be shocked at all," Gwyn said. "A structure of such magnitude? Quite expensive to build."

Her brother's expression altered, and for a moment interest glinted in his eyes. "Indeed it is. Which is why it still remains unfinished."

"A ruined ruins," Grey said acidly. "I have several of those on my estates, but we call them 'tenant cottages.'" When Beatrice shot him a quick glance, he added, "My father was rather lax in keeping up his property, something I am determined to change."

"Yes, yes," Gwyn said with a dismissive wave of her hand, "we know all about your grand schemes to make improvements, Grey. But these are deliberate ruins, created just for show. I've heard of the English doing them, but never thought I'd be near one." She smiled at Joshua. "I should very much like to see these ruins."

"I doubt a lady as fine as you would consider it entertaining," Joshua said.

Gwyn lifted an eyebrow. "Even fine ladies can have unusual interests, sir. But then you might know that if you ever came to visit us."

Joshua narrowed his gaze on her. "You would welcome a visit from your half brother's gamekeeper, madam?"

"My half brother's *cousin,* sir." Challenge glinted in her eyes. "That makes you family."

"You and I aren't related, Lady Gwyn," Joshua said in a hard voice. "Thank God."

"Trust me, Major Wolfe," she said with a coy

tilt to her head, "I'm as delighted as you to hear that we are in no wise related."

Joshua appeared momentarily rendered speechless.

Beatrice nearly crowed her pleasure aloud. She would love to learn *that* trick. Never mind the come-out lessons—perhaps Gwyn could give her a lesson in how to handle prickly brothers, since the lady managed to keep her own mostly in line.

"In any case," Gwyn went on, with a fluttering of her lashes, "I would be simply ecstatic if you would show me the estate ruins, sir."

"You could go there yourself," Joshua said. "I'll tell you how to find it."

"Then I'd miss the informative commentary you're sure to provide," Gwyn said. "I wouldn't hear of it."

When Joshua drew himself up as if preparing for battle, Sheridan stepped in. "Please forgive my impatient sister. She has a passion for old buildings. She fills notebooks with rapt descriptions of their artistic characteristics and their ancient part in history. When we were children, she was incessantly dragging me, Thorn, and Heywood down some secluded street in Berlin to see a house she thought was 'splendid.'"

Gwyn sniffed. "It was good for you. None of you have an adequate sense of the beauties of architecture."

As Grey rolled his eyes, it dawned on Beatrice that this might be a good chance for her to show him and Sheridan that she wasn't bothered by the prospect of witnessing the site of Uncle Armie's demise, since it happened to be close to the ruins. But it would only work if she could make sure that Joshua was left out of it.

"*I* can take you to see it." Beatrice broadened her gaze to include Sheridan and Grey. "It's a few miles away—we could all walk or ride there."

"Only if Major Wolfe joins us. What do you think, sir?" Gwyn asked Joshua. "Shall we go now?"

The direct request for immediate satisfaction struck terror into Beatrice's heart. She figured she could govern her own reaction at seeing the spot where Uncle Armie had died, but how was she to govern Joshua's?

A muscle worked in Joshua's jaw. "You seem to have forgotten, madam, that I came here merely to fetch my sister home."

Beatrice watched his face. A mask had come down over it that made his expression unreadable. But if she had to guess, she'd say he was none too happy at the prospect of accompanying guests out to the ruins.

She glanced over to find Grey equally interested in her brother's reaction, blast him. "It's growing late for it, anyway," Beatrice said. "By the time we got there, it would be too dark to see anything."

"Then let's visit the ruins tomorrow," Grey said.

"A capital idea!" Gwyn cried. "We can make an excursion of it, bring a picnic lunch and everything."

"But Gwyn," Aunt Lydia put in, "what about the lessons?"

"If I don't have a chance to be outdoors for at least one day, Mama, I shall go mad," Gwyn said. "We have months for our lessons. And you know how I like looking at such things."

"Then it's settled," Beatrice said. "I'll come for you at ten tomorrow, and we'll go visit the ruins."

"*We* will come for you," Joshua said firmly. "I can put off my business in Leicester for one day."

Beatrice gaped at him, surprised that he seemed to like the idea.

Then Joshua bowed to the company. "But Beatrice and I will leave you now so we can make plans for this 'excursion.' "

His tone brooked no refusal, so with a nod, Beatrice said her farewells to the others and left with her brother.

She waited until they were well away from the hall before she ventured, "Are you sure you want to spend tomorrow at the ruins?"

"Why wouldn't I?" he asked, though he kept his gaze fixed upon the path. "You've been nagging me for weeks to spend more time with our relations."

"Yes, but . . . well . . . it's so near where Uncle Armie died."

He shrugged. "Why would that matter? Don't tell me you miss the old bastard."

"No, of course not." She tried to read something from his expression, but it showed nothing. And the fact that he wouldn't look at her might not mean anything, either. She knew better than anyone how difficult navigating a gravel path was for him. "Uncle Maurice was much preferable to Uncle Armie. And Sheridan is even nicer."

Her brother grunted, taciturn as usual.

"Indeed," she went on, "they're all very nice. But I'm only too aware how you dislike being forced into their company. So if you prefer not to go—"

"I know what you're trying to do," he growled. "You're itching to spend another day with your precious Greycourt, and you want me out of the way while you do."

"What? No!" She hadn't anticipated this turn to the conversation. And how on earth had Joshua guessed that she and Grey . . . "That's ridiculous."

"Is it? You talk about his opinions and pronouncements more than you realize. That's why I came over today in the first place—to see for myself how the two of you are together." He skewered her with a glance. "Then I overheard what he said about how *he* wouldn't be put off so easily if he were a man wanting to dance with

204

you—and I saw how you blushed. The two of you together . . ." His features hardened. "It worries me."

"Why?" Heat rose perversely in her cheeks. Really, must she blush every time she thought of Grey? She marched ahead of Joshua so he wouldn't notice. "Do you think me incapable of attracting such a man?"

The breath left him in a great whoosh. "Damn it, Beatrice, it's not about attraction. Men like him and Uncle Armie chew women up and spit them out, just for their own pleasure. Then they actually *marry* some more suitable female."

Every word stamped on her heart. "You think I don't know that?" she cried, her throat raw with unshed tears. She whirled to face him, stopping him in his tracks. "Do you assume I have no sense at all?"

The pain behind her words must have registered with him, for he blinked. "I don't mean—I wasn't saying—" He swore a vile oath. "I just want to protect you. Father didn't leave you so much as a farthing for a dowry, and as you pointed out the other day, our relations are liable to toss us out of the dower house the first chance they get."

She winced. Those fears had been somewhat allayed in the past week, when it became obvious that her aunt and Gwyn cared too much about her to do such a horrible thing. Even Sheridan didn't seem to have the heart for it.

Joshua went on. "Not to mention Uncle Armie, who . . ."

When he trailed off, a cold wind blew through her. "What about Uncle Armie?"

"Nothing." He rubbed a hand over his tight jaw. "The point is, no one, including me, has given you anything to live on that comes near what you're worth. The others didn't, and I can't. But the one thing I *can* do is keep you safe. And I mean to do it, whatever it takes."

If ever he'd come close to admitting what he'd done, it was now. She gulped down her fear. "You don't need to keep me safe. I can keep myself safe."

He snorted. "Right. Last time I checked, your shooting skills left something to be desired."

That caught her off guard. Uncle Armie hadn't been shot. Why was he talking about guns? Was he just speaking generally? She tried to read something from his expression, but it showed nothing.

"In any case," he added, "I'm going with you tomorrow whether you like it or not."

"What about your business in Leicester?"

"It can wait." His gaze met hers, then softened. "I know you don't believe it sometimes, duckie, but nothing is more important to me than your future."

The kind words were bittersweet. Again, she considered confronting him with her fears. But she couldn't, when he'd just said more to her and their relations than he had in weeks.

Very well. Perhaps she should confront Grey and Sheridan with what she'd overheard and demand to hear what they knew. And if they had evidence to go with their suspicions, she would argue for why Joshua must have done it. If, after knowing the depths of Uncle Armie's degradation, they could still pursue Joshua, then she would urge Joshua to flee.

Because if it came to a choice between her relations—or Grey—and her brother, she would choose Joshua every time.

Chapter Fifteen

After Beatrice and her brother left, Grey suggested that Sheridan join him in the study for a brandy so they could talk privately. The door had scarcely closed when Sheridan asked, "What did you think of my cousin, now that you've had more time to assess him?"

Grey thrust his hands into his pockets. "I didn't like how he was looking at Gwyn."

"What are you talking about?"

"Didn't you see the two of them? She was flirting with Wolfe, and he was clearly looking her over with lust."

"*Lust?* I sure as hell didn't notice *that,*" Sheridan said.

Grey had—he'd recognized the covetous look in Wolfe's eyes every time the man stared at Gwyn. It reflected the same craving Grey felt every time he saw Beatrice. Which meant Gwyn was playing with fire.

As he was himself, come to think of it. Those Wolfes were a potent pair. "I'm just saying that if you're right and the major has his eye on the dukedom, he might be looking for a wife to complete the package. Someone like our sister."

Sheridan laughed outright. "Then my cousin has chosen badly. Gwyn is too clever to marry a penniless gamekeeper, no matter what his rank in the Royal Marines."

"If you're right about him and he's trying to gain the dukedom for himself, then he wouldn't *be* a penniless gamekeeper when he set his sights on her, would he?"

"The only way Joshua will gain the dukedom is if he kills both me and Heywood without anyone noticing. And that won't happen, since you and I are going to stop him first. So it doesn't matter *how* he looks at Gwyn. She'll never marry him as things stand now. He's not rich enough for her."

Grey wasn't so certain. But then he wasn't sure he knew her at all. He hadn't been around when she was growing up. Hell, he'd barely been around since the family's arrival in England. And the letters from his parents hadn't done her justice. How could they? Gwyn was in a class of her own. Of course Wolfe was drawn to her. Who wouldn't be?

"Never mind, then," he told Sheridan. "Perhaps I imagined their mutual admiration." Though of course he hadn't. "On another subject, this place we're going to tomorrow . . . are these the same ruins you said were near where your uncle died?"

Sheridan nodded. "Did you see Joshua's expression when Gwyn mentioned having him take her there? If ever that's an indication of guilt—"

"He's the one who brought up the ruins in the

209

first place," Grey pointed out. "He'd hardly do that if he were guilty." Of something other than lusting after their sister, that is.

"All the same," Sheridan said, "tomorrow we should manufacture a way to bring him right to the site and witness his reactions."

"Not 'we,'" Grey said. "Me." When Sheridan drew breath to protest, Grey added, "While Wolfe is preoccupied with this excursion, you're going to go up by the bridge and see if you can locate the pieces of the railing that fell into the river with Father. Finding them will go a long way toward confirming whether the bridge was damaged. While Wolfe is elsewhere is the perfect time—no need to answer any questions."

Sheridan's expression cleared. "Good point."

"Have you searched the site of your uncle's death?"

"I have. I didn't see anything. But if there had been evidence of foul play, Joshua had plenty of time to get rid of it. We only made it back to England weeks after Uncle Armie's funeral."

"If there's anything to be found, surely one of us will uncover it."

"And if we don't?"

"Then there's naught to find."

Sheridan crossed his arms over his chest. "Are you sure Bea's pretty blushes and sweet smiles aren't influencing you to ignore the obvious?"

Grey bristled. "If you'll recall, I was skeptical

of your suspicions from the beginning, when I'd barely met Miss Wolfe."

A shadow passed over Sheridan's face. "Sorry, old chap. I'm just . . . frustrated we haven't discovered anything concrete."

So was Grey. But he didn't want to tell Sheridan what he'd noticed about *Beatrice's* reaction to things until he had more confirmation.

The next morning, Grey was surprised when Beatrice entered the foyer alone. "Where's your brother?"

"I could ask the same thing about yours," she said archly. "And by the way, for a man who has supposedly been helping me improve my manners the past few days, you could use some improvement in yours. A 'good morning' is the usual greeting, I've been told. Not 'where's your brother?' barked at the first person to enter your current abode."

She'd managed a passable version of his tone when he was demanding something. It was disconcerting, to say the least. "Do forgive me, Miss Wolfe," he said, his lips twitching. "Good morning. How are you today? Where, pray tell, is your brother?" He lifted an eyebrow. "Is that a sufficient greeting for you?"

Biting her lip as if to keep from smiling, she said, "I suppose. And to answer your question— Joshua is outside with the foxhounds."

"Ah, the dogs again. If you're hoping they'll

keep me at bay, it didn't work very well last time with the pointers."

A blush seeped into her cheeks. "What nonsense. I merely thought they could use the exercise." When he chuckled, she tipped up her pretty chin. "Where is the rest of *your* family, Your Grace?"

"So we're back to 'Your Grace,' I see." When she made no reply to that, he stifled a curse. "Sheridan won't be joining us. He has too much work to finish before meeting with his solicitor. Gwyn is still getting ready and said to tell you she'd be down shortly. Mother wanted to join us, but forgot that she'd already scheduled a fitting for a new mourning gown."

Today Beatrice wore the same practical bonnet she'd worn the day they'd walked together before, but this time she'd paired it with a black wool redingote that would be perfectly presentable for a woman in mourning—except for one addition—a green knit scarf wrapped about her neck.

"You look like a rose in bloom." He had no idea where the idiotic words came from except she *did* look like that with her cheeks aflame and eyes alight. Not to mention the scarf. "It's the green," he said, gesturing to it. "Reminds me of . . . a stem. You know."

When her color deepened, she looked even *more* like a rose in bloom. "I couldn't find my black one, I don't have a white one, and it's chilly today."

Her words spilled out in a rush, as hers often did when she was nervous. He didn't mind that as much as he ought. He was so used to society women who governed every syllable that he relished being with someone who never did.

"Trust me, I'm happy to see it. I'm growing tired of everyone wearing unrelieved black with only bits of white here and there." He smiled. "And I doubt the dogs will care whether you follow the mourning attire rules to the letter."

He'd hoped to make her laugh, but her curt words yesterday proved she was still unhappy with him over their intimate encounter. So he wasn't surprised when she said nothing.

Not that he blamed her. He'd as much as told her he could never marry her, and without giving her a reason. But how could he tell her of the years he'd spent hardening himself to resist his uncle's torments and manipulations? That giving a person power over him—even a wife—was too much to bear? That letting someone in, letting them twist his emotions, however unwittingly . . .

No, he couldn't.

Yet he hated how nonchalant she'd been about their encounter last week: *I bear you no ill will, sir. I merely think it wise we do no more dancing in private, if you take my meaning.*

He took it, all right. She wasn't about to indulge

in that sort of behavior with a man who wouldn't marry her. And though it was no more than he'd expected—and he liked to think he would never prey on her in such a way, anyway—it chafed him. Because it meant she could rid herself of her desire for him more easily than he seemed able to rid himself of his for her.

Her continued silence irritated him, prompting him to say what he shouldn't to get a rise out of her. "I suspect that Mother's real reason for absenting herself today is to play matchmaker by allowing Gwyn to have your brother all to herself. And me to have *you* all to myself."

At last he got a reaction. The stare she gave him would have frozen steam. "You should have told her that wouldn't work. As you've made quite clear, you're not looking for a wife. Or at least not one like me."

That was *not* what he'd intended her to think, and she knew it. "Damn it, Beatrice—"

Gwyn chose that moment to hurry down the stairs. "I'm coming, I'm coming!" She walked up to kiss Beatrice on both cheeks. "Do forgive me for being late. My maid was having *such* a time fixing my hair. Every little lock of it went whatever direction it wished, no matter how hard she worked. And she's usually a magician. But then, it *takes* a magician to control my unruly curls."

"At least you have curls." Beatrice smiled.

"My hair lies flat and straight no matter what I do."

Gwyn shook her head as the footman helped her on with her black pelisse. "Your hair is lovely as always." Then she glanced about. "Where is your brother?"

"He's outside with the dogs. We decided—"

"Now see here, Miss Wolfe," Grey broke in, his temper finally boiling over, "why didn't you give *Gwyn* the lecture about asking where your brother is?"

Beatrice lifted one eyebrow. "Because she greeted me properly *before* she asked the question."

His sister chuckled. "Let me guess: You arrived and Grey started barking commands disguised as questions. Is that about right?"

"You know your brother so well," Beatrice said, smirking at Grey.

Gwyn sniffed. "I hope you gave him what for."

"Of course."

"Oh, for God's sake," Grey muttered, annoyed with their game. "I'm standing right here, you know."

Gwyn sauntered up to him. "Aw, poor Grey, forced to be with women who don't drop into frantic curtseys every time he enters a room."

"Careful, you impudent rebel," he warned, "or I'll scandalize society by asking you to dance at a ball."

"Pish-posh, I don't care," Gwyn said. "I'll dance with my brother if I please. A little scandal never hurt anyone."

Beatrice's face fell. "I do hope you're right. Because with me they'll have more than a *little* scandal to gnaw on."

"Of course I'm right, Bea." Gwyn linked her arm through Beatrice's to lead her toward the door. "We'll take on society as the vestal virgins of the *ton*. The gossips might whisper about us behind their hands, but not for long. We have three dukes on our side—no one will dare spread scandal about us or give us the cut direct."

"Gwyn has a point, Miss Wolfe. You'll be surrounded by dukes."

"Two of whom are infamous themselves, Bea," Gwyn said archly, "so no one will be talking about *you,* I promise. They'll be too busy gossiping about Thorn and Grey even while throwing their daughters into my brothers' paths at every turn."

"Won't they be doing the same for Sheridan?" Grey asked.

Gwyn laughed. "Of course. But any gossip about *him* will be about his saintly character."

"Right," Grey said with a bit of sarcasm. Saint Sheridan. His younger brother would hate that moniker, although it suited him.

"Now," Gwyn said, patting Beatrice's hand as

they walked to the door arm in arm, "what's this about dogs?"

Grey followed the ladies, but heard not a word of their chatter. He doubted that the gossips would focus on Sheridan's saintly character if the man uncovered a plot by his relations to murder his father and uncle. That would rouse a different sort of rumors.

And Beatrice would pay the price.

The thought disturbed Grey. He hadn't considered what would happen to her if her brother was accused of murder. Even if she hadn't been involved in the plot, she would never again be able to raise her head in polite society. The gossips would dredge up the old scandal about her father's death by duel, then say that his son had followed in his violent footsteps. They'd add nasty remarks about the major's lameness, too. When they were done with him, they'd turn to tarring and feathering *her* for being related to the heinous fellow.

And if Wolfe went to prison? She'd become even more of the poor relation than she was now. Mother could champion her all she liked, but eventually Beatrice would sink into oblivion in the wilds of Lincolnshire, forced into spinsterhood because her brother was a notorious criminal.

Grey wished he'd never become embroiled in this investigation. He was fairly certain Wolfe hadn't murdered Maurice—the man had no motivation for doing so. And if the major had murdered Armitage, a devil who took advantage of any woman in his orbit . . . well, that was a different matter. Grey hadn't met a single person who mourned the fellow.

Getting Sheridan to give up his foolish pursuit was the least Grey could do to repay Beatrice for upsetting her life.

Beatrice walked down the steps with Gwyn, ignoring the fact that Grey was behind them. How dared he make comments about his mother matching them up? He had no interest in her as a wife, yet he persisted in pursuing her, probably wanting her as a mistress, the scoundrel.

The barking of the dogs at the bottom of the steps drew her attention in time to catch the way Joshua gazed up at Gwyn breezing down the steps beside her.

Beatrice hid her joy at the sight. At least she hadn't imagined Joshua's interest in Gwyn. Now, if only something came of it, Beatrice wouldn't have to worry about her brother so much. Gwyn was, after all, a very nice lady. If anyone could break through Joshua's melancholy, it was the merry Lady Gwyn.

Indeed, it was Gwyn who gave a cry of pleasure and knelt down at Joshua's feet to pet one of the foxhounds. "Oh, look at the little darlings! Your pups are adorable." Gwyn smiled up at Joshua.

"They're hardly 'pups,'" Grey gritted out. "They're foxhounds."

Beatrice didn't know what was irking Grey, but he'd seemed put out with his sister ever since she had come down.

"I *know* that," Gwyn said. "I only meant that they're charming." She batted her eyelashes at Joshua. "I do love dogs."

"As I recall," Grey said, "you used to hate them."

Gwyn rose to glare at her brother. "That was a long time ago. Before you left home, I did indeed hate them . . . but only because they terrified me. What did you expect? I was *six*. But then I grew up and Mama got Snuggles, and my entire opinion of dogs changed."

"What sort of dog was Snuggles?" Beatrice asked, determined to shift the conversation away from Grey's absurd overprotectiveness.

Gwyn turned to her with a warm smile that transformed her face. "He was the sweetest little pug you've ever seen, Bea. You would have loved him. It nearly broke my heart to leave him behind in Berlin, but he was getting too old to survive the trip. Fortunately, Mama says we can find another pug for me in London next time we go."

"Let's hope you don't name that one 'Snuggles,' too," Joshua muttered.

"I'll second that thought," Grey said.

Gwyn laughed. "You men! Mama was the one to name our pug, actually. *I* wanted to name him Pugsy."

The two men groaned.

"The poor lad probably wanted to crawl under a chair with mortification every time he was around his fellows," Grey told Joshua. " 'Snuggles,' indeed."

"And Pugsy?" Joshua snorted. "You might as well hang a lace ruff around his neck. A male dog should be named something manly, like these two lads—Mercury and Zeus."

"Ah," Grey said. "I take it you're the one with the penchant for the classics?"

"I named every dog in that kennel. If I'd allowed it, Beatrice would have named them all Sunny and Brilliant and Elegant."

"I never chose any such names!" Beatrice protested.

"And what's wrong with them, anyway?" Gwyn asked, warming Beatrice's heart by standing up for her. "Those names sound very sweet."

"The dogs are foxhounds, not pugs," Joshua said. "Their purpose is to hunt. They shouldn't have 'sweet' names."

Beatrice gazed coldly at her brother. "Well, who names a dog Mercury and Zeus? Dogs aren't characters in a Homeric odyssey, for pity's sake!"

The man actually blinked. "And what do you know about Homeric odysseys?"

Beatrice sniffed. "I *can* read, you know. I merely choose to read different things than you. And just for that, you can walk both dogs. Perhaps you'll get lucky and they'll do their manly business on your boots! Grey and Gwyn and I will meet you at the ruins." She lifted her skirts. "Come on, you two. Let's leave my brother to his foxhounds."

"You go on with Grey." Gwyn cast a furtive glance at Joshua. "I'll keep your brother company."

"Suit yourself," Beatrice said. "Though I hope you don't end up throttling him for being a *bloody arse* before you get there."

And with that wholly unladylike remark, she marched off down the drive toward the path through the gardens that led to the ruins.

Grey headed after her. As soon he'd caught up to her and they were out of earshot, he asked, "What was that about?"

No point in hiding the truth. "My brother infuriates me. Gwyn was being nice, and he still couldn't resist poking holes in her enthusiasm. He does the same to me, all the time. Him and his *manly* names. They're *dogs*. They don't care what they're called."

"You're certainly taking this dog-naming business seriously."

"The dogs are just part of what has put me in a temper." She was more angry about all the sacrifices she'd made for Joshua, all the secrets she'd kept. And for what? He didn't seem to care whether he got hanged for murder. And she began to wonder why *she* cared.

Except that she couldn't help caring. It had been just the two of them looking after each other ever since he'd come back from the war. It annoyed her that he couldn't see how much that mattered to her.

I know you don't believe it sometimes, duckie, but nothing is more important to me than your future.

She sighed. Clearly it mattered to him, too. Which made her only more determined to protect him, even if he wouldn't protect himself.

"Walk faster, will you?" she muttered to Grey.

"Whatever you wish, minx. Why are we in such a hurry, anyway?"

"I need to talk to you. And I need to make sure my brother isn't privy to it."

A darkness descended over his features. "I see."

From then on, he made no remark as she marched down the path toward the spot where she'd determined she could get him alone.

As soon as they reached it, she tugged Grey through what looked at first glance like a thicket of bushes, but what really shielded a path into a large clearing with a stone bench and more.

He glanced around, obviously taking in the carefully constructed arbor on one end, overgrown with pink Ayrshire roses. "What is this place?"

"It was one of Uncle Armie's first smaller projects created by his landscape fellow." She shuddered to think what her uncle had probably used it for, but she knew of nowhere else that couldn't be seen from the path, nowhere else they could talk privately.

"Does your brother know of this spot?"

"No. *I* wouldn't know of it if not for helping my uncle sort out the bills for the landscape fellow." It began to dawn on her what had prompted the question. "Why do you ask?"

"No reason." The wariness in his eyes belied his words.

"Tell the truth—you're asking because you believe Joshua stood here," she hissed. "That he lay in wait for Uncle Armie the night of his death."

Grey crossed his arms over his chest. "Why would I believe *that?*"

She stared him down. "At least have the courtesy not to pretend ignorance to my face. I overheard you and Sheridan discussing my brother the day you and I danced privately together."

As Grey released a coarse oath, Beatrice drew in a long, ragged breath. "You believe that my brother murdered my uncle."

Chapter Sixteen

Damn it all to hell. She'd known all this time?

To Grey's relief, at that moment they heard Wolfe and Gwyn talking as they made their slow way down the path past the entrance to the clearing. So he and Beatrice were forced to keep quiet, which gave him time to gather his shattered thoughts.

He should have seen this coming. Initially he'd been afraid that Beatrice might have heard him and Sheridan discussing her brother. But after days had passed and she hadn't said or implied anything, he'd been lulled into believing his fears were unfounded. He'd simply assumed that her cool manner stemmed from his refusal to consider marrying her. Clearly, he'd been wrong.

As the sound of Wolfe's and Gwyn's voices and footfalls receded, he murmured, "I'm sorry, Beatrice. I didn't mean to—"

"Blame my brother for someone's accidental death?" She crossed her arms over her chest. "Of course you did. Never mind that he served his country—and this estate—admirably. He was a decorated officer before he was wounded. Now he's practically a hermit and snarls at everyone, so he's the logical choice for a villain. *If* one is looking for a villain, which apparently you two are. Though I can't imagine why."

"Can't you? You certainly do your best to avoid talking about him, as well as your uncle."

She looked away. "I just . . . I don't know what to say about him. Joshua is obviously unhappy. But that doesn't mean he killed Uncle Armie!" Wrapping her arms about herself, she gazed at him. "And I don't like talking about Uncle Armie because I don't want to speak ill of the dead."

That again. "You didn't mind speaking ill of the dead when you were telling me of your uncle's lording it over you and your brother."

"Those were *your* words, not mine. It was an *accident*." She sounded as if she was trying to convince herself. "I brought you in here to tell you that you're wrong about Joshua. He isn't guilty of anything but being a grump." Her breath grew ragged, hoarse. "So you can stop your flirting and your compliments and your . . . your cozying up to me and all of that. It's not going to make me c-confirm your suspicions. Because they're not true."

"What the hell?" He stepped up close to her. "I didn't 'cozy' up to you because of Sheridan's suspicions. Good God, what kind of man do you think I am?"

When she thrust her face up to his, he saw the hurt glittering in her eyes, and it fairly slayed him.

"I think," she choked out, "that you're a man used to doing whatever he must to get what he wants, even if it means saying . . . lovely things to the ridiculous sister of . . . the man you suspect." She bit her lower lip. "To your brother's . . . 'self-conscious, awkward cousin.' "

Holy hell, this was worse than he'd thought—she'd actually heard Sheridan's guesses about why Grey would never marry a woman like her.

He grabbed her by the shoulders. "Those were Sheridan's words, not mine. And I have never thought you awkward or ridiculous. You can't really believe I pretended to desire you just to learn more about your brother."

That impertinent chin of hers came up again. "*You* were the one who told your brother: 'How the devil do you expect me to find out about Wolfe's involvement with the deaths if I can't speak to Beatrice alone?' " She glowered at him. "Your so-called desire was all part of your scheme to help my cousin learn the truth. Although I daresay he wouldn't approve of the tactics you used in trying to find it out."

"No," Grey bit out, "he wouldn't approve. And neither would I. I'd never use a woman in such a fashion. Which is why I *tried* to resist my worst impulses with you." His gaze dropped to her trembling lips. "But I failed. Even now, I want only to kiss you until you see exactly what nonsense your assumption is."

Jerking free of him, she strode across the clearing to stand next to the stone bench. When she turned her back to him, her shoulders shook. "That would hardly prove anything. You've already demonstrated you're perfectly capable of feigning desire when it suits you."

"Damn it, I was not fei—" He dragged one hand down his face. Stalking up to her, he slipped an arm about her waist from behind and lowered his voice. "I know you felt the same things I did when we were dancing."

Her body trembled in his arms. "Yes, you're a master at seduction, so good that you get caught up in the illusion. But if you had a choice, a man with . . . with your experience would not—"

"My experience is what has taught me how rare a woman you are."

Damn, he couldn't believe he was spouting these things. How his brothers would laugh! Yet the thought that she believed herself incapable of tempting a man beyond reason, that he could have wounded her so deeply . . .

He tightened his hold on her, aware she didn't resist as he wrapped his other arm about her waist to pull her against him.

Her voice fell to a ragged murmur. "I'm a nobody to you."

"Clearly not." He untied her bonnet, then stripped it from her head and dropped it onto the bench so he could nuzzle her hair. "Do you think I tramp about the woods every day with nobodies? Or spend hours teaching them how to dance?"

"When it suits you," she whispered.

"Initially, Sheridan wanted to be the one to help with your come-out lessons, so he asked me to spy on your brother. I persuaded him to let *me* help teach you instead of him. Do you wish to hear why?"

"Not particularly," she said with a sniff.

"Because you'd already made me want to know you better, with your teasing and tart remarks and impudence." And later, her sympathy for his feelings. "How could I *not* be intrigued by a woman with so many talents?"

She uttered a self-mocking laugh. "What talents? The ability to train dogs? I daresay you have twenty such men in your employ. And I've already shown that I'm woefully inexperienced in social etiquette."

"Anyone can learn such niceties." He bent his head to kiss her ear, then her cheek, reveling in the stuttering breath that escaped her. God, she made him harder than stone. How could she not see that his desire for her was genuine? "But your other talents are part of your character. Like your loyalty to family, your deft ability to manage tradesmen, and your knowledge of how an estate works. You've kept this household going ever since our family came here and without antagonizing any of them. Given the fractious nature of my relations, that's quite a feat."

As she softened against him, he gave in to the urge to cover one of her breasts with his hand. He rubbed it, then lowered his other hand to rub her between her thighs.

When she moaned, he caressed her more eagerly through her clothes. If only he could strip them from her, urge her onto that bench, and seduce her like the heedless rakehell some thought him to be. "I desire you with a maddening intensity."

She laid her hand over his as if to move it aside, but instead urged him to stroke harder, her body undulating against him. "If you desire me . . . it's only because you wish . . . to make me your . . . mistress."

"God forbid."

She pivoted in his arms to glare at him. "So I'm not even good enough for that."

He caught her head in his hands. "You're *too* good, more like. You deserve better than ruination."

"How can you say that when you can't even bring yourself to offer marriage?"

The pain in her voice tore through him. "*Won't* bring myself. There's a profound difference. It's a choice I'm making because . . . because . . ."

"Of Joshua," she whispered, her expression shadowed.

"That has naught to do with it. I just know I

can't be the husband you want and need. No matter how much I might wish to."

Temper flared in her wide, soulful eyes. "Then why do you keep touching and kissing me, knowing it will come to naught? I can see only one reason—you're hoping to get me to betray my bro—"

"It's because I can't keep my hands off you, damn it!" he cried, then cursed himself for admitting so much. "Do you think I'm proud of that? I assure you I am not. I'm known for my self-control. It's the reason the gossips spin tales about me—because they're hoping to see me squirm."

Bending his face to hers, he murmured, "Yet each time you and I are together, I want . . . I need . . . I have to have . . ." He took her mouth in a hard, hungry kiss before pulling back. "You. With me."

At his words, Beatrice felt a flutter in her chest, then despaired at her susceptibility. How could the man so easily melt her bones? She wanted his mouth on hers again, his hands stroking her, she wanted . . .

The same things he wanted, apparently. If she dared believe him.

He continued in a hard rasp, "And it has nothing to do with your brother or Sheridan's theories about murder." He slid a hand down the front of her, skimming her breast, then her ribs, then her hips before snaking it behind her derriere to tug her against him so she could feel the arousal in his trousers. "It has only to do with you and me. How much we desire each other." Brushing her lips with his, he murmured, "How much we desire *this,* as unwise as it is."

This time when he kissed her, he took no quarter, drowning her in a need as forceful as a wave pounding the shore. His tongue claimed every inch of her mouth even as his hands roamed and stroked and explored.

She grabbed at his shoulders, then his neck, going up on tiptoe to drug him with her own kisses. She didn't care if she could never be his duchess. All she knew was he was taking her mouth with the desire of a man who had no rank, no expectations . . . except that she yield to him. And, Lord help her, she was.

Through the fog of her pleasure, she felt him tug her scarf from around her neck and drop it on the bench next to her. Then he broke the kiss, only to drag his parted lips down her cheek to her neck, where he tongued the hollow of her throat, making her pulse jump and her blood run so hot that she didn't at first notice him inching her redingote and petticoat up her thigh on one side.

But she definitely noticed when he slipped his hand behind her knee and pulled her leg up so he could prop her foot on the bench. It opened her thighs in a most scandalous fashion, which he instantly took advantage of, settling her redingote and petticoat on her bent leg so he could get at the same place he'd been fondling earlier—her honeypot, as she knew men sometimes called it.

Now she realized why, for when he ran one finger down the cleft, she realized she was slick as melted honey there, in the spot that ached for him. "Grey . . . I'm not sure this is . . . wise."

"No, not wise." He nuzzled her throat. He dipped his finger inside her, and she gasped, which made the cursed fellow chuckle. "You like that, do you?"

"Yes . . . oh yes . . . Grey, please . . . *please* . . ."

"Don't worry, sweetheart," he said, his voice deliciously husky. "I will show you delights beyond compare. If you'll let me."

She clasped his shoulders. "Right now, I'll let you do anything you want," she admitted shamelessly.

"Don't say that," he growled, though his mouth found hers, pausing a moment to hover there. "Because what I want would take hours, and your brother is bound to come looking for us eventually."

That should have been a warning to her, but his fingers caressing her blotted out anything except her need to have him fondle her down there. "Hours?" she asked, half-aware of pushing herself against the hand caressing her below.

232

"Days," he muttered. "Weeks, if I had the chance."

He covered her mouth with his again, and kissed her with a savagery that called to her own. She wanted him; he wanted her. What could be wrong about that?

Oh, so much. Yet she rose to the kiss like some bitch in heat, needing him to take her, to show her those delights he hinted at. And show her, he did. His fingers plucked deftly at her, finding some hard, yearning spot that throbbed and ached beneath his touch.

What a devil. Even now, he knew how to intoxicate her.

"Touch me, too, sweetheart." He urged her hand down to where he was rigid in his trousers. "Here. *Please* . . ."

His voice sounded as needy as she felt. So as he rubbed her, she rubbed him through the fabric, reveling in the catch in his breathing, the way his fingers stroked harder than before, stoking a fire in her that she never knew existed. The glorious sensations inflaming her were almost unbearable.

Before long, she was gripping his arm with her free hand, desperate for more . . . greater . . . fiercer, until she felt the flames leaping inside her, burning away every inhibition, turning her moans and sighs into loud groans and gasps.

"Grey!" She erupted in a wild explosion that

shattered her from the inside out. "Oh . . . my *word!*"

In the next instant, he swept her hand away and clutched her to him. "Holy hell, sweetheart!" His eyes slid shut as he threw his head back. His body shuddered against hers. "Dear sweet . . . Beatrice . . . God help me but . . . you've made me . . . go too far."

She wasn't sure what he meant until he fumbled for a handkerchief and shoved it inside his trousers as his breath came in the same urgent gasps as hers. She gazed up into his taut features and felt a surge of satisfaction that she could make this handsome, desirable man feel such things.

He lowered his head and stared at her through heavy-lidded eyes for a long, tense moment. "Do you finally understand? *This* is what you do to me, just by being yourself. So never again say to me that my desire for you is feigned . . . for *any* reason. It is no more feigned than yours is for me."

They stared at each other a long moment, both caught up in the snare of their waning carnal urges. Then, to her horror, she heard the voice of her brother.

"Beatrice! Damn it, where are you?"

Chapter Seventeen

Grey hadn't intended to make matters more difficult for Beatrice. Yet obviously he had, judging from how hastily she dropped her foot from the bench, then rushed to smooth her skirts and hunt for her bonnet and scarf.

"Beatrice—" he began while hastily shoving the handkerchief in his pocket and buttoning up his greatcoat.

"Hush now, Grey. I can't let my brother find us here together. Not like this."

As if to punctuate her fears, Grey heard Wolfe calling, "Where are you?" from not far beyond their secluded space.

"A pox on him," Beatrice hissed as she frantically tied on her bonnet and wrapped her scarf about her lovely throat. "He didn't give us enough time."

Damn it to hell—this was what came of wanting a woman beyond endurance.

"Stay here," she murmured as she headed for the entrance.

"Wait," Grey said in a voice low enough not to be heard by anyone on the path. Having already lost control of his body, he didn't intend to lose control of his mind, too. He still hadn't learned what he'd come out here to discover, after all.

When she paused to stare at him, he said, "Tell the truth—Did your brother kill your uncle Armie?"

She sighed. "I honestly don't know." Then she hurried out onto the path.

Biting back a curse, Grey heard her meet with her brother and Gwyn, heard the major demand to know where she had gone and where Grey was.

Damn. She was a terrible liar. God only knew what she might blurt out if her brother pressed her too hard. Grey schooled his features into nonchalance and strode out onto the path.

"Miss Wolfe, this is quite an amazing—" Grey pretended to be shocked to see her brother standing there. "Oh, there you are, Major Wolfe. I assume you know about this wonderful enclosure built by your uncle. Your sister was just showing it to me. It's quite a feat of landscaping."

Wolfe's dark eyes narrowed on him. "What the devil are you talking about?"

Grey gestured to the hidden pathway. "The arbor back there. I thought you were aware of it."

"I damned well was not." Wolfe glanced at his sister. "What is he babbling about?"

Shooting Grey a grateful glance, Beatrice said, "Uncle Armie had a sweet little enclosure built in the woods. I was showing it to His Grace, since he'd already expressed an interest in the ruins and other landscape features."

"Oh, I want to see!" Gwyn cried. "Where is it?"

"This way." Beatrice led them all into the clearing. "It was my uncle's first experiment in creating secret spots for . . . um . . . contemplation."

The major gazed about the clearing with obvious suspicion. "How did you know about this place, Beatrice?"

"As I explained to His Grace, I saw all the bills for its creation. So I used to come here to get away from everyone. After Uncle Armie died, that is."

Gwyn cast Grey a veiled glance. "How kind of you to give my brother a look at it. He so enjoys secluded places."

Grey glared at his sister.

"I daresay he does," Wolfe gritted out as he swept the area with an eagle eye.

Beatrice said quickly, "If you enter the arbor there and go to the end, you'll find a well with whimsical creatures carved into its sides."

Brightening, Gwyn grabbed Beatrice's hand. "You must show it to me, my dear!" She tugged Beatrice through the arbor.

As soon as the ladies were out of earshot, Wolfe faced Grey with a hardened stance. "Don't think I'm blind to what you're about, sir."

"Oh?" Grey asked, feigning ignorance. "What is it that I'm 'about,' exactly?"

"Enticing my sister into your snare." Wolfe's

face darkened with rage. "Seducing her with your compliments and suave city manners."

"I was unaware I even *had* suave city manners." Indeed, Grey was perilously close to using his not-so-suave fist to bash the major's face in.

How dared Wolfe accuse *him* of anything? None of this situation would even exist if not for the man's possible criminal acts and Sheridan's subsequent suspicions.

"This may be a joke to you," Wolfe snarled, "but I'm warning you, Greycourt: Stay away from my sister!"

Grey stared him down. "Or what?"

That seemed to take the major aback. Then, with a scowl, he rested his weight on his good leg and brandished his cane at Grey. "I'll call you out. Duke or no, you will *not* take advantage of Beatrice. And don't think my bad leg has impaired my shooting ability. I assure you, it has not."

Grey was about to point out that the challenged party got to pick the weapons, and he would certainly pick swords, if only to put a swift end to Wolfe's foolish idea of dueling. Fortunately, the ladies returned before he could utter words the proud major would probably find intolerable.

Moving to Wolfe's side, Gwyn said flirtatiously, "You really should go look at the well, sir. It's rather amazing."

Keeping his gaze trained on Grey, Wolfe said,

"Another time perhaps. Beatrice and I are going home."

Beatrice set her shoulders. "But we haven't had our picnic. Why, Grey hasn't even seen the ruins yet!"

"I don't care about any damned picnic!" Wolfe cried, then stiffened when both Gwyn and Beatrice scowled at him. "I'll take you on a picnic another time, duckie," he went on sullenly. "And Lady Gwyn can show His Grace the ruins."

Gwyn looked from Wolfe to Beatrice, whose face had gone pale. "I think Grey can find the ruins all by himself. They weren't that impressive anyway." She offered her hand to Beatrice. "Let's return to the house, shall we? Mama is probably tired of dealing with the dressmaker and ready to continue our come-out lessons."

Wolfe stepped between Gwyn and his sister. "She doesn't need lessons from your lot. She can find a husband on her own, right here in Lincolnshire."

Gwyn looked as if she might answer, but Beatrice stepped around her brother to join her friend and said, "What if I don't *want* a husband from Lincolnshire? This is not your choice to make. No matter what you think, I could use their help in making a decent match." Beatrice slid her hand in Gwyn's arm. "Come, let's go find your mother. I am more than eager to continue preparing for my debut in London."

As the two women flounced off, neither casting

Grey even a backward glance, Wolfe looked momentarily unsettled, as if he hadn't anticipated this turn of events. Grey hadn't either, so he understood exactly how the major felt.

Nonetheless, he would take advantage of the ladies' exit. "Perhaps *you* should show me the ruins, sir," he drawled.

Wolfe looked nonplussed. Then he snapped, "I'm afraid you'll have to tour them yourself. I put off important matters so we could go on this little expedition." With the merest bow of his head, he added, "Good day to you, Your Grace. And remember what I told you: Leave my sister be."

Grey wished to counter with a warning to the same effect—that Wolfe should leave *Gwyn* alone. But Gwyn had a mind of her own. If she wanted the major, Grey's interference—hell, Sheridan's interference—would only make her want the man more.

So he let Wolfe walk away without making a similar threat. There was no point. As Sheridan had said, Gwyn knew better than to choose a man like Wolfe.

A man who might be a murderer. It bothered Grey that Wolfe had refused to go near the site of his uncle Armie's death. Perhaps Grey should view the spot himself, see if he could find anything Sheridan had missed.

But when he searched the area, Grey found

nothing of significance. So he headed back to the manor, part of him wondering if he might see Beatrice. His pulse quickened at the thought, damn it.

Why did she do this to him? No woman in society had even raised his temperature, yet some country chit made his blood heat and his mouth water? It made no sense. Even in his wild days of wine, women, and song, he'd always managed to enjoy himself without losing control. Or yearning to see any woman more often.

Yet he couldn't deny his disappointment at discovering that Beatrice had left Gwyn and his mother not long after she'd arrived back at the hall. He turned to asking about Sheridan, but his half brother hadn't returned to the hall yet. So after changing his clothes for dinner, Grey waited for him in the study. And was rewarded for his diligence when Sheridan appeared a couple of hours later.

"Where the devil have you been?" Grey couldn't help asking.

Sheridan glowered at him. "You were supposed to keep Joshua out of my way so I could do some exploring. But as I was searching the river, he appeared on the bridge. I had to hide from him." He looked irate. "*Hide,* mind you! I never hide from anyone."

"Aren't you fortunate?" Grey had spent half his life hiding—from his aunt's and uncle's machinations, from women who wanted to snag him as a husband . . . from himself.

"What the devil is *that* supposed to mean?" Sheridan asked.

"Nothing. Anyway, today's expedition didn't turn out quite as planned."

Sheridan rolled his eyes. "Obviously. But I discovered something important all the same." He went to pour himself some brandy. "After I left the area, I decided to see what the gossips in Sanforth might have to say about Joshua. And that's when I learned that Uncle Armie was planning to sell the dower house. Right out from under Joshua's feet."

A chill ran down Grey's spine. "Not just Joshua's. His sister's, too."

Looking suddenly uncomfortable, Sheridan downed some brandy. "It was well known in town that Uncle Armie wanted to sell the dower house to help pay his debts. And supposedly Joshua knew it, too. So the murder might have had nothing to do with the dukedom. Joshua might simply have decided to kill Uncle Armie to keep the man from selling his home."

"Possibly," Grey said grimly. "Though that theory doesn't explain your father's death."

"Actually, it might." Sheridan stared down into his glass. "I'd forgotten about it, but at some point after we took up residence here, Father mentioned that if worse came to worst we could always sell the dower house."

Grey suddenly found it hard to breathe. "Could Wolfe—or even Beatrice—have overheard Maurice?"

Sheridan shrugged. "I honestly have no idea. But if Joshua did, whether from her or from town gossip—"

"Then it gives him a motive for wanting both men dead."

Grey's heart sank. It gave Beatrice a motive as well. And though he still couldn't see her riding out to murder two men, *she,* not Wolfe, had known of the little hiding place not far from where their uncle Armie had died.

Still, Grey doubted she had the strength—or the will—to pull a man off his horse and break his neck, even a man in his sixties. She would need her brother to help her. Despite Wolfe's bad leg, the two of them might manage it between them.

But to assume that, Grey would have to believe he'd been entirely wrong about her character, had mistaken every word, every blush . . . every sweet, hot caress. Could he really have been *that* wrong about her?

Staring off into space, Grey examined her behavior since they'd met. Until today, she'd actively avoided being around him, especially whenever he brought up her brother or uncle. Even today, she'd probably only taken him aside so she could keep him from seeing Wolfe's reaction to the spot where her uncle had died.

All this time he'd assumed she might have another reason for her evasions, but what if she hadn't? She'd accused Grey of cozying up to her . . . but what if all this time *she* had been cozying up to *him,* just more subtly and effectively than any woman he'd ever met? What if she'd been trying to allay his suspicions by tempting him into madness? Trying to find out what he knew, what Sheridan knew . . . if Sheridan was planning to sell the dower house?

If she *had* been such a schemer, she was even more manipulative than his aunt and uncle, which he had trouble believing.

The more he thought about that possibility, the angrier he got. What if, in his . . . foolish infatuation for her, he'd simply played into the hands of a murderer and his accomplice?

"Grey. Are you all right?"

"I'm fine." Grey rose. "But I need to go. There's something I must check on."

As Grey headed for the door, Sheridan said, "I almost forgot—what happened with you and Joshua on the trip to the ruins? Did he react to seeing the spot where Uncle Armie died?"

"We didn't get that far," Grey said.

No, they hadn't. Because Beatrice had made sure that they hadn't.

Beatrice was eating her supper when a pounding came at the front door. What on earth? It couldn't be Joshua. He wouldn't knock, and anyway, by the time she'd returned from Armitage Hall, he'd already ridden off to Leicester. At least that was what their maid-of-all-work, their only servant these days, had told her before going home to her family.

Leaving Beatrice alone here. Which made her reluctant to let anyone in now that night had fallen. She told herself it was probably a servant from the hall, come to fetch her for some reason, but still . . .

"Open this door!" demanded a voice she recognized only too well.

Him.

She hesitated a moment longer. Grey sounded angry. And given how they'd parted, perhaps he had a right to be. She'd as much as admitted he had good reason for his suspicions, even though she wasn't sure of that herself.

Still, she knew him too well to think he would just go away and leave. And when he cried, "Wolfe, damn it, I want to speak to you now!" she ignored the butterflies in her belly, strode to the door, and swung it open.

"What do you want, Your Grace?" she asked, fighting to sound unafraid. It was hard not to be afraid when he was looking so ducal in his evening attire.

He seemed startled to see her standing there in her nightdress and wrapper. Then he collected himself. His gaze took in the empty room behind her. "Where's your brother?"

"I believe we had this discussion before," she said tartly. "The appropriate greeting—"

Temper flared in his face. "I don't give a damn about social rules just now. I want to speak to Wolfe!"

"He's not here." She started to close the door. "Go away and come back tomorrow."

Grey stuck his foot in the door to prevent her from shutting it. "Not until I get some answers. Where is he?"

Grey wasn't just angry—he was well and truly furious.

She shuddered. "Joshua is in Leicester. He was supposed to go this morning, but he put his business off for our outing. Why are you asking? What has happened?"

"Your brother has left you, a woman, alone at night?" He ran his gaze down her, obviously taking in the flimsiness of her attire.

"Our maid-of-all-work generally stays with me if he's gone, but her babe is sick, so I told her to go home. It's safe enough on the estate." And she kept a loaded pistol on the console table near the door, though she didn't have the best aim. "Joshua will be back tomorrow."

He leveled a hard gaze on her. "Are you sure he's *coming* back?"

What an odd question. "Of course he's coming

back. When he goes to Leicester on business, he's rarely gone more than one night. Now please go and leave me to my supper."

Instead, he shoved open the door and entered. "Then I will talk to you in his stead."

As he shut the door behind him, she swallowed hard. "This is most inappropriate."

"I don't care." He tossed his hat onto the console table and caught sight of her pistol. "You shoot?"

"Not very well, no," she admitted, then realized perhaps she should have kept that detail to herself. Though honestly, she couldn't see herself shooting a duke. Particularly this one. "I keep it there for protection."

"From whom?"

"People like you who barge into my home without an invitation," she bit out.

A faint smile crossed his face before he squelched it. He picked up the pistol and turned the handle toward her. "Then go ahead—feel free. Though it won't help you or your brother advance your aims in the same way that pushing someone off a bridge might have."

She felt all at sea as she took the pistol and carefully set it back on the table. "Advance our aims? What do you mean?" Then it hit her. "Uncle *Maurice?* Now you suspect my brother of murdering him, too?"

"Your brother," he said coldly. "Or you."

"Me!" She burst into laughter. The idea of her killing anyone was ludicrous.

But Grey's grim expression showed that he didn't find it so, and at once her amusement vanished.

She stared him down. "Why in God's name would I murder Uncle Maurice? I *liked* him!"

"He was planning to sell this house out from under you and your brother." Grey cast her a triumphant look as if he'd finally unveiled all her secrets.

"Yes, and so was Uncle Armie."

The triumph in his face vanished. "You're not *denying* that you knew about it."

"Why would I?" This conversation got stranger by the moment. "Everyone in the whole blasted town of Sanforth knew. I daresay half of London knew. Even if I hadn't heard about it from several people eons ago, I wouldn't have been surprised to learn of it. Since this parcel of the estate isn't entailed, selling it was one of the few ways left to my uncles to shore up a failing dukedom. Indeed, I assumed that the reason for my come-out lessons was that Sheridan was planning something of the sort himself, so your mother figured she'd best find me a husband and quick."

Grey looked as if she'd sucked the wind right out of his sails. "So you weren't concerned about it."

"Well, yes. But it's not as if I could do anything." She cocked her head. "I certainly wouldn't have tried to murder anyone in a futile attempt to prevent it." She shook her head. "You actually thought I would . . . kill your stepfather over such a thing."

"It crossed my mind." He ran his fingers through his hair distractedly. "But no. Not really." His gaze shot to her. "Your brother is another matter entirely, however."

"He would never have murdered Uncle Maurice," she said stoutly.

"But you're not so certain about his murdering your uncle Armie."

So they were back to that, were they? Her hands grew clammy. "H-He wouldn't have done it over *that,* to be sure."

The moment the words left her mouth, she could have cursed her quick tongue.

Especially when Grey's eyes focused on her with great intensity. "Not over *that?* Then over what, pray tell?"

Her stomach sank. She should have known from his questions this afternoon that he wouldn't let his suspicions slide. Especially after her parting words in the clearing.

Not sure what to do or say, she headed back toward the kitchen. "My supper is getting cold."

He followed her, his presence looming behind her like a thundercloud. "By all means, don't let me keep you from supper. It's not as if we're discussing anything *important*."

As she entered the kitchen, she asked, "Have you eaten? There's still some beef stew, and I think—"

"Leave it." Taking her arm, Grey pulled her around to face him. "This afternoon you said you didn't know if Joshua killed your uncle Armie. But if he did, what reason do *you* think he'd have for doing it?"

"I'd rather not go into it," she murmured, though his threatening visage made it clear he wouldn't let that go. "Why does it matter, anyway? Uncle Armie was an arse and now he's gone."

"It matters because Sheridan thinks your brother is after the dukedom—that he killed both your uncles and is plotting to kill Sheridan and Heywood so he can become duke himself."

She gaped at him, but clearly he was serious. "Joshua doesn't care about the dukedom. He doesn't care about much of anything these days, except for his stupid trips to Leicester . . . and perhaps protecting me."

"Perhaps?" He relaxed his grip on her arm and softened his tone. "Trust me, he definitely cares about protecting *you*. He made that painfully clear this afternoon."

A pox on her brother. "Did he say something to you? Oh, Lord, what did he tell you? I suppose he warned you away from me."

"He threatened to call me out if I didn't leave you be."

"What?" Pulling free of him, she balled her hands into fists. "I will thrash that devil myself. How dare he suggest a duel, after the way Papa died?"

Grey lifted an eyebrow. "You can't blame him, considering what you and I were doing in that clearing. Any fool could have seen through our excuses. And your brother is no fool. Not to mention that he seems determined to protect you from any man who—"

He halted, a look of horror spreading over his features. "So *that's* what you meant when you said he wouldn't kill over the sale of the dower house. Because you know there's only one thing he *would* kill over. You. Keeping you safe."

She turned away, unable to bear his expression. He knew. Or rather, he suspected the truth.

And all at once, her years of embarrassment and shame came flooding back.

Chapter Eighteen

"Bastard!" Grey growled.

Beatrice shot him a wary glance. "Who? My brother?"

"No. Your uncle Armie."

When Grey saw the color drain from her, he couldn't breathe, couldn't move. He felt rooted to the floor. What kind of monster did . . . what that arse must have done to her to make her brother wish to murder him?

Thorn's remark came back to him once more. *I suspect that Miss Wolfe is more worldly wise than you think.*

Grey should have put it together when the servants were talking about the man's peccadilloes, but he hadn't thought the fellow would . . . "Please tell me your uncle Armie didn't take your innocence."

"What? No!" A blush stained her cheeks. "I mean, he did, but not in the way you mean. He just stripped it from me word by filthy word." She moved to the stove and started filling a plate with stew, as if the action could anchor her in normalcy.

There was nothing normal about this. Grey's very blood ran cold at the thought of her enduring whatever her uncle—her *uncle,* for

God's sake—had dished out. "So he . . . never touched you."

Her back went rigid. "Well, of course he *touched* me. But he always tried to disguise it as . . . perfectly natural. A hard hug that pressed my breasts against him, a 'friendly' slap on the behind, a lingering kiss to my cheek so he could get close enough to look down the front of my . . . gowns."

"*Gowns?* So he made a regular practice of such attentions."

"Oh yes," she said in a guilt-ridden voice that infuriated him on her behalf.

When she fell silent and came over to place a heaping plate of stew opposite hers on the table, then stood there slicing bread to add to his plate, he resisted the urge to pepper her with questions.

"Tell me everything, sweetheart."

When she continued to say nothing, he approached her from behind. It disturbed him that she wouldn't look at him. She had no reason to be ashamed.

He curled his hands into fists, wishing her uncle Armie wasn't dead so Grey could beat him to death. "How old were you when it started?"

"I don't know—sixteen? My grandmother was still alive."

She'd been only a girl, for God's sake. Grey could hardly bear to think of it.

"After his wife, my aunt, died," she went on,

"it was just me and him most of the time. And the servants, of course. Grandpapa was gone, Joshua was posted abroad, Grandmama was consumptive, and Uncle Armie was lord of the manor in every way you might imagine. It made it hard for me to escape him."

So the bastard had used his power over her to try forcing her to his will. Grey's every feeling revolted to think of what she'd suffered, but he kept silent, wanting to give her the freedom to talk about it. It was important to discuss such things. He'd never had that chance during the time his aunt and uncle had tried bending him to *their* will. He'd felt all alone . . . until Vanessa had grown old enough to listen.

Even then, he hadn't told her everything, not wanting to poison her feelings for her parents, since they'd never treated *her* ill.

He shook off the memory. This wasn't about *his* suffering but Beatrice's, which he genuinely wanted to understand. He said nothing, but simply laid a comforting hand on her shoulder.

"It started with him commenting on my clothing—whether it enhanced my breasts, whether it showed my . . . bottom to good effect." As Grey swallowed his disgust, she left him to roam the kitchen like a caged sparrow seeking a way out of her prison. "Then he began . . . trying to kiss me on the lips, but I mostly managed to avoid that. He was, after all, a good bit older than I, so I was usually able to evade his . . . attentions."

"You shouldn't have had to."

"No. But he was my uncle. He had me . . . under his thumb, so to speak."

Other questions occurred to him. "Didn't your grandmother try to put a stop to it?"

"I didn't tell her." She stared down at her hands. "Grandmama already thought me a 'naughty saucebox,' so I was afraid she would blame *me* for what he did."

"And that would have been wrong, too," he said hoarsely.

Startled, she glanced up at him. "Do you truly think so?"

Her reaction made him want to weep, and he'd never wept in his life, even when Uncle Eustace had been at his worst. "His behavior was intolerable, sweetheart. And he forced you into hiding it by making you think that knowledge of it would wound his mother, your grandmother."

"It would have," she said with her usual bluntness.

"Perhaps. But from what the servants told me, his wife had known about his 'dalliances.' So your grandmother might already have known, too."

She poured claret in a glass and set it by the plate. When he ignored it, she drank some herself. "The maids suffered much the same treatment as

I, so she might have seen that. Though he was careful to keep his behavior toward *me* from being seen by anyone."

"I'm not so sure about that," he said softly. "One of the maids told me your uncle wasn't 'circumspect' about his dalliances. And when I remarked that he surely hid them from *you,* she said, 'A man like that don't hide his true character from nobody.' At the time I thought she meant he was open about his mistresses around you, but now I realize she meant that he . . . showed his true colors with you, as well."

Shame suffused her cheeks with scarlet. "Oh, Lord, what the servants must have thought of me!"

Instantly, he regretted having roused that particular fear in her mind. "They *thought,* and still think, that you are, and I quote, 'a fine woman, always considering the needs of others without any reward.' And I can't be sure they knew, anyway. The maid didn't say anything about that in particular."

Her throat worked convulsively. "I never encouraged his behavior, you know."

"I assumed that you didn't."

She stared down at the wineglass. "Yet you asked the servants about me. And him."

"Not about the two of you together, for God's sake. I had no idea . . . I never dreamed . . ." When he paused, thinking through his next response, she lifted a questing gaze to him.

He drew in a harsh breath. "After the maid said you were his hostess and he was a philanderer, I had some notion you might have seen things—" Damn, he was digging the hole deeper with every word. "You can't blame me for wanting to learn more about what makes you who you are," he finished feebly.

Her pretty eyebrow shot up. "Is that really why you asked about me? Or was it just to determine how easily you might tempt me into betraying my brother?"

Holy hell. She always got right to the point, didn't she? "It's not as if the servants would ever reveal such a thing to me. They're loyal to you."

Now he fervently wished he'd remembered that before he had come over here half-cocked. Because the scheming seductress he'd conjured up in his fevered imagination—between when he'd spoken to Sheridan and when he'd confronted her—bore no resemblance to the woman the staff at Armitage Hall had described. Or the woman he'd come to know himself.

Clearly, *that* woman had been caught in a cruel trap. And he was only making matters worse. "But we were talking about your grandmother and what she knew."

"Right. And why I didn't tell her."

"It might have been better if you had. At least then she could have called your uncle out for it." He wanted to take her in his arms, reassure her.

But now he wasn't sure how she'd regard such an act. "It wasn't your responsibility to protect him."

"Trust me, it was never about protecting *him*." She glanced away. "If you're right and Grandmama did realize what he was up to, then it might not have made a difference if I'd told her, anyway," she said glumly. "I was almost afraid to find out."

He could understand that. And she might be right—it might not have made a difference. But that was neither here nor there. Beatrice should never have been abused in such a fashion in the first place. "Your brother was still gone, I take it."

"He didn't return until six years after my aunt died but shortly before Grandmama's death."

"Did matters improve once your uncle knew you had a protector nearby?"

"A little," she said, which told him all he needed to know.

That her uncle had continued to be an arse. That the man probably hadn't considered Wolfe a threat because he was wounded and a mere poor relation.

"For a year after Joshua's return," she went on, "he required a great deal of care. His limp is only the most visible manifestation of his wounds. Beyond his damaged leg, he has scars . . ." She set her glass down. "Anyway, since we were living here and not at the hall, I could often use the excuse that I had to go home to look after Joshua. That helped me avoid Uncle Armie many a time."

The fact that she'd had to resort to such an excuse made him want to howl his anger on her behalf. "You never told your brother about what your uncle was doing?"

Her gaze shot to his. "Of course not. At first, it was because Joshua was struggling to survive, and I didn't want to compromise that. Then it was because I knew how he would react. Just look how he was with *you*. How could I risk his confronting our uncle?"

"Yet you think he might have done so, anyway."

Her shoulders slumped. "I honestly don't know. I've never been sure if Joshua realized what was going on. I mean, if he killed Uncle Armie as a result of finding out what the man was doing, my secretive brother would be unlikely to tell me the truth about it. And if Joshua *didn't* kill Uncle Armie . . ." She released a long breath. "Then he'd hate me for suspecting him of such a crime in the first place."

"Still . . . You would have been within your rights to seek your brother's aid."

"Yes, but truthfully, by then I was able to handle it." She kept her gaze averted from him. "I had learned how to keep from being alone with my uncle. I usually claimed I had to be elsewhere, or I threatened to tell Joshua. That worked fairly well. Until . . ."

When she trailed off and her eyes got a faraway look in them, his stomach churned. "Until?"

"Well, a year ago, I started hearing that Uncle Armie might be planning to sell the dower house." She cast Grey a sheepish look. "As you said earlier, I was concerned. When I finally got up the nerve to ask him . . ." Her voice grew haunted. "He told me he wouldn't sell *if* . . . I'd agree to be his mistress. He said Joshua and I could live in the dower house as long as we wished, but in exchange I'd have to . . . do as he pleased."

The fury rising in Grey burned clear down to his soul. Which was probably why he spoke so unwisely. "If your uncle Armie were still alive, I'd kill him myself for that."

The words seemed to startle her. "You don't blame me?"

He blinked. "For what?"

"Attracting his attentions. Perhaps dressing too . . . I don't know, provocatively? Though I really didn't think I did."

"Of course you didn't. *He* was the culprit. He was the one who thought he could make use of you, whether or not you wished it." It reminded him of his own relations trying to make use of him. He understood all too well what it was like to be little more than a child at the mercy of one's family.

"I did try to keep him from touching me, even when he pretended it was innocent affection in front of the servants. And I always ignored the lascivious remarks he hissed under his breath when he passed me in the hall." She slumped. "Though that only seemed to make him say worse things. He seemed determined to get a rise out of me."

Grey tried to swallow past the bile rising in his throat. "Certain men thrive on the challenge of seducing a woman who won't pay them any mind." He reached out to caress her cheek, then thought better of it and dropped his hand. "Your uncle wanted to win you, as vile as that sounds. And if he'd done so, he would have discarded you soon enough for the next new attractive female who resisted him."

"Attractive?" Her brow furrowed. "I always just figured he chose me because I was close at hand and easy to bully."

"Not so easy. Thank God."

She glanced away. "He has a string of former mistresses scattered about Sanforth, you know. I've always wondered how many of them actually *chose* the position. He also has a by-blow he never provided for."

"That isn't a surprise, given his tendencies. You were wise to put him off."

"Was I?" She shook her head. "When I refused his vile 'offer,' it's possible he resorted to telling

Joshua his demands. Because not long after I refused to let him blackmail me into being his mistress, Uncle Armie . . . um . . ."

"Met his demise?"

Her wince was answer enough.

"So you suspect that your brother resorted to murder."

"I'd like to think he wouldn't have. And he said he was in Leicester that night. But . . ."

"You can't be sure."

She shook her head no. Then she faced him with squared shoulders. "However, I do know for a fact that Joshua didn't murder Uncle Maurice. Joshua was with *me* the night your stepfather died. We'd promised Uncle Maurice we would ready the gamekeeper's accounts for his meeting with the family solicitor the next day. I'm not certain why, but he wanted us to make sure they were up-to-date and there were no errors. So Joshua and I were going over them together."

Grey narrowed his gaze on her. "And you spent the whole *evening* doing that? You were with your brother the entire time?"

She nodded. "We were still working on it in the wee hours of the morning when a servant came to fetch Uncle Maurice back to the hall. That's when we learned that he'd headed over here earlier and hadn't been seen since. We told the footman, and a search was begun immediately." Tears welled in her eyes. "They found Uncle Maurice washed up on the bank the next morning."

Which meant that if Joshua had killed their uncle Armie, it could only have been to stop what the man had tried to force her into.

As if she'd read his mind, she muttered, "It's merely Uncle Armie's death I'm not sure about. Joshua might have . . . it's possible that he—"

"To be honest," Grey said slowly, "I would hope your brother *did* murder him if the only other choice was seeing you become the man's mistress. Hell, I'd shake your brother's hand for it. Your uncle *deserved* death for what he tried to force upon you."

Her gaze swung back to him. "You can say that, even though he was a duke? And related to your half brother?"

He snorted. "Contrary to popular opinion, there's no code of ducal honor that we all follow." His voice hardened. "And if there were, I'm sure your uncle broke it by trying to make you commit incest."

The ugly word made her flinch. "Good point."

"I make them occasionally," he quipped, to inject humor into an increasingly difficult discussion.

At least it brought a smile to her lips. "Yes, you do."

"In between my attempts to seduce you. If I'm to be honest, I had no more right than your uncle to—"

"Do *not* compare yourself to Uncle Armie. He never gave me a choice. You always did, even when you were suspicious of me and my brother. A lesser man would have used the situation to blackmail me into his bed." She stepped closer. "You never resorted to such a thing."

"I don't believe in blackmail," he admitted.

His uncle Eustace had tried to blackmail him into signing papers, and Grey had refused to be bullied. So he sure as hell wasn't going to try the same tactics on anyone else. Especially a woman like Beatrice, who'd always been at the mercy of her relations.

Even early on, he'd sensed they had that in common. And now that he *knew* they did, it made him desire her even more. Which, given all she'd told him about her situation, was unconscionable.

He cleared his throat and tried to remind himself of his real purpose here. "Much as I desired you, I promise I would never have resorted to force to get you into my bed."

"I know." A blush suffused her cheeks again. "I never thought of you as pushing your attentions on me. And certainly not in the way my uncle did."

He stared hard at her. "All the same—"

"No!" She pressed a finger to his lips. "I won't let you see it as comparable. Until you came along, I regarded marriage as only a way for a woman to find financial security. I thought relations between men and women must surely be dirty and unpleasant. I couldn't imagine finding enjoyment from a man's caresses."

When she paused, he rasped, "And now?"

Her beautiful brown eyes shone up at him. "Now I know it's possible to find pleasure in touching a man, in being with a man. Knowing a man so intimately that—"

He kissed her. He couldn't help himself. Having feared that his actions had only added to her fears, it humbled him to discover he'd managed to alleviate them a bit. And when she looped her arms about his neck so she could kiss him back, his pulse thudded hard and fast in his veins.

She had a mouth like an angel—a seductive angel with a penchant for claret. Yet the taste of it on her tongue wasn't nearly as heady as the intoxication of kissing her and holding her, knowing that she *wanted* to be there.

Which only made it harder for him to resist touching her. Her floor-length wrapper was chaste as a muslin gown—made of starched linen and finished off with frilly ruffles at every collar, cuff, and hem. But when he gave in to the urge to let his hands roam beneath it to her nightdress . . .

God, but that thin piece of worn cotton shielded nothing. With no corset to hinder him, he could plunder her pert breasts to his heart's content, reveling in their softness. And the feel of her nipples hardening beneath his fingers through the fabric made him ache to explore more.

He pulled back. "Forgive me. I didn't mean to take advan—"

She cut off the words with her lips. That was when he knew he was in trouble. Because randy devil that he was, he couldn't stop himself from kissing her sumptuous mouth again.

Chapter Nineteen

Beatrice was in heaven. Dear Lord, but His Grace knew how to kiss. Grey knocked her right back on her heels with the sensuous plunges of his tongue, the sweeping strokes of his hands, and even the heady scent of cologne in his hair. Her body quaked from the surfeit of so many pleasures at once.

Still, what was she doing, tempting a man who could lead her only to ruin? Why, he'd thought her capable of murder!

Yet she wanted him. *Needed* him. Wished to climb all over him, to find out what he felt like beneath his clothes. To have him inside her.

And not just his fingers, like this afternoon. No, she wanted him entirely, filling her up until the past was no more. It might be only temporary, but for tonight she wanted to know how it felt to be desired for who she was, by a man whom she actually desired in return.

She tugged at his coat until he shrugged it off, and in return he stripped off her wrapper and tossed it over a nearby chair. Now she wore only her nightdress, and she didn't even care.

"You realize this is madness. Pure insanity," he said even as he worked loose the buttons of her nightdress. Perhaps he didn't care either.

"Is it?" When he spread hot kisses down inside the opened placket, she nearly fainted from the anticipation of what he meant to do. "Feels perfectly sane to me."

With a heartfelt groan, he seized one breast in his mouth, and she melted. He teased and nibbled, licked and sucked. Lord, she was on fire. Her nipple ached from the decadent enjoyment she'd barely sampled before. She clutched his head close, praying for more, and he answered her prayers by treating her other breast to the same wonderful treatment.

He clapped his large hands around her hips and began to caress her curves as if trying to memorize every one. All the while his mouth plundered her breasts like a ravisher of old.

Except she didn't feel ravished. She felt worshipped.

"You taste like honey," he murmured, "like the angel you are." To her vast annoyance, he drew back to gaze into her eyes. "Which is one more reason I should stop. You deserve better."

"Stop saying that!" The words frustrated her. "I don't care what I deserve, *who* I deserve." She unbuttoned his waistcoat, and though he cursed under his breath, she didn't stop until she had it undone. "Every time you touch some part of me that my depraved uncle tried to sully with his words, you dim the memory. When you caress me, I no longer feel dirty; when you kiss me, I no longer remember his slobbering mouth on my lips. You have no idea what a gift that is."

She lifted her gaze. "I have no idea what the future will bring for me—if I'll ever find a husband or be with a man who makes me . . . yearn and soar as you do." Fisting her hands in his waistcoat, she said, "So I want my first time to be with you."

Though an unholy fire leapt in his face, he didn't return to what he'd been doing. "Sweetheart—"

"No!" She dragged his waistcoat off. "Don't say whatever you mean to—about how I should keep my virtue intact or whatever rot true gentlemen are schooled to tell a respectable female like me." She tossed his waistcoat aside. "Do you desire me?"

She held her breath, half afraid to hear the answer, but his face showed it all. "You know that I do." As if to prove it, he tightened his grip on her hips.

"Then take me to bed."

"You will come to regret it."

"I won't." She gazed at him uneasily. "But will you?"

His eyes turned a molten blue-green. "How could I? You're giving me everything I want and asking nothing in return. Unfortunately, the consequences aren't the same for a man as they are for a woman." He caught her head in his hands, forcing her to look at him. "What if you have a child?"

"I thought one could prevent such things."

That seemed to surprise him. "You did, did you?" He slid his hands down to her shoulders. "How, pray tell?"

She met his gaze, startled by the glint of amusement in it. "I have no idea." She worked to loosen the elaborate knot of his cravat. "But when I refused Uncle Armie's offer, he said if I was worried about bearing . . . a bastard, there were ways to stop that from occurring. He just didn't bother to tell me what they were."

His amusement vanished. "God, the man really was an arse."

"Was it a lie?"

Lifting his eyes heavenward, he muttered, "It's not that. There are ways, but—"

"You don't know what they are." With a sigh, she gripped either end of his cravat. "I assumed you *would,* given your reputation, but if you don't, perhaps we could figure it out together. I mean, I'm fairly familiar with how breeding is managed for dogs and horses."

"Yes, I'm well aware of your extensive knowledge in *that* area," he said, looking as if he were choking on the words.

"But the only way I know of to prevent animals from breeding is not to let them mate in the first place."

"Mate?" he echoed, one eyebrow shooting up. "Is that how you see what we would do together? *If* we were to do anything?"

"No, of course not. We'd be sharing a bed."

He shot her a black look. "Sharing a bed," he repeated.

She felt her cheeks heat. Blast it, she hated her tendency to blush. "Isn't that what you want?"

"What I *want* is to make love to you. What I want is to show you what it feels like to need someone so desperately that nothing else makes sense, that the mere thought of seeing that person makes one's heart race." He caught her by the waist and pulled her close. "What I want is to banish your uncle's memory from your thoughts."

"That's what I want, too!" she cried, delighted that he spoke of desperation, although she knew it was a mere thing of the moment.

"Except that afterward—"

"I don't care about afterward. If you *do* know how to prevent my bearing a child, there's no problem, right? We can just . . ." She leaned up to brush his lips with hers and whisper, "Be together in my bed."

He stared at her with eyes like the churning river nearby. "You make it hard to resist you, my dear Beatrice."

The words were a balm to her wounded vanity. No man had ever called her irresistible

271

before. "Good," she said, her heart in her throat. "Because you do the same to me."

This time when he kissed her, he didn't stop. Still kissing her, he backed her up to the kitchen table, then took her by surprise when he lifted her onto it, his eyes gleaming at her. "I need sustenance, sweetheart."

"Oh! I forgot about your food—I do hope it's enough."

When she tried to scoot out of his arms to get it, he grabbed her back, laughing. "Not *that* kind of sustenance." He lifted her nightdress to her knees, then paused. "Are you *sure* your brother will be gone until morning?"

"*Early* in the morning, but yes."

"So we have the entire night together."

She caught her breath. "If you wish."

"I wish, I promise you." The look in his eyes said exactly what sorts of things he promised, and her excitement ramped up just wondering what those might be. He tugged her forward until she was close to the table's edge. "It will take me all night and more for a proper lovemaking."

"Well, then," she said as she set about undoing the buttons of his shirt, "since we don't have 'more,' we'll have to settle for an *improper* lovemaking."

Chuckling, he dropped to his knees. "Well put. Which is my cue for taking my sustenance."

Catching her by surprise, he pushed her legs wide. "I'm going to taste you, all right?"

Ohhh, that's what he meant by sustenance. And now he was staring right at her privates, heating her blood and rousing her body.

Especially down there.

He glanced up at her. "Do you trust me, sweetheart?"

She certainly trusted him when it came to bedsport, no matter what he claimed about having a pristine reputation. She bobbed her head.

That seemed to be all the answer he needed, for hunger leapt in his face. "Then close your eyes. Just concentrate on how it feels."

The moment she did so, he began kissing her inner thigh, little nibbling kisses that made her squirm and ache for . . . a release like the one he'd given her in the clearing earlier. The higher his mouth went, the hotter it grew until her blood felt like steam and her body like jelly.

She began to moan. And that was when he used his fingers to part her curls so he could lick— *lick*—her tender flesh!

"Grey!" Her eyes shot open and she grabbed his head. "Dear Lord, *Grey* . . ."

Now *his* eyes were closed. He said nothing since his mouth was otherwise engaged . . . in kissing and licking and sucking her in a *most* provocative manner.

Then his tongue slid inside her, and she arched

up on the table's edge. "I don't think this is how . . . lovemaking is done," she managed to gasp. "Not from what I . . . understand." Surely he needed to use a different part of his body to—

All thought abruptly left her mind. Because he was . . . oh, heavens, what he was doing with his mouth and . . . and teeth was . . . *wonderful*. She wanted more of *that*. She pushed against him, and his tongue caresses grew more intense. Soon she was keening and swaying until with a cry she vaulted over into madness.

He gave her only a moment before he wiped his lips on her nightdress, then drew back, his face wrought with tension.

"Where's your bedchamber?" he asked.

Too replete with pleasure to think, she stared at him. "Why?"

"I'll embarrass myself again if we don't go there now. And I'm not about to take you for the first time on a kitchen table. So where is it?"

"Upstairs."

He groaned. "Of course it is."

Rising from the floor, he reached behind her to swig some claret from the glass she'd set down. Then he swept her into his arms and carried her through to the entranceway. As he climbed the staircase, she grabbed his neck to keep from falling. Not that he seemed likely to drop her. Dear Lord, he must be very strong to be managing this.

"I'm quite capable of walking, you know," she said, though something about being carried up by him sent a thrill through her.

As he reached the top and saw the three open doorways, he growled, "Which one?"

All she could do was point, still drowning in the amazing aftermath of his carnal caresses. He hurried through the doorway she'd indicated, then set her down on her bed so he could pull off his cravat and unfasten the fall of his trousers.

As she knelt on the bed, she noticed his member swelling in his drawers through the open fall. It should have frightened her. After this afternoon, it did not. She'd never imagined being able to arouse such a man, who could have any woman he pleased.

Uncle Armie had been aroused by anything in skirts, but she'd watched Grey with the maids, and even the pretty ones hadn't drawn his gaze. She began to think he might really *prefer* her. Well, at least he preferred her to the maids.

His heated gaze seared her as he kicked off his shoes. "Take off your nightdress, sweetheart. I want to see you naked."

Uh-oh. It was one thing to let him see parts of her at a time, but to allow him to see her plump bottom and freckled back and small bosom altogether . . .

"Heavens, but you're bossy." She folded her

arms over her chest. "I haven't even seen *you* naked yet."

"You want me to go first?" He lifted an eyebrow. "Very well."

He shucked off his trousers, which left him in only his stockings, his prominently bulging drawers, and his shirt, which he dragged off over his head and tossed aside, too.

Her breath got stuck in her throat. For a duke with leisure time to spare, he certainly had a magnificent chest, with firmly defined muscles and a patch of black, curly hair spreading between them before narrowing to a thin line that led down to a lean stomach so perfect she wanted to bite it.

Bite it? Had she really had such a thought?

"Like what you see?" he asked in a low rumble, reminding her of their first kiss.

She nodded, incapable of forming words at the moment.

A smug smile flashed over his face. "Want to see more?"

"Yes, please," she choked out.

"Then take off your nightdress, sweetheart."

"But—"

"Let me guess—you're balking because you have warts on your belly."

She eyed him askance. "Don't be silly—no one gets warts there."

His eyes twinkled as he pulled off his stockings. "You have the pox then?"

"Of *course* not!" She huffed out a breath. "I only . . . it's merely that . . . well . . . I'm no more a beauty naked than I am clothed."

Just like that, his amusement vanished. "Who the hell told you that you weren't a beauty?" When she chewed on her lower lip, his face darkened. "Ah, right. Your arse of an uncle, I suppose." Walking up to where she stood by the bed, he caught her chin in his hand. "Let's get this straight once and for all. You are not merely a beauty—you're the *queen* of beauties."

She glared at him, her throat aching at the blatant untruth. "There's no need to lie, Grey. You're already in my bedchamber. It's not as if I'm going to kick you out."

"I'm not lying." He scowled. "Didn't we agree to always speak the truth to each other?"

"We did."

"And haven't I done so?"

She cocked her head. "You didn't tell me you were investigating my brother."

"Because you didn't ask. Not once have I lied to your face. I've probed, I've urged, and I've coaxed. But I haven't lied. I'm telling you the truth now, as I always have." He skimmed his fingers over her cheek. "With enough fine clothes and subtle cosmetics and a lady's maid to dress her hair to greatest advantage, anybody can be a beauty."

He stared her down. "But only a few have

beauty bred in the bone. And you, my dear lady, even in your mourning clothes, with your lovely locks simply dressed, are one of those. I daresay once you have your debut, in your fine gown, with your hair dressed properly, you will be positively *majestic*." A faint smile crossed his lips. "Indeed, I shudder to think how many men I shall have to thrash just for looking at you."

"Grey . . ." she said, hardly able to fathom his compliments.

"Take it off." His eyes shone a smoky green in the firelight. "Let me see what those fellows will never get the chance to. Not if I have anything to say about it."

The words were nearly a promise. She wanted to believe him, even if he only meant it for this one night. So she took off her nightdress. What else could she do? She wanted him in her bed, and he wanted her naked.

Though if there had been even a flicker of disappointment in his eyes, she would have bounded out of there, naked or no. But the only thing she saw was heat and want and need. And desire. Lots and lots of desire. He skimmed his gaze down her neck past her shoulder to her breasts, lingering there only a moment before he took in the rest of her, including the part between her legs that still throbbed from his ministrations.

Then he lifted his eyes to her face and cupped her head in his hand. "Majestic, I tell you."

He bent his head as if to kiss her, but she jerked away. "My turn," she said, and reached for the buttons of his drawers.

His eyes solemn, he caught her hand. "Tell me one thing—are you doing this only to drive out memories of your uncle?"

She considered the question, unsure what to say. That was part of it, yes, but not by any means all. Yet she was afraid to give him the real answer—that she was starting to fall in love with him.

So she settled on another perfectly honest reason for wanting him to take her to bed. "No. I'm doing this for me."

Apparently, he recognized the truth of that, because with a shuddering breath that resonated through her, he quickly unbuttoned and shucked off his drawers. "God help us both if that's a lie."

She got only a glimpse of the heavy ballocks between his legs and his rather large staff, thrust out with typical masculine impudence, before Grey was tumbling her down upon the bed.

In moments he had her panting for him again. With only a few caresses of her breasts and a stroke or two between her legs, he made her as eager for him as he obviously was for her. Which only proved how shameless she was, at least when it came to him.

And now at last he was . . . he was . . . *forging*

up inside her? That was the only word she could think of for how it felt to have that . . . massive "yard" of his pushing steadily forward.

She was rather disappointed. She'd expected something different, something more . . . well . . . glorious. And she couldn't even bring herself to look at him for reassurance, since their position was—"It's rather awkward, isn't it?"

He made a strangled sound she would have *sworn* was a laugh. Then he brushed her temple with his lips and whispered, "That only means . . . I'm doing it wrong."

"How is that possible? You must have had plenty of practice." All at once his remarks about how his reputation was undeserved flooded her mind, and she jerked her gaze up to him in shock. "You *have* done this before, right?"

She *knew* he was laughing when he bent his head to hers, his shoulders shaking. "A few times, yes. Just not with an untried maiden." Then his shoulders stilled, and his voice gentled. "And certainly never with a woman I wanted as much as I do you."

The tender words softened her, which oddly enough, made it feel like his flesh inside her wasn't quite so intrusive. "Do you mind if I . . . um . . . move a little?"

He groaned and muttered something that sounded distinctly like, "God save me," before adding, "Move as much as you please if it helps.

Actually . . ." He pulled one of her knees up and murmured, "Better?"

"I . . . I think so." She lifted up her other knee and shifted experimentally beneath him. With a moan, he slid farther inside her, sparking the most amazing sensation down there. Quite . . . enjoyable. "Ohh, *yes!* Much better."

He gazed down at her with a sly satisfaction. "More of that?" he rasped, rocking against her in a *very* provocative manner that had his member going in and out of her.

She was panting now and clutching his arms. "Much, *much* more."

Because the more he thrust inside her, the better it felt. The heat of it stunned her, made her arch up against him. And that delicious feeling along her nerves from their encounter earlier in the day had begun again, somewhat muted at first, but still there beneath the surface like an echo of pleasure in her bones.

"You feel like heaven to *me,*" he choked out. "An angel come to earth."

"An angel wouldn't . . . do this," she couldn't resist pointing out.

"Then, a fallen angel," he said roughly, nuzzling her hair. "Fallen right into my arms."

She undulated against him, and the delicious feeling became a crackling lightning in her blood, so wonderful . . . so *heavenly.*

Perhaps he was right—this *was* like heaven . . .

and she was falling . . . falling so far, so fast that she couldn't catch her breath . . . couldn't think, couldn't do anything but hold on to him and let the rushing wind take her down . . . down into—

"I'll catch . . . you," he whispered as he pounded her harder and deeper with each successive thrust. "Trust me, sweetheart. Just . . . let . . . go."

So she did. She gave herself up to the glory that was Grey inside her, and she let him tug her down with him into insanity. It was *marvelous*. And as she reached her release again, her body shook and quivered like an earthquake in the soul.

Only Grey could make her quake. Judging from the cry he gave as he drove deep into her and then strained against her, she was the only one who made *him* quake, too.

"My fallen angel," he breathed as he spilled himself inside her, then slumped atop her. "I've got you now."

He certainly had.

And when that dawned on her, to her horror, she began to cry.

Chapter Twenty

Concern gripped Grey. Had he hurt her?

He still shook from the power of his release—beyond anything he'd ever known—and it was all he could do to drag himself out of his pleasure to take care of her.

"Beatrice . . ." he murmured. "What's wrong?"

She seemed to fight to catch her breath. "I didn't expect it to be so . . . so . . ."

"Uncomfortable?" he prodded.

She shook her head no. "So wonderful!" she wailed.

It took him a moment to realize what she was saying. Then with relief, he rolled off her and stifled a chuckle. Propping his head up with his hand, he lay on his side to stare at her. "Sorry, sweetheart. I was afraid I'd bungled things."

He left the bed to dig his handkerchief out of his trouser pocket, then crawled back next to her and handed it over.

She took it gratefully, blotting her eyes and blowing her nose. "I *never* cry, you know," she said, her sniffling belying the claim. "Not over anything, not since Papa died. This is *so* embarrassing."

"Not for me." He frowned. "Though it's rather sobering to make a woman cry in bed. Perhaps I *should* be embarrassed. Or . . . something."

"You think this is funny," she accused him.

"No." He knew better than to admit that. He took the handkerchief from her and wiped away a tear she'd missed. "I'm merely humbled that the experience affected you so deeply. That's not the usual reaction."

She turned on her side to face him. "What *is* the usual reaction?"

Holy hell. He probably shouldn't have alluded to other women.

When he said nothing, trying to figure out how to answer, she added, "You've had more than 'a few' women in your bed, haven't you?"

He sighed. "Do you really want to know?"

Her lovely throat trembled. "I suppose not."

Turning onto her back, she stared up at the ceiling with an unreadable gaze.

Could she be comparing herself to those other women? Because that was absurd. Next to them, she was a goddess. Even now, he couldn't get enough of her body. Golden skin, golden-brown hair above and below, a pouty belly that made him want to lick and caress and fondle. Her body was perfect, no matter what she thought.

He'd never been one for big breasts; he preferred a big bottom, which she had. Not to mention her big wit and her big character and her big soul. Those were what he liked the most about her.

Certainly her attributes went beyond those

of the carefully coiffed society ladies he knew. He liked that she was utterly natural, with her freckles and tanned skin and hair that didn't conform to rules.

Her *character* that didn't conform to rules. Because *he* never conformed to rules unless they made sense. It was always his choice. That's what he loved about her. She refused to be bullied into following the rules.

Or letting her uncle make her his mistress.

Grey scowled. Damn that man. It drove him mad just to think of how her uncle Armie had tormented her. It drove him mad that she was withdrawing from him. Again. And all over some perception of how he'd lived his life.

Or perhaps because Grey hadn't yet made the offer of marriage that he knew he must. It was the only recourse when a gentleman ruined a woman. Despite his behavior this night, he *was* a gentleman.

But first he'd better rid her of the perception he'd given her by alluding to his other intimate experiences, like a fool. "You needn't worry about the women I've had in my bed."

"Oh? Why not?"

"Because they stopped being part of my life years ago. Once I figured out that sowing wild oats only gets you weeds, that sort of indiscriminate behavior lost its appeal."

She eyed him uncertainly. "*Years* ago?"

"More or less. To be honest, I'd rather pleasure myself than go into the stews and risk theft and disease. I've had a couple of dalliances with merry widows, and I briefly kept a mistress, but . . ." He met her inquisitive gaze, and his tone softened. "I found such experiences eminently less satisfying than our short acquaintance has proven to be."

He was glad he'd admitted the truth when her eyes lit up. "Really?"

"I told you—I've never lied to you."

She digested that a moment. "Perhaps. But until this evening you never revealed that you thought I'd taken part in both my uncles' murders, either."

God save him. His sins were coming home to roost. "That was a temporary madness born of Sheridan's discovery this afternoon that your uncles were planning to sell this place. Directly after he told me, I marched over here without stopping to think. But honestly, sweetheart, once my saner impulses asserted themselves, I knew it was absurd."

She ran her fingers over his chest. "So you didn't *really* think I could have murdered them both."

His impulse to convince her warred with his impulse to tease her. The latter won out. "Of course I did." When she gaped at him, he added blithely, "Your dogs will obey your every command, so you probably spent months teaching them how to drag your uncle Armie from his horse and break his neck. Then when my stepfather came along, you taught them to shove him off a bridge. It's clear as day to me now."

"Grey!" she cried, though she was obviously suppressing a laugh.

"You did brag to me about how well you trained them."

She swatted his shoulder with her hand. "I didn't train them to *kill,* for pity's sake."

"Ah. There goes *that* theory."

When he grinned at her, she rolled her eyes. "You really are incorrigible."

"You've got me confused with Thorn."

"I have not." Turning serious, she cuddled up next to him. "You may hide your tendencies better, but you and Thorn are more like each other than you will admit."

That gave him pause. "Do you think so?"

"I do." She stared into his eyes. "What made you separate yourself from your family for so long, anyway?"

He tensed. This was exactly what he'd been afraid of—letting someone he cared about into his inner sanctum. Letting that someone see his weaknesses. "They lived in Prussia. I lived here. That should be obvious."

She searched his face. "It's more than that."

Damn her for being so perceptive. Why was it that the rest of his family hadn't hit upon the truth? Why was it only her?

He couldn't let her see his deepest fears. "You're imagining things."

"I don't think so."

Leaning over to stare down at her, he murmured, "I don't want to talk about my family. Or yours, for that matter. If we have all night, I mean to spend it in more enjoyable pursuits. Like this." He slid his hand down to cup her below. "I ache for you again." God save him, but it was true. "Do you ache for me?"

She softened. "You know I do."

This was how to keep her from guessing his shameful secrets. All he need do was keep her in bed.

A noise brought Grey awake. He was momentarily disoriented. Where was he?

Then he felt the warm body next to him and realized where. With Beatrice. In *her* home. Which meant he'd fallen asleep. And so had she. Judging from the light coming in the window, it was early morning. Damn, damn, damn. Long past time for him to go.

He would have leapt from the bed except that in that exact moment a sound registered in his sleep-drugged brain: that of a gun being cocked.

"Get up! Now!"

Holy hell. Grey knew that voice. And this was not going to end well.

Beatrice roused beside him. "What's happening?"

"Your lover is about to die, my dear sister," Wolfe said in a voice of such deadly calm it sent alarm down Grey's spine. "You should probably bid him farewell."

"Joshua?" Beatrice sat up in bed and clutched the covers to her breasts. Thank God that sometime in the night, they'd climbed under the bedclothes. "Joshua, put that thing away!"

Grey stifled a curse. He'd intended to be gone before now, if only to preserve her reputation in front of her brother until he could make her a legitimate offer of marriage. But the murderous glare Wolfe was giving him meant Grey would probably pay for that oversight with his life.

Wolfe ignored Beatrice. "How *dare* you?" he growled at Grey. "She's my sister, for God's sake!"

Before Grey could even muster a defense for what was indefensible, Beatrice spoke. "I *chose* to be with him. Why do you care? You're not here most of the time anyway."

Grey groaned. The last thing she should do is provoke her brother with reminders of how he'd failed her.

And Wolfe clearly felt it, for he lowered the muzzle of his rifle to Grey's head.

"Stop that!" she said. "I wanted him here."

Wolfe's expression showed his uncertainty. "But Beatrice . . ."

"Go," she told Grey in a low voice. "I'll deal with him."

Grey wasn't about to allow that. Rising from the bed, he faced Wolfe down, unashamed of his nudity. "Beatrice and I are going to marry," he said, realizing the rightness of it the minute the words left his mouth.

That took Wolfe aback. But only for a moment. "You can't marry her."

"The hell he can't!" Beatrice cried.

"He's engaged to someone else, duckie," her brother said with a tenderness that gave Grey pause. Until the rest of his words registered.

Grey walked over to where his drawers were and drew them on. "I'm not engaged to anyone."

Wolfe tossed a newspaper onto the bed. "No? The *Times* says differently."

Picking up the paper, Grey skimmed what turned out to be an announcement of his betrothal. He swore under his breath. "This is a lie."

"Is it?" The major glanced at his sister. "It states that your lover is engaged to marry a woman named Vanessa Pryde."

Grey scowled at the major. "I'm not betrothed to Vanessa or anyone. She's my cousin. I have no intention of marrying her."

Beatrice snatched the paper from him. As she read it, her face fell. "That's not what this says." Lifting her heartbroken gaze to him, she wrapped the sheet around herself and left the bed.

Damn his aunt! Clearly the bloody woman had decided to take matters into her own hands, since Grey had resisted all attempts to yoke him to Vanessa.

"I swear on my father's grave that it's a lie," he told Beatrice as he pulled on his clothes. "Neither Vanessa nor I wish to marry each other. But my aunt is trying to force the issue because she thinks I would never stand Vanessa up and thus destroy my cousin's reputation. The only woman I wish to marry is *you*."

"Why?" she asked. "You haven't wished to marry me before."

"I took your innocence," he said matter-of-factly. "Which means I must marry you."

He knew he'd said the wrong thing when she flinched. "How flattering."

"Damn it, that's not what I meant."

She walked over to where her nightdress lay and managed somehow to don it while still protecting her modesty with the sheet. "Then what *did* you mean?"

"She doesn't want you," her brother said. "And she deserves better than you."

"Don't you think I know that?" Grey barked as he continued to dress.

That seemed to take Wolfe aback. Then he sneered at Grey. "Is that why you're betrothing yourself to some other woman?"

"I'm not!" He turned to Beatrice as he tied

his cravat. "I need to speak with you privately, sweetheart."

"The hell you will!" Wolfe growled.

Beatrice looked at her brother. "Let me talk to His Grace." When Wolfe stiffened, she said in a low voice, "Come on, Grey. We should hash this out before he shoots you."

Grey let her pull him into the hallway. But as soon as they were out of earshot of her brother, he seized her by her shoulders. "You *know* we must marry. I realize I've spent half the night acting like your uncle, but I'm unlike him in the one way that counts. I'm a gentleman."

Clearly remembering what she'd said about her uncle's *not* being a gentleman, she kept staring at him.

He went on. "The moment I came up here to bed you I knew I'd be offering marriage. I will not behave as some vile seducer who takes a respectable country girl to bed and then abandons her to her ruination. We must marry, and we *will* marry."

"You don't have to convince *me*."

"Oh." He released her to run a hand through his hair. "From the way you were behaving, I rather thought I might."

Beatrice rolled her eyes. "What I mean is, you don't have to convince *me;* you have to convince *her.*"

"Her who?"

"Your cousin Vanessa, you dolt!"

He let out an exasperated breath. "The Vanessa who'd rather have her tongue cut out than marry me? *That* Vanessa? Trust me, the only one who wants to see me and my cousin married is her mother."

"And no wonder. Her daughter is clearly a ninny in need of husbandly guidance if she can't see how lucky she would be to have you."

The compliment brought him up short. Gave him hope. "Vanessa is no ninny. But then, neither are you." Staring down into her uncertain gaze, he said, "And *that* is the real reason I wish to marry you."

"You mean, it's not because you ruined me?" she said, throwing his heedless words back in his face.

He winced. "I shouldn't have said that. The truth is, I would feel myself fortunate to have you for a wife." As long as she didn't expect too much from him. But that was a conversation they'd have to have later, once he ironed out this mess with his aunt. "And I pray you can believe that."

"I don't know what to believe, Grey," she whispered.

He stared down at the woman he'd only now begun to understand. "Then know this. Vanessa isn't the one I wish to marry. *You* are. I mean to come back here and do whatever I must to convince you of that. But for now I must go to London at once and unravel this Gordian knot my aunt has woven." He pulled her close. "I want to marry you, sweetheart, no matter what my aunt says and no matter what your brother says. You are the only woman for me."

She gazed up at him, her eyes shining. "I'll wait for you."

The simple words struck him in the chest, in the place he'd always thought of as hollow, missing a heart. She wanted him. She was willing to wait for him, to trust him to do right by her. No one had ever trusted him like that before.

"Good," he said, realizing that the word couldn't possibly convey how he felt. "*Good,*" he repeated.

She smiled at him. "Go. And do it quick. I'll handle Joshua."

Grey glanced back into the room, where Wolfe was still glowering at him through the open doorway. "I don't like to leave you alone with him, especially after we—"

"His bark is worse than his bite, believe me." When he eyed her skeptically, thinking of what they both suspected her brother had done, she added, "He won't hurt *me,* I promise. In his own gruff way, he loves me."

That was all he needed to hear. He brushed a kiss to her forehead. "I'll be back as soon as I can." Then he hurried off down the stairs.

Chapter Twenty-One

As Grey left the house, without his coat or waistcoat, which were still in the kitchen, Joshua growled, "Wait, where are you going, you damned bastard!" and stomped toward the hall, with his pistol in one hand and his cane in the other.

Though Beatrice was still reeling from all that Grey had told her, she blocked the doorway. "Let him go. You don't want to murder another duke."

Uh-oh. She hadn't meant to blurt out "another duke," but it was early morning and she wasn't thinking straight.

"Step aside, Beatrice. I mean to make sure that the scoundrel doesn't—" He paused to stare at her. "Wait, did you say, *another* duke?"

Blast. "I . . . um . . . well . . . You obviously misheard me."

"The hell I did! What duke am I supposed to have murdered?"

She winced. The cat had its paw out of the bag—she might as well pull it out the rest of the way. "Uncle Armie."

"What?!" As if realizing he still held a pistol in his hand, practically giving her a reason to accuse him, he carefully uncocked it and set it down on a nearby table. "Why would I murder

Uncle Armie? I didn't like the man, but I had no reason to kill him."

She sighed. His protests *sounded* genuine, but that didn't mean he was telling the truth. Perhaps it was time to shake him up enough to get him to admit it. "No reason? He said he would sell the dower house out from under us unless I agreed to be his mistress."

When the blood drained from her brother's face, she knew the truth. He had no idea what she was talking about.

"Oh, my God, *Beatrice*—" he began.

"Never mind," she said. Now she wished she hadn't let Grey believe Joshua might be guilty. "It doesn't matter."

Joshua continued to gape at her. "Clearly, it does." Apparently, her words were starting to sink in, for he sagged onto his cane. "So you're saying that Uncle Armie . . . that he . . . When did our arse of an uncle make such a vile threat?"

In that moment, she knew she could never reveal to Joshua all of what she'd revealed to Grey. Joshua would blame himself for not protecting her through the years, and he couldn't change the past anyway. He'd had enough pain in his life already without her adding to it.

Best to just keep it to Uncle Armie's blackmail, which was bad enough. "He made it right before he died," she said. "I thought you knew."

Joshua's eyes were wide with horror. "I had no idea! Why didn't you *tell* me?"

"Because I feared what you would do to him if you knew. And since I turned him down, it seemed pointless to mention it."

"Pointless?" Anger flushed his features. "It damned well wasn't pointless, because you're right, I *would* have killed him if I'd learned of it. And I assure you no one would ever have known I'd done it either, trust me."

She raised an eyebrow at him.

As he realized what he'd said, he cursed under his breath. "Ah. That's why you thought I'd killed him."

"That . . . and the fact that his death happened so soon after he threatened me."

Joshua scowled. "Now I wish I *had* murdered the arse. How dared he even think to—" He halted, his hand squeezing the knob of his cane. "Oh, God, duckie, please tell me that he didn't . . . That he never laid a hand on you in *that* way."

"No," she said firmly. It was the easiest lie she'd ever told. She didn't like lying, especially not to her brother. But it must be done.

He scrubbed his free hand over his face. "Thank God for that. I'd think you were lying except that you've always been so bad at it."

Not always.

She cast him a thin smile. "Anyway, it's in the past."

"Not entirely." He stared hard at her. "Did Greycourt make a similar offer—that he would convince Sheridan not to sell this place if you became his mistress? Is that why he was in your bed?"

"Are you mad? If I wouldn't give myself to Uncle Armie to save this house, why would I give myself to Grey?"

Her brother snorted. "Because he's handsome and knows how to flatter a woman. Better than Uncle Armie did, anyway."

"You're certainly right about that, but no, Grey didn't ask me to be his mistress. You heard him— he wants to make me his wife."

Joshua flashed her a pitying look. "Ah, duckie, wealthy dukes do not marry penniless—"

"He's not like that," she said stoutly, not wanting to hear him voice her own fears. "You don't know him the way I do."

"Don't remind me of the way *you* know him." His eyes narrowed. "I can still ride over to the hall and challenge him to a duel."

She planted her hands on her hips. "If you even try it, Joshua Wolfe, I will never speak to you again. Then I'll be forced to live in the streets, since you will be hanged and our aunt will want nothing to do with me after you kill her son."

Joshua walked over to a hall chair and sank heavily into it. "So you thought I had killed Uncle Armie." When she remained silent, not wanting to wound him further, he glanced up at her. "Did Greycourt think so, too?"

She debated how much to tell him. But he needed to know what he was facing. "He speculated that you might have. Except he thought it would be to thwart Uncle Armie in his plans to sell the dower house."

Joshua grimaced. "I hope you told him I would never kill anyone over property. Or did he merely use his suspicions to blackmail you into sharing your bed with him?"

She huffed out a frustrated breath. "You simply have to stop inventing ways Grey must have taken advantage of me. I told you—I wanted to be with him. If anything, I seduced *him*." When that made Joshua eye her askance, she added, "He is *not* the man you think he is."

A muscle worked in Joshua's jaw. "Meanwhile, you think your own brother is a murderer."

Going to kneel at his feet, she caught his hands in hers. "This is precisely why I never told you my suspicions. Because if they proved groundless I would have hurt you needlessly. But the truth is, I only suspected such a thing because I knew you would kill to protect me. Which merely demonstrates I know how much you care."

He stared at her. "Even when I don't show it? When I haven't yet found a way to make sure you're taken care of if something happens to me?" He dragged in a heavy breath. "When I may not even be able to keep a roof over your head, thus forcing you to sell yourself to a man like Greycourt?"

"I did not sell myself! I *love* him, Joshua."

When he blinked at that, she realized what she'd said. The words were true. She loved Grey, even with his reluctance to speak of his past and his suspicions. She loved his wit and his kindness and the fact that he didn't blame *her* for what had happened with Uncle Armie.

Until she'd met Grey, she had never felt free to say what she wanted when she wanted, even to Joshua. How wonderful that was!

How she wished Grey felt the same freedom with her. Clearly, he did not or he would answer her questions about his family. But for now, having him want her to wed him was enough.

"Does he love *you?*" Joshua asked.

"I don't know. You didn't give us much chance to sort that out, you know."

His expression hardened. "Yes. He was too busy trying to convince you he wasn't engaged to this Vanessa woman."

Jumping to her feet, she glared at him. "Fine. You're not going to believe what I say until you see the truth of it with your own eyes. So let's agree to disagree, shall we? He'll be back for me. You'll see." She bent toward him. "And when he is, you must promise you'll give your consent to the marriage."

"All right."

She straightened to eye him with rank suspicion. "You mean it?"

"Of course I mean it. Because he won't be returning. At least not without a new fiancée in tow."

"Ooh, you can be so infuriating!" Turning on her heel, she marched away to go back to bed.

"If you have any remaining doubt about the night Uncle Armie died, I can prove that I was in Leicester that night."

She pivoted to stare at him. "That doesn't prove a thing. You were probably in some inn where you had plenty of time to ride back here, pull Uncle Armie off his horse to break his neck, and ride back there before anyone realized you were gone."

"Actually, I was *not* in an inn. I was with a woman."

"A woman!" As she realized what sort of woman he must mean, her mouth dropped open. Poor infatuated Gwyn would be *so* disappointed!

"But it's not what you think," he said.

And with that, Joshua began to reveal why he traveled to Leicester so often.

Shortly before ten, Beatrice dragged herself from bed and got dressed to go over to Armitage Hall. Ten was the time she usually arrived for her come-out lessons. She was hardly in the mood today, after tossing and turning, thinking over everything Joshua and Grey had said and replaying her delicious moments with Grey. That made it very hard to sleep. It would make it even harder to be around people.

But if she didn't go to Armitage Hall, they would wonder why, and she didn't want anyone speculating about her and Grey having done . . . well . . . what they'd done.

Besides, she wanted to see how Aunt Lydia was taking the news of Grey's engagement. His family had to know *something*. Surely he wouldn't have left for London without telling anyone.

When she entered the hall, however, it was to find the place in turmoil. Because apparently that was precisely what Grey had done—he'd taken his coach off to London before anyone had arisen. She had no idea what to make of that. Footmen were scurrying off on errands, grooms were being questioned, and a maid was being tasked with bringing more tea to the ladies in the breakfast room.

She even overheard Sheridan in one corner dressing down the butler. "What do you mean, you didn't see him enter until early this morning? Where the devil was he?"

Hoping not to be noticed by Sheridan, she moved like a wraith through the bustling servants, then headed down the hall to the breakfast room.

The moment she entered, she was accosted by her aunt.

"Oh, Bea, it's too awful. I can't believe Grey didn't tell us a thing! And I was so hoping that you and he . . . that the two of you . . ." When Beatrice stared blankly at her, Aunt Lydia muttered an unladylike curse under her breath. "You don't know! Lord, I'm so sorry. I just assumed you saw the *Times*. But of course you haven't. Why would you have? I doubt that you and Joshua—"

"Grey is engaged to Vanessa," Gwyn said bluntly. "The sneaky bastard."

For once, her mother didn't correct her language.

"I know about Vanessa," Beatrice said. "Joshua saw a copy of the *Times* in town and brought it to me."

Gwyn's eyes flashed a sudden heat. "Oh, I'm just sure he did. He was probably delighted to malign my brother's character." She sighed. "Although right now, I would happily join him. How *dare* Grey lead us to think he cared about you, Bea, when all the time he was plotting to marry that little chit Vanessa?"

Beatrice was trying to figure out how to answer when Sheridan walked in. "Sheathe your claws, Gwyn," he muttered. "I'm sure matters aren't as they appear."

"Oh, you are, are you?" Gwyn crossed her

arms over her chest. "You four *men* always stick together. Well, he's gone too far this time, leading on a feeling young woman like our Bea here."

"He did not lead me on," Beatrice said, though Gwyn's concern touched her. "We're merely friends."

When the others snorted in unison, she bit her tongue. Really, could she not lie convincingly *at all?*

"Grey swore to me he had no interest in Vanessa," Sheridan said. "And I don't think he was lying."

"Besides," Aunt Lydia put in, "if he *had* proposed to her, I'm sure he would tell his mother." Her expression turned anxious. "Wouldn't he?"

This was killing her. She wanted to divulge everything, and she couldn't. She should have stayed away. "Perhaps I should go home. It doesn't seem as if we'll be having our usual lessons."

They ignored her. Sheridan poured himself some tea, then fixed her with a dark look. "Did you happen to see Grey last night? When he left here, he said he had something to take care of. Then he stayed out for hours. I got the distinct impression he might be going to talk to you."

All eyes turned to her. Blast. She considered lying, but that hadn't been working well for her lately. "Um. Yes. I did see him. He came looking for Joshua, and I told him my brother was in Leicester. So I imagine he went off there." That was true. Mostly.

Sheridan's expression cleared. "That makes sense. It would explain why he was out all night."

"He was out *all night?*" his mother said. "Whatever for? Why couldn't he just speak to Joshua when the man returned?"

It was Sheridan's turn to look uncomfortable. He stirred some sugar into his tea. "I would imagine that he . . . Perhaps Grey had some notion . . ." He set down the cup of tea. "Honestly, I have no idea. I'll see if anyone else has a guess."

And he was out of the room before they could stop him.

"That was odd." Gwyn gazed after her brother. "I think he knows more than he's letting on. I'm going to find out what it is." She too marched out the door.

When Beatrice stood there awkwardly, wondering if she could now make her escape, Aunt Lydia gestured to the table. "Come have some breakfast, my dear. Don't leave yet. Keep me company, if you don't mind."

Stifling a sigh, Beatrice said, "Of course, Aunt. I'd be happy to."

As her aunt slid into a chair, Beatrice went to fill a plate at the sideboard. She could practically feel her aunt's gaze boring into her. *Oh, dear.*

"Tell me, Bea, and I want you to be honest," her aunt said. "Grey hasn't done anything to . . . hurt you, has he?"

Not yet, he hasn't.

Beatrice paused with her plate in hand. Then she pasted on a big smile and faced her aunt. "Don't be silly. Everyone has been more than kind to me, including your son."

Her aunt seemed to take that at face value. "Well, he hasn't been very kind to his *mother,* drat him. And quite frankly, I can't believe he would marry Vanessa, of all people. I mean, I gather that she's been more like a sister to him than a cousin, and one doesn't marry one's sister."

Sister? The word lightened Beatrice's mood.

"I worry that he'll break her heart," Aunt Lydia went on. "He's so . . . closed to love, so afraid to trust anyone."

Even Beatrice had noticed *that.* "It could . . . explain the engagement," she said. "A cousin he sees as a sister would be a safe and sensible choice. He wouldn't have to give his heart." Even as she said the words, she realized they made sense. "During his days of living with the Prydes, he probably grew close to the family."

"I doubt that." His mother gazed out the window at the lawn. "I'm fairly certain his life with them was not a happy one."

Beatrice had guessed as much, but to hear it stated so baldly by Grey's own mother sent an arrow through her heart. "How do you know?" She came over to sit next to her aunt with her plate, but food didn't interest her just now. "Did he tell you?"

"He didn't have to. Ever since our return, he has acted strangely toward me. He's kind one moment, then avoids me the next. And from things Thorn has told me, I fear Eustace . . . treated him ill."

"What sort of things?"

"Grey left the Pryde house at twenty-one and never returned. He couldn't avoid seeing his aunt and uncle in society, of course, but Thorn says he barely talked to them."

"I thought he helped with Vanessa's debut."

"He did. He threw a ball at his town house to introduce her in society, knowing that having a duke behind her would help her move in loftier circles. Thorn attended it. He said Grey hardly spoke to her parents, and as soon as it was over, Grey said he was well shut of them. Of course, now that his uncle is dead, Grey only has to deal with the aunt."

Beatrice stared down at her plate. "Thorn didn't happen to know *how* he was mistreated, did he?"

"Thorn never exactly said Grey was mistreated—just that he suspected it. And Grey has never said anything to me. I think he wants to spare me the details."

"That's probably wise, don't you think?"

Beatrice reached over to take Aunt Lydia's hand. "You wouldn't want to know."

"I suppose. But I worry that . . ." After squeezing Beatrice's hand, her aunt released it. "I truly hated to give him up, but that stupid will said I had to. We even considered breaking it, but Eustace seemed so understanding when he came to fetch Grey, and Maurice said it would do Grey good to learn proper ducal behavior. Besides, Grey seemed eager to go. I thought it was best for him."

With pain etched on her face, Aunt Lydia sipped some tea. "It nearly killed me to let him leave. I wasn't sure when we'd see him again. I never dreamed it would be so many years, between wars and my husband's career and the children. Thorn told me once Grey came into his majority, he refused to leave his properties, for fear his uncle might try to step in and run them. Thorn said Grey didn't feel easy until Eustace died a few years ago."

Beatrice sighed. Aunt Lydia had left her with more questions than answers. "So Grey never told you about it himself."

Her aunt slumped. "He never tells me anything important."

He never told Beatrice anything important either. He skirted the issue, hinted at memories. It frustrated her.

Could she live happily with a man who

wouldn't show her his inmost feelings? A man who could never say he loved her, who kept his past private?

Sadly, she didn't know. What if she couldn't? What would happen to her?

Perhaps she should find out. "Aunt Lydia, I've heard rumors that the family might sell the dower house. Is that true?"

Her aunt's brow was furrowed. "Sheridan has considered it, yes. The dower house isn't entailed, so selling it would give us a much needed surplus of funds." Aunt Lydia took Beatrice's hand. "But if that happens, you and Joshua will always have a place in this house."

Beatrice's relief at hearing that was overset by her worry that Joshua would never accept such charity. So if Grey's offer of marriage wasn't genuine . . .

Life for her and Joshua was about to become far more complicated.

Chapter Twenty-Two

Since Grey had told his coachman to drive like the wind and the man had taken him at his word, they reached town before the *Times* offices closed for the evening. Thank God. As they'd careened down the rutted roads to London, Grey had come up with a plan for saving Vanessa's reputation that he thought might work, as long as the *Times* would agree to it.

Fortunately, the moment Grey arrived, the clerk ushered him right in to see the general editor. There were *some* advantages to being a duke, after all, even if Beatrice and her brother were too foolish to realize it. Grey made a few threats, followed by an offer of a great deal of money, to gain the general editor's cooperation.

Then he headed to his aunt's London town house to beard the lioness in her den. As the coachman drew up in front of his aunt's house, Grey's stomach began to churn. He hadn't been here since he'd reached his majority and fled the place, but it still held painful memories.

But he was doing this for Beatrice and Vanessa. That thought alone propelled him out of the carriage and up the steps. At least he wouldn't have to return again until Aunt Cora was in the grave with her damned husband.

When he entered, the butler tried to convince him she was not "in" to callers.

"I'm her nephew, the Duke of Greycourt," Grey said in his most dictatorial voice. "And when your mistress dies, this place will be mine. So unless you wish to incur my wrath—"

The man hurried off to do Grey's bidding.

Before Aunt Cora appeared, Vanessa slipped out from the music room to take him aside. "You have to *do* something. Forgive me, but you and I simply cannot marry!"

"I agree." He chucked her under the chin. "But I've taken care of it. Don't worry—it will all work out."

"How? Mama has already had it put into the paper without my knowledge, and that means—"

A voice he'd hoped never to hear again broke in. "I see that you've come to visit your fiancée." His aunt descended the vaulted staircase wearing an elegant dinner gown and a cat-in-the-cream smile.

"Mama!" Vanessa cried. "How could you *do* this to us? If Grey doesn't marry me, we'll all be humiliated, and I'll never be able to gain a husband!"

"Forgive me, pet, but that's the point," Grey said to Vanessa with the utmost nonchalance. Because like a snake, Aunt Cora always struck when she sensed any hesitation or fear in her opponent. "Your mother decided we weren't getting to the business of marriage fast enough, so she made it so we *had* to marry."

His aunt sidled up to him. "I don't know what you're talking about. I'm sure the *Times* merely mentioned the prevailing gossip."

"As it came right out of your mouth, you mean." He stared down at the woman who'd never shown him an ounce of familial affection. Who'd ignored him while her husband bullied him, and who, after her husband died, had taken it upon herself to get what she could for her daughter out of Grey's connection to her, whether her daughter wanted it or not.

For the first time, Grey noticed a hint of fear in her eyes. She wasn't as sure of herself as she seemed. She had played her card, but she wasn't certain it would win the hand. And the fact that she'd risked her daughter's reputation in the process infuriated him. It damned well wasn't fair to Vanessa.

"Vanessa," Aunt Cora said, as if she'd read his mind, "why don't you go upstairs while my nephew and I work this out?"

"Stay, Vanessa," he ordered, making his aunt scowl. "This involves you, so you should hear the whole of it."

Vanessa glanced anxiously from him to her mother as Aunt Cora circled him, looking for a place to strike. "What is there to hear? My daughter is right—unless you want to destroy her reputation, you have to marry her. The announcement is in the *Times*. There's naught you can do about that now."

"You think not?" He chuckled, feeling a moment's triumph when that gave his aunt pause. She'd gambled on what she saw as his weakness—his tendency to protect Vanessa.

Fortunately, she'd forgotten that once he'd left this house to assume the title, she had lost all power to bully him, even through her daughter. "It's a pity you didn't bother to consult me before running over to the *Times*. Because then you would have learned I am already engaged to Miss Beatrice Wolfe."

"Sheridan's cousin?" Vanessa exclaimed.

With a nod, he leaned down to meet his aunt eye to eye. "So I informed the *Times* they should have spoken to me first, and if they didn't want a lawsuit on their hands, they would print an errata revealing they had mistaken the name of my cousin for the name of my real fiancée. They were kind enough to agree. And that is the news appearing in the newspaper *tomorrow* morning."

He knew his arrow had hit the mark when her face turned gray. "You will regret this. I will deny it to all my friends. I will say you led my Vanessa on and now you wish to marry your mistress. I will blacken—"

"You will do no such thing, Mama!" Vanessa cried. "I told you, neither of us wishes to marry the other. And if you speak such untruths about me or Grey, I will be standing right beside you claiming them to be lies."

Her mother scowled at her. "Hush now, you foolish chit. He's a duke!"

"Leave her be," Grey snapped. "If I ever hear of you spreading tales again—like, for example, the one you started concerning my 'secret cabal of dissolute bachelors'—"

What could he threaten that wouldn't come back to hurt Vanessa or someone else he loved? His aunt had no scruples.

Perhaps it was time to appeal to Aunt Cora's greed. He could afford it, after all. Though he hated to reward her for her machinations, this madness had to stop.

"What if I double Vanessa's dowry?" he said. "Then she can acquire whatever husband she wishes."

Even Vanessa's poet, although Grey still thought that a most unwise choice.

"Double?" Aunt Cora squeaked. He could practically see her calculating the amount in her head.

"Double," he confirmed.

"But Grey, you shouldn't have to—" Vanessa began.

"Quiet, girl," her mother ordered. "If he wants to throw his money around, let him. Lord knows we deserve it after his ingratitude through the years, despite all we did for him when he was a boy."

"Did for me?" The past came flooding back in all its ugliness, and a red haze filled his vision. *"Did for me?* We both know what you and my uncle did—and didn't—do for me. You never took my side, never offered me affection or solace." His hands curled into fists. "You never once put the needs of a small boy ahead of your greed."

Clearly startled by his vehemence, his aunt took a step back. "I'm only saying—"

"I suggest you stop talking, Mama," Vanessa said. "Before Grey forgets that we're his relations."

Vanessa's low voice reached him in the midst of his fury, drawing him back to the present. Grey struggled to breathe, to calm himself . . . to keep from throttling the woman who'd done nothing—*nothing*—to protect the ten-year-old him from his uncle.

"Mama, go upstairs," Vanessa ordered as she watched him fight to contain his temper. "I will finish this . . . negotiation."

When her mother hesitated, Grey choked out, "Best to listen to your daughter, Aunt Cora."

Alarm creasing her aging face, she whirled to hurry up the stairs. But she paused halfway up to look down at him. "You said double her dowry! Don't forget!"

She hurried the rest of the way up the stairs and disappeared from view.

Vanessa laid a hand on his arm. "I'm aware Mama and Papa were always pretty . . . dreadful to you. Still, perhaps it's time you put the past behind you."

"Perhaps," he said noncommittally. How was he to put behind him a youth full of mistreatment and heartbreak? Even now he could barely think of it without rage boiling up within him, a feeling exacerbated by being back in this damned house again.

"Surely your new wife will help with that." Vanessa searched his face. "You *were* telling Mama the truth, weren't you? That you're marrying Miss Wolfe?"

An image of Beatrice rose in his mind to calm his temper further, and he couldn't stop the smile that spread over his face. "Yes. As soon as it can be arranged."

"You look as if you're terribly in love with her."

"Terribly," he lied, not wanting the inquisition that would follow if he said otherwise. Or was it a lie? He wasn't as sure anymore. "She's different from any woman I've ever met. She has a mind of her own, and she's not afraid to speak it."

"Even with you?"

"Especially with me," he said dryly. "She's rather like you in that respect."

"Oh, dear. Then I wish her all the luck in the world. She'll need it." When he frowned at her, she laughed and said, "Seriously, though, will I like her?"

He raised one eyebrow. "I'm fairly certain you two will become as thick as thieves. I shudder to think what trouble you'll get into together."

Beaming at him, she relaxed. "Oh, wonderful! I could use another bosom friend." She leaned close to whisper confidentially, "Especially with Mother in the temper she'll be in over my having lost you."

"Remind her you never had me, and you'll be fine."

Vanessa tipped up her chin. "I'll remind her of that doubled dowry, and *then* she'll be fine."

He pressed a kiss to the top of her head. "Now don't go spending that dowry too quickly. And *don't* give it to some damned poet."

"Is that a condition of your doubling it?" she asked with narrowed eyes.

He sighed. "Would it make a difference if I said it was?"

"No."

"That's what I thought." He glanced up the stairs. "Do you think your mother has personally told anyone in society of our supposed engagement? Because if she has, my plan won't work. So I need to know who else's silence I must buy while in town."

"I don't believe she has told a soul. I refused to go anywhere with her until you arrived to salvage things. And since you were fairly quick—"

"It's not as if she gave me a choice. You can only imagine how my prospective wife regarded the news that I was engaged to another."

"Oh no! Poor Miss Wolfe." She winked at him. "But I'm sure a dissolute fellow like you will know how to turn her up sweet."

He bloody well hoped so. "Speaking of that, I must return to Sanforth at once to soothe her fears." And get this whole matter of who'd killed whom—if anyone even had killed anyone— wrapped up once and for all, so he could start his marriage to Beatrice with a clean slate for them both.

"Of course!" She hugged him. "And *thank* you. I can never repay you for not . . . well . . ."

"Letting you be forced into marrying me?" When she winced, he chuckled. "I don't know whether to be flattered or insulted. But if you ever need me again, try something less dramatic than a betrothal announcement in the papers."

"I will." She flashed him a minxish grin. "But I'm not making any promises."

On that note, he chose to leave. Vanessa was going to lead some fellow a merry dance once she married. Thank God it wouldn't be him.

Still, as his coachman drove off into the night,

he couldn't get her words out of his head: *But perhaps it's time you put the past behind you.*

For the first time, he realized he wanted to. He wanted to stop the anger and resentment, wanted to stop hurting every time he thought of those early days. He had a feeling if he didn't, he would lose Beatrice, perhaps not now but eventually.

After all, a man with a hollow chest where his heart should be wasn't likely to keep a woman like her happy for very long.

When Grey returned to Armitage Hall in the morning on the day after he left, he was surprised to find Sheridan waiting for him.

"It's about damned time you got here," Sheridan snapped. "What's this nonsense about your being engaged to Vanessa? You told me—"

"It was a mistake in the paper. I had it corrected."

That brought Sheridan up short. "What do you mean, 'a mistake'?"

"Read today's *Times* when it arrives, and you'll understand." Grey surveyed the entrance hall. "Is Beatrice here?"

"No. She sent a message saying she was staying home today."

Grey headed for the door. All he wanted to do was find Beatrice and reassure her they could marry. He didn't want her to see the paper until he could properly propose.

"Grey, wait!" Sheridan cried. "I have new information about Father's death."

That arrested him. "What kind of information?"

"While you were in London, I located the bridge rails washed up from the river. I also discovered that the man who built the bridge lived right in Sanforth. So I had him examine the bridge and rails." Sheridan ran a hand through his hair. "He said the structure had definitely been damaged deliberately beforehand so as to make it dangerous if someone fell against the rails."

Ignoring the frisson of unease sweeping over him, Grey eyed his brother skeptically. "What else would he say? He fears if the bridge is faulty, he'll be liable for Maurice's death."

"I don't think that's it. He showed me what he was talking about. It was convincing enough that I mean to take the information to our local constable. Then he can question Joshua himself."

But Wolfe had an alibi, though Grey could hardly say that without revealing how he knew. Even so, Sheridan was unlikely to put much stock in Beatrice's word. He seemed determined to pursue his suspicions to the bitter end.

Sheridan went on. "You'll remember that Joshua was the one who summoned Father to the dower house."

Grey had forgotten that. And Beatrice had not said anything about a summons.

"He also had good reason to murder Father,

given what I learned about Father's plans to sell the dower house. Which could also explain why Joshua might have killed Uncle Armie, although I can't prove that. Yet."

Grey's heart sank as he thought of the much more plausible reason for Joshua to want the scoundrel dead.

"Before you go to the constable, I want to question Wolfe," Grey said. "I want to hear what he has to say about his whereabouts that night."

Sheridan stared at him. "Fine. But don't take too long. I can't risk the possibility Joshua will flee once you speak to him."

"For God's sake, I need not let him know of your accusations in order to question him." Although since Beatrice knew everything, that might be a bit difficult.

"But if he's guilty," Sheridan said, "any questions on the matter will spook him. I know you have a soft spot for Beatrice, but I cannot let Joshua's actions stand."

"I realize that. Just let me talk to him before you run off for the constable. I'm heading over there now, anyway." He stared Sheridan down. "I suppose I should let you know. I don't merely have a soft spot for Beatrice: I mean to marry her."

Sheridan gaped at him. "You realize she has no dowry and no prospects beyond what small portion I might provide for her one day as her relation. She'll bring little to the marriage beyond herself.

Given how hard you work to increase your wealth, I would have thought you, of all people—"

"Beatrice 'herself' is plenty enough for me," he snapped, annoyed that his brother saw him as so mercenary. "I work to increase my wealth so my children and grandchildren won't be saddled with crippling debt the way you now are, but I don't need a rich wife for that. I'm only telling you of our impending marriage so you'll know that if this irrational obsession of yours with blaming her brother harms her in any way—"

"I would never intentionally harm Bea."

"Good. Because if you do, I will stand with her. Even if it means standing against you."

Sheridan rubbed a hand over his jaw. "I see. Then I suppose I'd best get to the bottom of this quickly."

"Be sure that you do. Because I *will* make Beatrice my wife. And I'm hoping not to make an enemy of my brother in the process."

"That will never happen, Grey," his brother said softly.

But as Sheridan swept past him on his way out, Grey wasn't so sure. Then again, Grey had been bereft of his brothers and sister for many years. He could live without them again if he must. Because if it came to choosing Beatrice or his family, he would choose Beatrice, no matter what her brother had or hadn't done.

That much he knew.

Chapter Twenty-Three

Beatrice was at home, trying not to worry about Grey, when Joshua glanced out the window and cursed under his breath. He then grabbed his pistol, loaded it, and limped through the door.

She followed him out. "Grey!" she cried, seeing him coming up the walkway. "You're here!"

The smile he flashed her was positively beatific. "I told you I'd come back for you." Then he saw Joshua's pistol, and his smile vanished.

Joshua cocked the pistol. "I was too blind to see what Uncle Armie was trying to force my sister into. But I *know* what you're about, and I damned well won't stand for it."

"Joshua, put that pistol down before it goes off!" she cried. "He has come back to marry me!"

"I have indeed," Grey said, his eyes never leaving the pistol.

"Damn it, Beatrice," Joshua grumbled. "He's betrothed to another woman."

"Not anymore." Grey lifted his gaze to meet her brother's. "And I don't blame you for killing your uncle Armie. If the man were here right now, I'd kill him myself."

When that seemed to take Joshua aback, Beatrice slipped around him to stand between her brother and Grey. "He didn't kill Uncle Armie. He was away in Leicester."

"Or so he says."

She crossed her arms over her chest. "He can prove it, actually." Glancing back at her brother, she said, "Tell him. Tell him where you were and why."

"I don't have to tell him a bloody thing!" Joshua growled. "It's none of his concern."

Grey glared at him over her head. "It is if you expect me to help you escape the hangman's noose. Because Sheridan is hell-bent on bringing you to justice. And I damned well do not wish to have to tell him about your uncle's behavior toward Beatrice unless I must. Your waving that gun at me every chance you get isn't exactly convincing me of your innocence, either."

Her heart hammering, Beatrice pivoted to face her brother. "Put the blasted pistol down, and tell him the truth!"

Thankfully, Joshua uncocked the pistol and lowered it. "I don't understand why Sheridan is all riled up. Uncle Armie's death was an accident."

"It may very well have been," Grey said, "but he thinks you have motive for it. That you killed the man to keep him from selling this place."

"Joshua?" Beatrice prompted him.

Her brother sighed. "I was in Leicester at a

healer's when Uncle Armie died. I go to her every time I have business in that town."

"Her?" Grey asked, an eyebrow raised.

Joshua scowled at him. "She's seventy years old if she's a day, so just get that nasty thought right out of your head. She would no more share a bed with me than . . . well . . . any woman would." A flush rose in his cheeks. "Why do you think I've been going to her? I want to be able to find a better, more secure position, so some woman will marry me without having to endure this"—he tapped his calf with his cane—"useless lump of flesh."

Beatrice saw the flash of pity in Grey's eyes and prayed that Joshua didn't see it.

Fortunately, Grey masked it swiftly. "And are her efforts helping?"

Joshua stiffened. "Not that I can see, despite all the blunt I've given her. I should have known. Nothing helps."

Ready to cry at the hopelessness in her brother's voice, Beatrice said, "The point is, he was with the healer all evening. The price for a night of her ministrations included lodging, since her method of healing was to wrap his leg in an herbal poultice overnight, then remove it in the morning. He's certain she will testify to his being there, too. She has no reason not to."

"Why the hell didn't he just tell you this?" Grey asked.

Beatrice sighed. "Because he's Joshua, the proudest fellow this side of the Channel. God forbid anyone learn of his willingness to do almost anything to gain a wife . . . or that he'd turned to some questionable healer for his cure, even though the surgeons said they'd done all they could."

"Damn it, Beatrice, why don't you just tell *all* my secrets to His bloody Grace?" Joshua muttered.

"It's better than seeing you hang," Beatrice said.

"And understandable to a man as proud as you," Grey said. "What about Maurice?"

"What about him?" Joshua stepped up to her to murmur, "What's he talking about?"

She wanted to throttle Grey for that. "Sheridan thinks you might have killed his father," she told her brother.

"You knew he suspected me of that, too?" Joshua shook his head. "Is that why you took Greycourt into your bed? Because you thought I was a double murderer?"

She rounded on him. "I have told you over and over that I seduced him. But you won't believe me!"

"Because I know how men like him are." He shoved the pistol into his coat pocket. "And you aren't the type to do something so foolish on your own."

"Stop painting me out to be a dissolute rogue!" Grey snapped. "Yes, she and I got carried away and went too far, but I mean to do right by her, whether you murdered my stepfather or not. She'll be safe, I promise you."

Joshua swore under his breath. "For God's sake, what the devil do you chaps think I am—some sort of master criminal? I haven't murdered anyone, and certainly not Uncle Maurice. Why would I? He was good to us."

"But he was planning on selling the dower house," Grey pointed out. "You could have decided to get rid of him once you learned that."

Beatrice rolled her eyes. "This is absurd. I already told you Joshua and I were together all night."

Grey looked uncomfortable. "What else are you going to say, sweetheart? He's your brother."

Her mouth dropped open. "Are you doubting my word?"

"I'm merely saying I wouldn't blame you if you wished to protect him. It's admirable, but you're forgetting there are things he hasn't accounted for. Like the matter of his having summoned Maurice here that evening."

"I didn't summon anyone," Joshua protested. "Beatrice and I were here doing the books all night. I had no reason to call him here."

"That's not what my mother says," Grey retorted.

"No surprise there." Joshua leaned heavily on his cane. "Has it occurred to you *she* might have killed him? The woman has been widowed three times and managed to gain something out of it every time. Don't you find that a tad suspicious?"

Grey's eyes turned the color of arctic ice. "Now see here, you bloody arse, my mother would never—"

"That's enough, both of you." Beatrice stepped between them. It was time to put an end to this. As long as her brother kept provoking Grey, she couldn't make Grey see reason. "Joshua, go inside. I need to speak to His Grace alone."

"The devil you will!"

"You can watch from the window. It's not as if he's going to ravish me on the lawn in broad daylight."

Joshua narrowed his gaze at Grey, who was still seething. "Make it quick," he said, and went back in the house.

She pulled Grey far enough away to be sure her brother didn't hear them through the open door. "Why are you doing this? You know he's innocent. He might kill someone in defense of me—like Uncle Armie—but he'd never murder your stepfather for property. And even if you're right and he was concerned about losing the dower house, your mother said Sheridan is considering selling it, so Joshua would have to kill him, too, without being caught. Then

Heywood would inherit, and he'd want to sell it . . . The whole thing's ludicrous."

"Beatrice—" he began in that soothing voice that could be so condescending.

"I might be biased toward my brother, but I'd never cover up a murder for him if I thought he'd done it for money. I was the one to tell you I feared Joshua might be guilty of killing Uncle Armie. Why would I do that, then turn around and lie about his alibi for the second death? It makes no sense."

"Perhaps you were afraid I wouldn't wed you if I knew he'd murdered my stepfather." When she bristled at that, he went on hastily, "But I stole your innocence, so I *will* marry you, as I promised."

That inflamed her. "So marriage to me would be like taking your medicine. How flattering."

He winced. "That's not what I meant."

"You must have a really low opinion of my character if you think I'd lie about my brother's alibi just to make sure you wed me." She planted her hands on her hips. "But I suppose I shouldn't be surprised. Your aunt tried to trap you into marriage, and your mother gave you away to your uncle who seems to have treated you badly. You're cynical about families in general. You think they all want something from you. And perhaps some do. But some are just muddling through. Like your mother. She did her best, yet you blame her."

"What do you know about it?" he growled.

"I talked to her at length yesterday. She wishes she could have handled matters differently, but she was trapped by your father's will. Your resentment of her wounds her deeply."

His face closed up. "I don't want to talk about my mother."

"You don't want to talk about anything— your feelings about being sent away . . . what happened between you and your uncle. How can you even think to marry me when you keep everything important to you hidden from me?"

Aware of Joshua watching through the window, she lowered her voice. "For that matter, how can you marry me when you believe I'd lie about my brother to secure you? How would you feel if I accused you of covering up some crime of Sheridan's? You certainly didn't like it when my brother accused your mother of murder. But then, only dukes are honorable and just, right? The rest of us are merely trying to get what we can."

"I was only saying—"

"That you don't trust my judgment or my character." Her breath caught in her throat. "Well, I can't wed a man who won't trust me. Who clearly doesn't know me at all."

"Now see here, are you *refusing* my offer of marriage?" he asked, clearly unable to take that in.

"I know you think that's unfathomable, but yes,

I am." She held her head high. "Good day, Your Grace."

Then turning on her heel, she stalked back into the house, her heart breaking a little more with each step.

"Bloody arse," she mumbled under her breath as she entered. "Insolent devil thinks he's God's gift to women. I'll show him and his brother they can't mess with us. I will damned well—"

"That's quite a mouth for a duke's grand-daughter," Joshua drawled. "He certainly got on *your* bad side."

She glowered at him. "Shut up. Because of you, I turned down an offer of marriage from the man I love. So I am *not* in the mood for your nonsense."

And leaving him gaping after her, she hurried up the stairs. She wasn't going to shed a single tear for that arse. She was *not*.

But as she reached the top, she felt the tears burning her throat and knew that once again Grey was going to make her cry.

Damn his soul to hell.

Grey stood staring after her, feeling as if he'd been bludgeoned. What the devil? She'd *refused* him? It was the first time in his life he'd ever proposed to a woman, and she'd turned him down.

He'd ruined her, for God's sake! She couldn't refuse him. It was madness.

Wolfe appeared in the doorway only long enough to slam the door shut. And that was that.

The hell it was. Grey scowled. Her every word had pierced him, especially the ones about his not trusting her. The woman certainly knew how to give a man what for. Even when he didn't deserve it. He'd done the honorable thing, behaved like a gentleman.

So marriage to me would be like taking your medicine. How flattering.

All right, so perhaps not quite like a gentleman. Still, he was a duke! She'd be daft to turn him down.

Then again, Beatrice *was* a little daft. She preferred long walks in the woods to dancing a minuet. Like him, come to think of it. She disliked pretension and lies. Like him. She was perfect for him in every way. And all she asked was that he let her look inside his very soul.

He should let her. It meant nothing, right?

It meant everything. It meant sharing his secrets with her, taking hers on faith, trusting her to hold his heart in her hands and not crush it, the way everyone else had. Because apparently he did have a heart if he were to judge from the searing pain in his chest.

He glanced at the dower house but saw no sign of Beatrice. She certainly wasn't running out here to beg him to ignore her refusal and marry her.

He sighed. She might not ever ask that of him. He might have lost her for good.

The searing pain in his chest spread outward until it felt as if his entire body was on fire. No wonder he had sought to protect himself from any emotion that might provoke heartbreak. Because heartbreak was wretched.

But there was no point in staying here and mooning after her like some forlorn swain, so he headed back to the hall. He must do something to fix this. The only thing he could think of was to save her brother for her. That would require convincing Sheridan to at least postpone arresting Joshua until the authorities could look into the summons thing and talk to Wolfe's healer in Leicester.

When he entered Armitage Hall sometime later, however, it wasn't Sheridan he found in the foyer but his mother.

"Grey! You're back! After I saw the *Times*, I felt certain you wouldn't return from London for a while. I need to talk to you."

Damn. He wasn't ready for this. "Where's Sheridan?"

"He's somewhere around here, I'm sure." She took Grey by the arm. "And this cannot wait."

He hesitated, but since the Wolfes had essentially run him off, he hadn't been gone long. Perhaps if Sheridan didn't see him, he would assume Grey hadn't returned yet. Besides,

Mother might be able to shed some light on the summons Maurice had received the night he died. So Grey followed her into the drawing room.

"Do you want some tea?" she asked.

"I don't have time for tea."

She sniffed. "You never have time for tea. Or your mother." The injured look on her face said volumes.

"I'm making time for you now." He waited until she sat down on the settee, then took a seat beside her. "What's this about?"

"Your betrothal to Vanessa."

Damn. Mother hadn't seen the errata in the paper yet. Not that it fit the circumstances now that Beatrice had turned him down.

He stiffened. Not for long. He would convince her to marry him if he had to beg. He would do whatever it took, even make peace with his mother. Because he had to have Beatrice in his life.

With that decision made, he felt a strange calm steal over him. Vanessa's words swept through his mind: *Perhaps it's time you put the past behind you.*

Perhaps it was.

"I'm not betrothed to Vanessa," he said. "The *Times* made a mistake."

Her expression brightened. "Oh, that explains so much. I did think it odd you would marry her when you've never expressed any interest there."

She stared down at her hands. "Then again, even if you had, I wouldn't know, would I? You barely speak to me."

"Mother—"

"Was sending you away so very bad?" she asked, lifting a teary gaze to him.

Leave it to Mother to get right to the point.

But she wasn't finished. "I truly thought giving you to your guardian so he could prepare you for your role as duke was the right thing to do."

Just like that, his bitterness came pouring out. "Yes, and having one less child underfoot certainly made it convenient, didn't it?"

Shock lined her features. "Is that what you think? That we just wanted to fob you off on someone else?"

Damn, he hadn't meant to say that. He sounded like a petulant child. "No, of course not." He crossed his arms over his chest. "But you could have broken the will. You could have sent my uncle packing and accepted the consequences."

"Those consequences would have affected only you, my dear."

"Going with him affected only me. What was the difference?"

That sparked his mother's temper. "Now see here, Fletcher Pryde. Your leaving affected us all profoundly. Gwyn cried herself to sleep for a week. Little Heywood kept asking for his 'Gwey' while Sheridan went around stabbing things with a stick. Thorn wanted to know when you were coming back. And Maurice walked about in a fog as if he'd lost his will to live. As for me . . ." She dabbed at her eyes with her handkerchief. "For months, I couldn't think or speak of you without bursting into tears."

The vivid image she painted of his family mourning his absence was balm to his wounded heart. "Then why did you send me away?" he asked hoarsely. "I didn't give a damn about learning to become a duke. I merely wanted to stay with all of you."

"You say that now, but at the time you seemed quite content with the plan."

He thought back to his ten-year-old self *before* his uncle had disillusioned him. In a flash, he remembered his excitement at going to England. He'd envisioned a world where he was important, where he wasn't treated like a child. Unlike his parents, Uncle Eustace had treated him like a man.

Little had he realized what a façade that was. But he'd learned soon enough. "I suppose I *was* eager to go. What did I know? I was a child."

"Exactly. Which is why you didn't realize that if we'd broken the will, you would have lost a fortune in unentailed property and stocks to your uncle. Maurice and I couldn't bear to cripple your financial future that way."

As his entire world shifted sideways, he stared at her. All this time he'd focused on where and to whom they'd sent him instead of *why* they'd sent him. He'd taken at face value their remarks that they wanted him prepared to be duke, without probing more deeply. He'd just stewed in his resentment and anger without trying to understand.

He should have tried harder to understand. "Why did you never tell me this?" he asked softly.

She shrugged. "You were ten. You wouldn't have understood the financial particulars."

"I might have. I certainly understood them when Uncle Eustace started trying to—" He halted too late.

"Trying to what?"

"It doesn't matter." He took her hand in his.

"Obviously it does, or you wouldn't be so angry with me even after all these years."

"I'm not angry with you. I'm angry with myself." For not listening, not asking more questions. For hardening his heart to his parents. For letting Maurice—*Father*—die without mending the rift.

Uncle Eustace, who had made such a show of liking him on the trip, had proved to be a bastard. But his parents couldn't have known that he would.

"Anyway," Grey said, "it's in the past. We should focus on making our present and future a happy one, don't you think?"

When he put his arms around her, she burst into tears. He let her cry, as his penance for making her so unhappy.

"I know now y-your . . . uncle was c-cruel . . . to you," she stammered. "Thorn t-told me he suspected it."

Damn Thorn. "I got through it," he said, not sure what else to say. He couldn't deny it. She'd know he was lying. His mother had always known when he was lying.

"Y-You . . . should have . . . w-written to us about . . . whatever he . . . was doing."

"I tried. But he was always the one to post the letters. So he read them first. And once I was away at school . . . He'd given up on forcing me into things." Mostly, anyway. By then Grey was too proud to turn to his parents for help. He was in the thick of a battle with his uncle and determined to win.

"So it w-wasn't *too* awful for you?" she asked, gazing up at him hopefully.

"No," he lied. She probably knew he lied, but he would bite off his tongue before he told her what his uncle had really done. "As I said, it's all in the past now."

Her tears began to die down at last, so he handed her his own handkerchief, since she'd soaked through her own. "I seem to have this effect on women, making them cry," he teased. "I don't know what I'm doing wrong."

His mother eyed him askance as she blew her nose and blotted her eyes. "You're breaking their hearts. Take Bea, for example. You know she's half in love with you already—and you encouraged that, I might add. So why on earth would you hurt a feeling young woman like her by sneaking off in the night and allowing her to think you were marrying Vanessa?"

Damn. He couldn't exactly reveal he'd bedded Beatrice—and proposed to her—the night before he'd gone to London. "Holy hell, Mother. You know how to hit a man where it hurts."

"Well? Answer the question."

He released a hard breath. "I did not put that announcement in the paper. My aunt did, trying to force my hand and make me marry Vanessa. But I straightened it out. I paid the *Times* to say they'd made an error in printing and my true fiancée is Beatrice."

Her face lit up, and she threw her arms about his neck. "Oh, Grey, what wonderful news! I'm so happy for you both!"

"Don't tell her about it, however," he said. "She accepted me at first, but then turned me down because I made an arse of myself over something her brother might have done. Now I have to fix that before she'll marry me. So I'm hoping she doesn't see the paper until I repair the situation."

"Oh, dear. That sounds serious. What exactly did Joshua do?"

He debated whether to tell her, but given it was her husband who'd been murdered, and Sheridan might ignore Grey's protests and run off to get the constable anyway, it was probably best Mother be prepared for what was to come.

So he summarized Sheridan's suspicions, his own attempts to confirm them, what alibis Joshua claimed to have, and Beatrice's reaction when Grey hadn't just taken her at her word concerning her brother.

"Now I see why she rejected you," Mother said hotly. "I'd reject you, too, if you sided with your brother against me and *my* brother."

"You don't have a brother."

"That's not the point! That woman is a jewel, which you obviously know already, since you wish to marry her. Her character is solid. She would never shield a murderer."

She did try, he wanted to say, but the situation had been very different. And he couldn't shame Beatrice by sharing her secrets about her uncle with his mother. She deserved better.

In any case, he agreed with Mother—he didn't really think Beatrice would lie for her brother. He shouldn't have said that to her. Why had he?

Oh, right. "Joshua did summon Father to the dower house that night. Yet he denies it."

A frown knit her brow. "It probably slipped his mind. Or perhaps he's embarrassed at having unwittingly been part of Maurice's death. The whole thing still might have been an accident after all."

"I doubt that, Mother. And so does Sheridan."

She snorted. "Sheridan is grieving. He's frustrated by the mess his uncle and Maurice left behind, and he's looking to blame someone for it." Drawing back from him, she smoothed her skirts. "And you have your own reasons for wanting his theory to be true, admit it."

Something in her solemn gaze gave him pause. "I don't know what you mean."

"Don't you? If Joshua is guilty, you don't have to compete with him for Bea's affections. Or worry she will take his side." As he stiffened, she caught his hand in hers. "You don't have to fear she'll leave you for him, the way we essentially left *you*."

"That's nonsense." But she was right. His mother, in her usual wise way, had struck to the heart of what ailed him. Even after all these years, she knew him so well.

Suddenly, Gwyn burst into the room. "Mama, I've been looking for you everywhere! Sheridan rode off to fetch the constable, babbling some nonsense about Joshua having killed Papa."

Holy hell. Grey rose. "When did he leave?"

"An hour ago at least."

Before Grey had even had the chance to talk to him. Damn Sheridan and his determination to avenge his father.

"I rode along with him for a while," Gwyn went on, "trying to make him see reason, but he wouldn't listen. So I came back here to get Mama." She set her hands on her hips. "And I see that *you're* back, Grey. I suppose you agree with Sheridan."

His mother looked at him, a question in her eyes.

It was the moment of truth. Did he want to go on not loving or being loved out of a fear he might be abandoned? Or did he instead want to take a chance on trusting Beatrice, the one woman who made him truly happy?

He knew what his answer must be. "No, I don't agree with Sheridan. But he's hell-bent on proving it." He leaned down to kiss his mother. "I have to go. Joshua needs to be warned."

"I'll go with you," Gwyn said.

"You will not," Mother said. "I need you here. And Grey needs to talk to Bea without your mucking things up."

Awareness dawned on Gwyn's face. "Ohhh, so it's *that* way, is it? But what about Vanessa and the announcement?"

"Please explain it all, Mother," he said, heading for the door. "I have to be off."

Grey just hoped he hadn't left things too late to save Joshua. Or he might lose Beatrice for good.

Chapter Twenty-Four

Beatrice, bleary-eyed and heartsick, was back in the kitchen helping the maid prepare supper when she heard the banging on the front door. Her pulse sped up. Dear Lord, had Sheridan already brought someone to arrest Joshua?

If so, what would she do? More importantly, what would *Joshua* do?

She didn't want to find out. Wiping her hands on her apron, she hurried to the front, but she was too late. Joshua was already opening the door.

It was Grey. Her heart's hammering only increased.

"What do you want?" Joshua growled, being his usual rude self.

"You have to leave now," Grey said.

Joshua scowled. "I'm not going anywhere."

Ignoring him, Beatrice approached the door. "Why must he leave?"

When Grey saw her, his expression softened. "Because Sheridan is on his way to fetch the constable to question Joshua. My half brother already has information that the bridge was purposely damaged, and he's convinced that Joshua did it, then pushed my stepfather off after summoning Maurice here."

"That's a pack of lies, all of it!" Joshua said.

"And I'd much rather stay and defend myself. If I leave, I look guilty."

"Not if you leave without them knowing you were aware of the situation. Beatrice can tell them you went to Leicester on business. Then they'll have to wait for your return or go after you there, where your healer can give them your alibi in person. Either way it will buy you time until we can prove you didn't summon Maurice."

Joshua rubbed his jaw. "I can't prove that. It's your mother's word against mine."

"And against Beatrice's. I'm hoping they'll take hers more seriously, given her reputation for being a woman of good character."

Beatrice eyed him suspiciously. "Why would they take mine more seriously when you don't?"

Remorse shadowed his features. "Ah, but I do, sweetheart. I merely had to be reminded of that by my mother."

His mother? He'd spoken of this to his mother? She hoped that meant something, but she was afraid to put too much faith in it. He'd already hurt her more than once.

Grey shifted his gaze to Joshua. "In any case, you'd best leave here before they arrive. Because as long as they don't see it as your fleeing to avoid them, they'll assume they simply missed you. I'll tell them I came to speak to you today, but you were already gone. And Beatrice can tell them—"

"You're out of your mind if you think I'll leave my sister alone with you," Joshua said. "You had no compunction about sporting with her in her bed before. I don't see why that has changed."

"For one thing, I'd have something to say about that," Beatrice said.

Joshua snorted. "You should have had something to say about it the first time, too, but you didn't, did you?"

His face darkening, Grey surged forward. "Careful, Major. I won't let you malign my fiancée even if you *are* her brother."

"She isn't your fiancée." Joshua thrust his chest out. "She refused you, remember?"

Gritting his teeth, Grey took a step back. "How about this? I'll take her over to my mother. Surely you trust your aunt with her. You can lock up this place, and when Sheridan comes here, he'll just assume he missed you both. If he goes back and asks what you said to me, I'll tell him you weren't here when I came by, but Beatrice was, and I brought her back to Armitage Hall." He wore a harried expression now. "Because once the constable gets you in his clutches, it'll be a scandal for you and Beatrice, even if in the end he decides you're innocent."

"Please listen to Grey." Beatrice was already taking off her apron and exchanging it for her wool cloak. "We've had to weather enough scandal in our lives. Your going to prison isn't one I want to weather."

Joshua leaned against the doorframe to glower at Grey. "I don't like the idea of you being still engaged to that other woman but telling my sister that you're—"

Grey bent forward to whisper something in Joshua's ear.

Joshua eyed him warily. "Is that true?"

"I swear it on my honor as a gentleman," Grey said. "My honor is unimpeachable." He smiled at her. "Or it was until I met your sister. Then I behaved in a rather ungentlemanly fashion. My only excuse is I fell hard for her."

While she was still basking in the promise hinted at in those words, Joshua glanced at her, then back at Grey.

Grey held out his hand to Joshua. "Just give me a chance to argue for your innocence. *And* give me your permission to make Beatrice my duchess."

The word "duchess" seemed to sink in with her brother. He blew out a breath, then shook Grey's hand. "If you're lying to me, I swear it will be pistols at dawn."

Grey nodded. "I would think less of you if it were otherwise." He looked back at the bridge. "But please make it quick. And take a route where you won't run into Sheridan and the constable."

With a quick bob of his head, Joshua gathered his coat and hat. He waited while Beatrice went to send the maid home through the servants' entrance, then fetched her bonnet and gloves. Once she was standing outside with Grey, Joshua locked the door. But he insisted on watching until she and Grey had crossed the bridge.

Turning to wave to him, she saw him head to where the horse and gig were kept. Only then did she let Grey take her past the road to Armitage Hall and onto the path through the woods.

She and Grey walked a few moments in silence. She was the first to speak. "Do you think this plan of yours will work?"

"For a while. And speaking of that, we should take our time returning to the hall, give him a chance to get away so he can reach Leicester before they do. But eventually he will have to talk to them. I'm just hoping I can convince them to accept your word concerning his alibi before that time comes."

That made sense. They walked a little farther in silence.

"What did you whisper to my brother?" she finally ventured.

"I'll get to that later," he said mysteriously.

"Well, whatever it was, you convinced him to go. So thank you for that. And thank you for what you're doing for him."

"No need to thank me. I'm doing what's right."

She lifted an eyebrow at him. "You didn't feel that way earlier today."

"Actually, I did. I just didn't want to admit it to myself."

"Why not?"

He cast her a rueful smile. "Because, as my mother pointed out, deep down I wanted you all to myself. I guess I wanted you to choose me over him."

"It wasn't a contest, Grey," she said irritably. "He was fighting for his life. I wanted you to help him, not hinder him. That's all."

"I realized that eventually."

She stared at the ground. "I also wanted you to trust me."

"I know. And I do. That's why I came back to try and save him."

He took her hand as they walked. It felt as much a declaration of his intentions as the one he'd made to Joshua, because anyone could come along and see them together. Apparently, he didn't care.

But that didn't resolve everything. Not by half. "I suppose you wanted me to choose you over Joshua because you felt your mother chose the rest of your family and your stepfather over you."

"Something like that." When she frowned at that obtuse reply, he added, "You said my mother did her best and yet I blame her. You were right. I did blame her. But I shouldn't have."

She lifted his gloved hand to her lips to kiss. "What do you blame your mother *for?* What happened between you and your aunt and uncle, anyway?" Would he finally answer her on that score, too?

He frowned, as if trying to figure out how and where to begin.

Then he drew in a heavy breath. "First, I should explain a few things about my return to England. When Uncle Eustace came to fetch me in Prussia, I was rather excited to go with him. I knew I was heir to a great estate, and my real father was an important man. But my mother and stepfather treated me the way all decent parents treat their children—as simply one of the lot, no better or worse than the others. The five of us fought for their attention, as children will do. Yet when someone on the outside tried to hurt any one of us, we all stood together against them."

"So, a typical family."

"And a happy one, although I was too much a child to realize how lucky I was until my family was lost to me." A shuddering sigh escaped him. "Anyway, at first, my aunt and uncle were kind. They indulged me, though I always sensed a sort of falseness in it." His voice hardened. "I found out why on the day Uncle Eustace brought some papers and asked me to sign and seal them."

She caught her breath. She could easily imagine

the drastic consequences that might have resulted from that.

"He fully expected me just to follow his bidding. And when I told him I needed a few days to read them over, he probably thought I was merely pretending to know what I was doing." He shook his head. "But my stepfather hadn't raised a fool. While I was unfamiliar with most of the financial terms in them, my uncle had a fine library, so I availed myself of it until I could make out what the documents said."

"Thank God," she whispered.

"Thank God indeed. Because he was trying to get me to sign away several significant, unentailed pieces of property. To deed them to him outright."

She gasped. "Could he have gotten away with that?"

"If I hadn't caught it? Probably. He was my guardian. If I'd been a less clever boy, by the time I'd reached my majority, I would have forgotten all about signing some pieces of paper. He would already have been handling the properties for some years, perhaps even selling them, and I would have assumed they'd always been his."

"So you didn't sign those papers."

"I did not." He stared off ahead of them, his voice dropping to a monotone. "And thus began our battle of wills. He tried cajoling me. I was unmoved. He tried caning me. That only made me more willful. He tried starving me. I refused to yield, even though it sometimes went for days."

Anger laced his words now. "Damned bastard knew that a boy that age is always hungry, so withholding food was his favorite method. He was *sure* I would give in." He gritted his teeth. "And I was determined I wouldn't."

"Oh, Grey," she said, her heart breaking for the child he'd been, forced into a battle not of his making. "How long did it last?"

"Off and on for three years, until I went to school. Thankfully, my real father did have the good sense to stipulate which school I was to attend at thirteen." When she muttered a curse on his behalf, he added, "But until then . . . my uncle would be nice to me for a while, to lull me into letting my guard down, I suppose. Then he would start some new method of trying to force my compliance."

"That's appalling!" she cried. She could hardly bear to think of young Grey going from a blissful childhood to one of such cruelty. "Why didn't you tell someone? Ask for help from someone?"

"How? Ask whom?" He gave her a sad smile. "He controlled that household entirely. He examined every letter I wrote before it could be posted. I knew no one in England, and I had no other guardian. My reckless fool of a real father never thought to designate a team of trustees as he should have done because he assumed that my mother would always be in England to look out for me. But then, I suppose my real father didn't expect to die of an ague in his forties, either, while I was still a babe."

He tucked her hand into the crook of his elbow. "Do you know what's ironic? I found out a few hours ago that the properties he was fighting to gain were probably the same ones I would have lost if Mother had broken the will and kept me with her. In standing against him, I made Mother's sacrifice worth it."

"But not worth it to you, I take it."

She felt his arm tense. This was obviously difficult for him, baring his feelings to her. Probably to anyone. He seemed to be a very private man.

"I honestly don't know anymore. Fighting my uncle made me strong, but missing my family was almost unbearable. So I . . . cut myself off from them because it hurt too much to think of all I'd lost."

She wanted to cry; she wanted to rage at his awful uncle. It wasn't fair. "I can't imagine going through such a thing and holding firm. You must have had a will of iron."

"You, too, to endure your own uncle's mistreatment without letting on to anyone else it was happening. We both had our secrets to keep and our reasons to keep them."

"Perhaps, but at least *my* torment didn't start until I was sixteen. You were so very young. How did you stand it?"

"Believe it or not, Vanessa helped me. She was just a baby, but I knew what babies were like. After all, my mother had borne four in rapid succession after she bore me. So at my uncle's, I used to sneak into the nursery and talk to Vanessa and listen to her babble. It felt . . . familiar. I could almost pretend I was home. I suppose the nursemaid felt sorry for me, because she told no one and tolerated my visits."

Beatrice ignored the quick stab of jealousy in her heart. "That's why you wanted to keep Vanessa from being hurt by that announcement."

He nodded. "And that's why she and I could never marry. In many respects, she's as much a sister to me as Gwyn. More, in fact, since I only really knew Gwyn until she was six, and I've known Vanessa her whole life."

"But your aunt didn't care that neither of you wanted to marry each other."

"No. Since my uncle never succeeded in gaining all the property they wanted from me, the next best thing for her was to have me wed Vanessa and thus have her become a duchess with access to all the wealth of the dukedom anyway."

Beatrice stared up at him. "So how did you

resolve the matter without making it look publicly as if you'd changed your mind about marrying Vanessa?"

"Before I tell you that, I need to ask you something." He halted in the middle of the path to glance around. "And here seems an excellent place to do it."

She followed his gaze to the huge log where they'd first kissed, and her pulse jumped.

He took her hands. "My previous proposals of marriage left much to be desired, so I'm going to try again." His tone turned solemn. "Dearest Beatrice, I cannot live without you. I'm in love with you. Please do me the honor of making you my bride."

She would swear her heart stopped. "You . . . you love me?"

His eyes sparkled. "More than life, sweetheart. I've been afraid to love for so long that I didn't recognize the feeling until I was in the middle of it. Then I panicked a bit. Loving someone means risking heartbreak. And I've always feared heartbreak more than anything."

"With good reason, I suppose, given how your wretched aunt and uncle treated you." She covered his hands with hers. "But without risk, there's no reward. Surely a man famous for shrewd dealings like yourself can see that."

"It took me a while, but yes, I see it now. I see *you* now, more perfectly than ever."

She couldn't breathe for fear this moment would vanish. "And what do you see?"

"The only woman who can match me word for word and deed for deed. The only woman who understands what it's like to lose family at a young age and yet has managed not to be damaged by it. And certainly the only woman I ever want to share a bed with." He brushed a kiss to her lips. "For as long as we both shall live."

That vow was enough to have her pulling him back for a more thorough kiss, which went on quite a while.

Then he broke it off to ask, in his usual peremptory tone, "Well? What's your answer, minx?"

The scoundrel was so sure of her. She would cure him of that. Touching a finger to her chin, she said coyly, "I don't know. I still haven't had my debut. It's possible I might find a better husband there."

"No," he said firmly. "I won't allow it."

"The debut? Or my finding a better husband?"

His eyes gleamed at her. "You can have all the debuts you want. But you accepted my marriage proposal once, and I will hold you to it."

"That's not a very persuasive argument," she teased.

"Perhaps not. But this is."

He kissed her again, only this time he also

hoisted her up and carried her over to the ancient oak trunk where they'd kissed the first time.

"Your Grace!" she cried in mock disapproval. "Do you mean to ravish me?"

"If you don't ravish me first," he said roughly. "I won't mind if that's your preference."

"Women can't ravish." They couldn't, could they?

"Of course they can." Setting her down by the fallen tree, he sat down on it and tugged her toward him.

"Grey!" she cried, thoroughly scandalized now that she realized he was serious about the ravishment. "It's one thing to kiss in public, but to do *that* . . . What if someone comes by?"

"When have we ever seen anyone come by on this path?" He arranged her cloak back over her shoulders until only the tie at the top showed in front. "Sheridan and the constable are sure to take the road in a carriage."

"Just our luck they will decide—*Grey!*"

He'd lifted her skirts and was sliding his hands up under them to cup her bare bottom. "Yes?"

She squirmed a little. "You are very naughty to ravish me in the outdoors."

"Nonsense. You're going to ravish *me*. And I'm going to let you." Grinning up at her, he unbuttoned his greatcoat with one hand while the other slipped up between her legs to fondle her, silkily and much too briefly.

"Hold these," he said, shoving her bunched-up skirts into her hands.

Like a fool, she did. She expected to feel embarrassed and painfully exposed with her entire bottom half laid bare for his perusal, but instead his gaze on her down there excited her.

While still staring at her exposed thighs and privates, he spread the bottom of his coat out over the tree trunk. As she stood shivering in anticipation, he unbuttoned the fall of his trousers and drawers and shimmied them down past his hips so he could sit on his coattails, allowing his rather prominent erection to push through into the air.

This time she got a good look at the impudent thing thrust up at her as if inviting her to envelop it. To *mount* it. Ohhh. So *that* was what he meant about having her ravish him.

When her gaze flew to his, she found him watching her face with a wicked glint in his eyes that sent a hot thrill straight through her. He slid one booted foot between her legs, then used his knee to open her. Once she realized what he was about, she parted her legs willingly.

This time when he reached back for her bottom, it was to pull her astride him so that her knees were planted on his open coat, and she was hovering over his aroused member. As she let go of her skirts to catch his shoulders for balance, he smoothed his hands up her thighs and said, "Ravish me, my love."

Delighted by the delicious prospect of being in charge, she let him guide her until she could slide down on him. "Whatever Your Grace wishes."

"Ah . . . my sweet Beatrice . . . this is *precisely* . . . what I wish."

He settled her more comfortably on him until she felt filled up with him, body and soul. It was a most glorious sensation, to have him beneath her, waiting on her to take control. No one had ever given her control in anything, and this generally high-handed duke of the realm was giving it to her in this. What a heady feeling!

"I'm mad for you, you know," she whispered as she rose up and came down on him again. "Out of my mind for you."

"So you love me at least a little?" he murmured.

She heard the faint uncertainty in his voice and drew back to stare at him. In that moment, she realized how deeply his mother's seeming abandonment and his aunt and uncle's changeable treatment had wounded him, made him afraid he couldn't be loved. That was at the root of his fear, if anyone dug deep enough to find it.

It made her heart bleed for him. "More than a little," she said earnestly. "I love you until death do us part and beyond."

"And you'll marry me."

He spoke it like a command, but she could indulge him in that. "Yes," she said. "Yes."

Chapter Twenty-Five

In that moment, Grey could feel the very air between them shift. She loved him. Beatrice, truly *his* Beatrice now, loved him. Joy rose in him like a mist of perfume, surrounding him in such a richness of feeling that he could hardly bear his own happiness.

She was smiling at him and riding him like the glorious goddess she was, and he thought he could die content right here in her arms.

"Now that I have . . . what *I* wish," he murmured. "What do *you* wish, my love? How can I improve your pleasure?"

Her pretty blush brought him to the edge of release, and he fought to hold it back.

"You could . . . touch me down there like . . . you did before." After choking out the words, she added hastily, "But only if you want."

He would have laughed if he hadn't been struggling not to come. "Like this?" he managed as he fingered her sweet little button.

"Oh, *yes,*" she breathed. "You're . . . very good at that."

With a surge of satisfaction, he kissed whatever exposed part of her he could reach—her chin, her throat, the lovely curve of her clavicle. He sank into the rosewater scent of her, so delicate, so feminine for a woman Sheridan had described as a hoyden. Grey wished he dared remove her clothes so he could fondle her pert breasts, but even he had no wish to tempt fate so blatantly.

After a moment, seeing her fully naked didn't even matter. She was writhing atop him with her head thrown back and her eyes closed, making him insane, and he was fighting to resist the pull of nature. Just as he thought he couldn't bear any more, she dropped down on him and cried, "Oh. My. *Heavens!*"

He came. How could he not? The feel of her engulfing him was pure ecstasy. As he poured his seed into her like the reckless fellow he was, she murmured, "You're mine now, Grey. *Mine.*"

The possessive note in her voice delighted him. "So are you," he choked out, his cock spasming and his body alert to every contraction of her quim. "Mine forever." When she collapsed against him, obviously replete, he nuzzled her throat. "And don't you forget it."

Even half-clothed and draped casually all over him, she was the most beautiful woman he'd ever seen. And his, all his.

It took some moments before they came fully to their senses. He began to notice dusk setting in, and the forest growing quiet in anticipation of the night. They should go. But he was loath to leave just yet.

"Mmm," she whispered. "That was wonderful."

He chuckled. "You are very easy to please."

She drew back to eye him askance. "Are you saying your lovemaking is inferior to that of other men?"

"And if it is? Would you still marry me?"

She looped her arms about his neck. "I would marry you if you were a complete incompetent at it. Which, by the way, you are not." She kissed his nose. "You make me happy. You understand me. I need nothing else, Grey."

That sent his heart soaring, an unfamiliar sensation for him. "Then perhaps you should call me by my Christian name."

"Fletcher? I prefer Grey. It suits you better."

He blinked. "You know my Christian name?"

"Of course I know it, silly. Sometimes your mother even calls you by it. Besides, it's written out in full with your titles whenever you appear in the scandal sheets." She adopted a pompous tone: " 'Fletcher Pryde, the Duke of Greycourt, was seen with opera dancer Whatever-Her-Name-Is. They were clearly quite intimate.' "

He rolled his eyes. "Don't be absurd. I have *never* had my name associated with an opera dancer."

"Are you sure?" She tapped her chin. "I could swear you have."

"Enough." He gave her a quick kiss. "You're teasing me again. Which, by the way, no one else, other than my family, dares to do."

"Only because everyone else is cowed by you."

"Except you, my love."

"Which is why you like me."

He laughed. "Also true." Then he sobered. "But as much as I'm enjoying this—"

"I know." She sighed. "We need to get to Armitage Hall, in case Sheridan is there."

"Precisely."

She slipped off his lap and worked to repair her clothing. "Are you ever going to tell me how you resolved the Vanessa issue?"

"Oh. Right." He rose and buttoned everything up. "I forgot." He explained what he'd had the *Times* print as an errata. "Will that do?"

A beautiful smile broke over her face. "That sounds *perfect*. Leave it to you to come up with such a brilliant solution."

The compliment pleased him ridiculously. "I'm glad you're happy. I wasn't sure you would be."

"It *was* rather arrogant of you to assume I would accept your proposal before I actually did," she said, though her teasing tone relieved him.

"I know. Why do you think I didn't tell you until I'd secured you?"

"I suppose I shall let it pass this time." She was clearly fighting a smile. "As long as you don't do it again."

"I can promise that easily. Although I must say Vanessa was very happy with my solution, especially since I promised her mother I would double Vanessa's dowry."

She frowned. "So you're rewarding your aunt for being despicable?"

"No. I'm ensuring Vanessa is unaffected by her mother's bad behavior."

"Oh. Well, that sounds wise."

He stared at her. Only Beatrice could see this as a practical way out, without jealousy or bias. Apparently, she loved him for his cleverness and wisdom. For his depth of feeling. For his character.

Considering that she'd turned him down when she thought *her* character was in question, he knew she loved him for himself, not for his dukedom. That meant more to him than he could possibly say. "I love you. Do you know that?"

She cocked her head. "I'm beginning to believe it."

He tried to take her back into his arms, but she wouldn't let him. "We must go. We have to convince Sheridan that Joshua is innocent."

"Right." He eyed her closely. "Is your brother always going to be a problem for us?"

"Dear Lord, I hope not." She cast him a minxish smile as she headed for the path. "I'm praying that your sister makes him less so."

"Keep praying," he muttered as he followed her. "Because that would require a miracle." He might not know his sister well, but he somehow suspected she wouldn't fall for the likes of Joshua Wolfe very easily, no matter how much she might flirt with him.

Once they weren't purposely dawdling, it didn't take them long to reach the house. But to Grey's alarm, Sheridan and the constable were already there.

"Where is Joshua?" Sheridan asked without preamble. "I went to the dower house, but he wasn't there."

Ignoring the constable, who stood solemnly watching the interaction, Grey shrugged. "He wasn't there when I arrived either. Beatrice said Joshua had gone to Leicester on business, so I brought her back here. I suppose that's where he is still."

"If you're lying to protect him—" Sheridan began.

Their mother entered the room. "Careful, Son. You're mistaken about your cousin. And accusing your brother isn't going to help matters."

Sheridan regarded her coldly. "Stay out of this, Mother. You may have forgotten, but Joshua summoned Father to the dower house on the night Father died."

"I'm sorry, Son, but you're wrong," she said. "Joshua didn't summon anyone. Or at least I don't think he did."

That gave all of them pause. "What do you mean?" Grey ventured.

She pulled out a piece of paper and an accounting ledger. "*This* is the summons Joshua supposedly sent to Maurice. When you spoke to me earlier about it, Grey, I thought perhaps I still had it, so I dug through my chest of drawers and found the note where I'd shoved it that night. Then I compared it to what Joshua listed as his expenses in his post as gamekeeper. The writing doesn't appear to match, at least to me."

"Let me see that." Sheridan glanced at the summons signature and then at the known signature of Joshua. "Damn," he muttered under his breath. He handed the note and the ledger to the constable.

After a moment's perusal, the constable lifted his head to stare at Sheridan. "Forgive me, Your Grace, but I agree with your mother. They clearly don't match."

"Perhaps Joshua got someone else to write it for him," Sheridan said.

"Who?" Grey asked. "The maidservant, who probably can't even read? Beatrice, whose handwriting could also be easily compared to the note? And wouldn't this person have reported him the moment Father turned up dead in the river?"

Sheridan scrubbed a hand over his face. "You're right. Even I can't accept such a farfetched idea."

When Beatrice sagged in relief, Grey looped his arm about her waist. At last, Sheridan realized he'd been wrong about Wolfe. Beatrice's brother might be a cantankerous son-of-a-bitch, but he hadn't killed anyone. Grey was certain of that.

So Grey had been right to trust Beatrice and her brother. Now he felt vindicated in his choice.

"I told you," she whispered in his ear.

"You did." He pulled her close. "And you were right."

She let Grey hold her a moment, then slipped away from him to face the constable. "Sir, I think you should know my brother was with me the night of Uncle Maurice's death. He couldn't have committed the murder even if he'd wanted to."

The constable nodded. "I will take that into consideration." He turned to Sheridan. "Your Grace? Are you satisfied that your cousin is not involved in your father's death?"

Sheridan huffed out a breath. "I suppose."

Then Wolfe himself sauntered in. "I'm here to profess my innocence." He crossed his arms over his chest. "I haven't murdered anyone, and certainly not Uncle Maurice."

Grey shook his head. Clearly, Wolfe had decided against following Grey's advice. Not that it mattered now.

Though it seemed to matter to Sheridan, for he narrowed his gaze on Grey. "You told me you hadn't seen him. So how did he know about my suspicions?"

Before Grey could answer, Wolfe said, "I heard you'd been asking about me in town, that you'd talked to the man who constructed the bridge, and that you'd brought the constable here to arrest someone for murder. It didn't take much to figure out whom you wanted to accuse."

When Sheridan eyed Wolfe askance over what truly was an outlandish claim, Grey said, "Don't listen to him. I told him to leave." He nodded to Wolfe, his soon-to-be brother-in-law. "Thank you for trying to help, Wolfe, but I don't want the smallest hint of suspicion hanging over your head. It's not fair to you."

Then Grey smiled at his brother. "I knew he was innocent, so I helped him. I wasn't sure you'd listen to reason about his alibi."

Sheridan crossed his arms over his chest. "I still think that *someone* murdered Father. Perhaps not Joshua, but someone else."

"I understand," the constable said. "And if you can provide some proof of that, I'll be happy to investigate."

"The note is the obvious place to start," Grey put in.

"True." The constable glanced at the people gathered there. "Do any of you have an idea of who might have forged the note summoning the previous Duke of Armitage to the dower house?"

No one offered any suggestions.

"Very well," said the constable. "If any of you discover anything, let me know. In the meantime, I shall be looking further into the matter."

Sheridan frowned. "Thank you, sir. We appreciate your efforts."

Even as the constable left, Gwyn strolled in. "The *Times* has arrived. There's a curious announcement in it." She flashed Beatrice a smile. "Apparently, the paper made a mistake in naming Vanessa Pryde as Grey's fiancée. It seems *you* are actually Grey's fiancée."

Beatrice brightened. "Let me see!"

"Ah, ah, ah," Gwyn said, holding the newspaper away from her. "First, tell me if you actually knew of this when we were going on and on about Grey's awful behavior to you."

"Leave her alone, Sis." Grey snatched the paper from her and handed it to Beatrice. "She wasn't sure of me yet, so she behaved cautiously. And I don't blame her for that." Especially since he was partly responsible for her caution in the first place.

Beatrice read the announcement eagerly, then handed it to Wolfe. "You see? I told you he really wanted to marry me."

Wolfe glanced at the paper, then at Grey. "So you weren't lying."

"Did you think I was?" he drawled. "That doesn't bode well for our future as brothers-in-law."

"Oh, hush, Grey," Gwyn said, tapping his arm with her fan. "You have a reputation. What did you expect?"

"An *undeserved* reputation," Beatrice said stoutly. "Do not think otherwise."

As Gwyn shot Beatrice a bemused glance, Sheridan laughed. "Oh, you have certainly got *her* wrapped around your finger, Brother."

"Trust me, no one wraps Beatrice around his finger," Grey said. "Which is precisely why I fell in love with her."

At the word "love," Gwyn looked shocked and Sheridan uncomfortable, but their mother beamed at Grey. "And that is certainly something to celebrate. Come, let's go to the drawing room. I'll send for champagne, and we'll toast the lovebirds."

When Beatrice blushed and smiled, looking already the part of a bride-to-be, Grey felt his heart beat faster. "We'll be right behind you," he said. "Just give us a moment."

Fortunately, his family had the good sense to go on without them. Then he pulled Beatrice into the cloakroom, where they could be more private.

"Thank you for seeing me for what I really am," he murmured. "You'll never convince the others of it, but as long as you believe it, it's enough for me."

She shook her head at him. "Give them some credit for recognizing the truth. Yes, they probably listen to the gossip about you a bit too much, but in time they'll realize how false it is. And they'll be right there to champion you when the gossips treat you unfairly. Because they love you. They may not understand you or even know how to treat you, but they love you deeply. You're as much a part of the family as anyone can be."

With his heart in his throat, he stared down at her. "You're marvelous, do you know that?"

"I do," she said lightly. Then she sobered. "But you, Your Grace, are more than marvelous. Because you saw the goodness in me and ignored the rest. For that, I will always love you, too."

Feeling his heart beat wildly in his chest, he kissed her. At last he'd found a woman who could not only know him thoroughly, but could accept him for what he was—a man with flaws and fears, but a man still capable of loving.

After a long moment of relishing the softness of her mouth and the tenderness of her heart, he drew back to smirk at her. "Does this mean you're not having a debut and hunting for a better husband after all?"

"Don't be silly," she teased. "My days as your mother's project may be over, but that only means I now have to show off how well I've learned my lessons. So I still need a debut, which means we can't marry for, oh, at least seven months, when the Season begins."

"The hell we can't. I am not waiting seven months to marry you, sweetheart."

"Six, then?" she said, clearly fighting a smile.

"Three, when your period of mourning is up."

She cast him a mock frown. "So you mean to deny me my debut, do you?"

"Not in the least." He grinned. "You'll just have to be presented at court as my new duchess." He leaned close to whisper, "And the great thing about being a duchess, my love, is you get to say whatever you want—just as your husband does. We'll be the outrageous Greycourts together."

She broke into a smile. "Ooh, I do like that idea. Does that mean I don't have to follow all those rules, either?"

He turned serious. "Except for one: You must keep on loving me."

She gave a dismissive wave of her hand. "That one's easy. Because I always will."

Epilogue

Of course, Grey got his way concerning their wedding. Three months to the day from the death of Beatrice's uncle Maurice, they got married.

Not that Beatrice minded. With so many relations around, she and Grey had never had the chance to be alone, so three months had seemed like three *years*. Especially since he'd been forced to spend time at his properties without her, arranging matters so they could go on an extended wedding trip in the Lake Country. Now all she had to do was endure this interminable wedding breakfast. Then she could have Grey to herself at last.

He and his family had honored her wishes— to be married at Armitage Hall. It was the only way to have her aunt and Gwyn and her cousins attend, since they were all still in mourning. Fortunately, no one considered it odd if a man like Grey married while in mourning, especially since the person who died had been his stepfather, not his father.

Grey came up behind her. "When can we respectably leave?" he murmured.

She laughed. "You're asking *me?* I have no idea what rule that is. Your mother was too busy planning this to give me lessons in wedding behavior."

Sheridan approached them accompanied by a stranger. "Heywood didn't get here in time for the ceremony, but at least he made it in time for the breakfast."

"Heywood? I would never have recognized you!" Grey said. "My God, I had no idea you were coming." He enveloped the fellow in a bear hug as Beatrice stood back enjoying the sight of familial camaraderie.

Heywood looked a bit like Sheridan, but more like his father, with Maurice's hazel eyes and high brow. And judging from the one portrait they had of a young Maurice, Heywood also had his father's light brown hair, except that Heywood's was streaked blond from his time on the Peninsula. He was as tall as Grey, though, which she could tell when the two men broke apart.

This was one important legacy of Grey's putting his resentment of his parents to rest. His relationship with his family had become easier. Even Sheridan had said only the other night that Grey was more like the adult version of his ten-year-old self than like the scary chap who'd first come to see them at Armitage Hall.

Her reply was that no one had bothered to dig beneath the surface. If they had, they would have found the same little boy cowering in the corner as she had, though it had taken her time to unearth him.

Grey drew back and clapped a hand on his brother's shoulder. "Beatrice, may I introduce Colonel Lord Heywood Wolfe of the Tenth Hussars, who is also your cousin and my half brother?"

"And my baby brother," Sheridan chimed in.

Heywood shook his head. "Sheridan always insists on saying that because he thinks it irks me. What he doesn't realize is it merely illustrates I'm younger than he is." He grinned at Sheridan. "Right, old man?"

"By one year," Sheridan grumbled. "That hardly counts."

"If you say so." Heywood bowed to her. "And it's a pleasure to meet the woman brave enough to marry Grey."

"I don't know where you got the impression that I'm some great terror to women," Grey drawled.

"From Sheridan," Heywood retorted, sparing a wink for her.

"I said no such thing, you damned trouble-maker," Sheridan shot back. "Now I remember why I was so happy to have you gone."

Heywood clutched at his heart. "That's a hard blow, considering that I took a leave of absence to come help you with this old pile."

"That's *not* why you came home, and you know it. You're only here because—"

"Boys, boys," Beatrice said, biting back a

smile. "Could you at least wait until the breakfast is over before coming to blows? Gwyn and your mother will hang you up by your . . . um . . . earlobes if you destroy the decorations they so carefully picked out."

"It's possible Gwyn would hang them by something decidedly lower," Grey said.

Beatrice gazed up at him. "I was going to say that, but I wasn't sure how serious you were about your duchess being able to speak her mind."

"Around this lot?" Grey snagged a glass of punch from a passing footman. "You have to speak your mind if you're going to compete with the likes of Heywood."

"Don't listen to him," Heywood said. "I'm an officer and a gentleman."

She patted his hand. "I'm sure you are. Grey is also a gentleman two days a week."

"What?" Grey cried in mock outrage. "It must be at least three. I'm certain of it."

Sheridan had been watching their bantering with an impatient look, and now took the chance to jump in. "I know you're itching to get out of here, Grey, but I have to talk to you privately about something urgent."

Grey raised an eyebrow. "Not a chance. The last time you wished to talk to me privately in the midst of a social situation, you were accusing Beatrice's brother of murder. So I think I'll pass. It's my wedding day, after all."

"Still, I need to speak to you."

"Anything you wish to say to me can be said in front of Beatrice. And surely you trust Heywood, too."

Sheridan glanced at Beatrice and sighed. "Very well. It's about that note summoning Father to the dower house. I'm not entirely certain, but I think it might have been given to Father by a footman who used to work here. He left the day after Father's death. I'd initially assumed he left because he saw the writing on the wall—that the staff was going to be reduced yet again."

"But leaving would have been unwise since he wouldn't have wanted to depart without a reference if he could get one," Beatrice said.

Sheridan turned to her. "Right. Clever of you to recognize that."

"My wife is generally clever," Grey said.

Oh, she liked the sound of that—"wife." And the "clever" part wasn't bad, either.

"But now I wonder at the footman's suspicious timing," Sheridan went on.

"So do I," Heywood said. When Grey looked at him oddly, he shrugged. "When I first arrived, Sheridan gave me a summary of his suspicions and what came of them."

"I didn't want to get into this today of all days," Grey said dryly, "but Wolfe said something the day the constable came that started me thinking.

He pointed out that if anyone had motive, it was Mother, since she'd had three husbands die, leaving her property, et cetera."

When his brothers bristled, he said hastily, "Don't worry, I set him straight on that score, but he had a point. Three husbands dead, two of them so close together that there were barely three years between their deaths? Two relatively young and all in good health? Perhaps this is about someone trying to kill Mother's husbands. It's odd, don't you think?"

He'd talked about this at length with her, but every time he did, a chill swept over her anew at the idea.

Heywood snorted. "That's absurd. Our father didn't die until he was a ripe old age, and he and Mother had been married for nearly thirty years."

"In Prussia," Grey said. "But only a few months here."

"What's that got to do with anything?" Sheridan asked.

"The first two deaths took place here in England," Grey said. "But after Mother married Father, they went to Prussia. The few Englishmen there stick out, so murdering Father would have been more difficult to hide. And perhaps the killer couldn't afford to follow them there. Or he had a family he couldn't leave or something. But Father came back only after your uncle Armie suffered an accident on horseback. Then

Father drowned a few months later in what we've already determined was *not* an accident."

"Yes, but *your* father died of an ague," Sheridan pointed out.

Grey sipped some punch. "That he supposedly caught from his infant son. Me. Yet I didn't die of it. Don't you find that strange?"

"What are you saying?" Heywood asked. "That your father was poisoned?"

"I don't know. I just think it's worth looking into." Grey shot Beatrice a veiled look. "We did suspect at one point that your uncle Armie might have been murdered, too, though we have no evidence to support that theory."

"Good God," Sheridan said. "This is . . . I am astonished. A span of thirty years in which someone systematically murdered all of Mother's husbands and Uncle Armie—that seems incredible. You've really thought this out, I see. Though perhaps you're drawing correspondences where there are none."

"That may be." Grey drained his glass. "Anyway, since you brought up Father's murder, I thought I'd mention it. But we won't solve the matter this afternoon, and I'm eager to take my wife off somewhere private, as you might guess."

"Then you'd better run fast," Sheridan said. "Here comes Joshua. And given that he still resents me, I think I'll go talk to Vanessa."

"She's the pretty one with the black curls,

right?" Heywood asked. "I do believe I'll join you."

"Holy hell," Grey muttered, "it's beginning. Now that Vanessa is free to marry whomever she wishes, the suitors are lining up to court her, especially since she's an even bigger heiress than before, thanks to me."

"An heiress?" Heywood said. "Even better."

He and Sheridan walked off arguing in hushed tones. Beatrice took Grey's glass and set it on a tray nearby, hoping they could sneak away.

But Joshua didn't give them the chance, walking up to them just then. "I . . . um . . . wanted to congratulate you both. And Greycourt, I wanted to thank you again for not letting them send me off to hang."

"Joshua!" she said. "Surely you could put it a bit less bluntly."

Her brother exchanged a glance with Grey. "See what you've done? She's all hoity-toity now, with her come-out lessons and such."

Grey held up his hands. "Don't blame me for that. Blame Mother."

"And Lady Gwyn," Joshua said with a scowl.

Beatrice bit her tongue to keep from pointing out that he'd had quite the hungry look on his face while he'd been watching Gwyn dance earlier. He would just deny it.

Joshua tugged at his cravat, looking decidedly uncomfortable. "I also wanted you to know that

I appreciate what you did by buying the dower house from Sheridan. At least I don't have to worry you'll turn me out anytime soon."

"He's not going to turn you out at all," Beatrice put in. "Not unless he wants me plaguing him for it."

"And I don't, trust me," Grey drawled.

"Well," Joshua said, "it may take me a while, but I'll pay you back. Somehow."

"You don't have to pay me back," Grey said. "You're my brother now. In fact, if you'd like a better position at one of my estates, I'm sure we could find one that would suit a man of your many talents."

Beatrice could have kissed him for that, but Joshua drew himself up proudly. "I don't need charity, Your Grace. I'm content in my position here."

"But Joshua—" Beatrice began.

Grey squeezed her hand to quiet her. "I understand, sir. If you change your mind, let me know." As her brother nodded, then limped off, headed for the door, Grey murmured, "Leave him with his pride. He thinks it's all he has."

"I still say he should take you up on your offer."

Grey smirked at her. "Ah, but then he'd have to move away from Gwyn."

That lightened her mood. "True. I hadn't thought of that."

"Oh, and look over there." He nodded across

the room. "Sheridan seems fit to be tied. Thorn just asked Vanessa to dance, and she accepted."

Beatrice eyed him askance. "It's not as if she could turn him down. Remember? That was one of my lessons—no refusing the dukes when they wish to dance with you at balls. As I recall, you drummed that lesson in very well."

"How else was I to ensure you never refused me when I asked you to dance?"

She tapped her fan against her chin. "That was quite devious of you. I ought to give you a severe tongue-lashing for it."

He cast her quite the lascivious look. "I tell you what. You give me a tongue-lashing, and I'll give *you* one." He dropped his gaze meaningfully to a particular part of her body, which instantly reacted to his offer. Then his voice turned husky. "What do you think of *that,* Duchess?"

She leaned up to kiss his cheek, then whispered, "I think we have finally figured out the appropriate time for the bride and groom to leave their wedding breakfast."

His eyes shone with both love and desire, sweetly intertwined. "And when is that?"

"Now, my love. *Now.*"

Then as slyly as a pair of children sneaking off to the fair, they slipped out the door.

About the Author

Sabrina Jeffries is the *New York Times* best-selling author of over 50 romance novels and works of short fiction (some written under the pseudonyms Deborah Martin and Deborah Nicholas). Whatever time not spent writing in a coffee-fueled haze is spent traveling with her husband and adult autistic son or indulging in one of her passions—jigsaw puzzles, chocolate, and music. With over 9 million books in print in 21 different languages, the North Carolina author never regrets tossing aside a budding career in academics for the sheer joy of writing fun fiction, and hopes that one day a book of hers will end up saving the world.

She always dreams big.

| Books are produced in the United States using U.S.-based materials | Books are printed using a revolutionary new process called THINKtech™ that lowers energy usage by 70% and increases overall quality | Books are durable and flexible because of Smyth-sewing | Paper is sourced using environmentally responsible foresting methods and the paper is acid-free |

Center Point Large Print
600 Brooks Road / PO Box 1
Thorndike, ME 04986-0001 USA

(207) 568-3717

US & Canada:
1 800 929-9108
www.centerpointlargeprint.com